In Search of Hope

ANNA JACOBS

Allison & Busby Limited
12 Fitzroy Mews
London W1T 6DW
allisonandbusby.com

First published in 2013.
This paperback edition published by Allison & Busby in 2017.

A CIP catalogue record for this book is available from
the British Library.

10 9 8 7 6 5 4 3 2

ISBN 978-0-7490-2144-3

Typeset in 10.5/15.5 pt Sabon by
Allison & Busby Ltd.

The paper used for this Allison & Busby publication
has been produced from trees that have been legally sourced
from well-managed and credibly certified forests.

Printed and bound by
CPI Group (UK) Ltd, Croydon, CR0 4YY

In Search of Hope

By Anna Jacobs

THE HOPE TRILOGY

A Place of Hope
In Search of Hope
A Time for Hope

THE HONEYFIELD SERIES

The Honeyfield Bequest
A Stranger in Honeyfield

THE PEPPERCORN STREET SERIES

Peppercorn Street
Cinnamon Gardens
Saffron Lane

THE GREYLADIES SERIES

Heir to Greyladies
Mistress of Greyladies
Legacy of Greyladies

THE WILTSHIRE GIRLS SERIES

Cherry Tree Lane
Elm Tree Road
Yew Tree Gardens

⊰◆⊱

Winds of Change

Chapter One

As Libby was carrying out the rubbish, the bag split. It was the final straw in a horrible week, during which her husband had been in a foul mood.

She was fighting to hold back the tears about the mess when she saw a stained and dirty letter among the rubbish . . . sticking out of an envelope addressed to her. It had been opened and thrown away without her even seeing it.

Her husband usually took out the rubbish, but he'd forgotten today, because he'd been too busy complaining about their four-year-old son's untidiness. His need for perfect order and tidiness was beyond reason, an obsession that was hard to live with. And poor Ned did very well for a child.

Steven always picked up their mail from their PO Box and she wasn't surprised that he'd opened her letter. It wasn't the first time it had happened. But why had he thrown this one away without letting her see it? This seemed to be a new step in their deteriorating relationship. Or had he been doing that sort of thing all along?

Grimacing at the mess of coffee grounds and vegetable

peelings which now decorated the letter, she took it out of the rubbish, wiped it and began to read.

> *Dear Mrs Pulford,*
> *You appear not to have replied to our previous letter, although it was sent by registered post and was signed for by someone at your address.*
> *In brief, your grandmother, Rose King, has died and left you a bequest of £20,000, plus some residual money which will come from a later sale of goods.*
> *If you will be so kind as to contact us, we will explain the conditions attached to your inheritance and arrange to have funds transferred to you once you have signed the agreement . . .*

Libby gasped and clapped one hand to her mouth. She hadn't seen her grandmother since she was twelve, when her mother had remarried and moved from Lancashire to Bristol, but she had very fond memories of Grandma Rose and had hoped to see her again one day.

It was her stepfather who had kept her away from her straight-talking grandmother. He'd claimed the 'old hag' was teaching his stepdaughter to be cheeky and answer him back. And anyway, since Libby was adopted, Rose wasn't really related to the child at all, so there was now no need for them to keep in touch.

There had been a few spectacular scenes, but in the end her mother had given in, as she always did, begging her daughter to let the matter drop and do nothing more to upset her stepfather.

Libby had written to Grandma Rose every year at Christmas, however, sending the letter secretly and getting the replies sent to various friends. But the replies had stopped after she got married and, when she asked, Steven had told her gently that her grandmother had died.

But that couldn't have been true, if her grandmother had only just died. It was just another of Steven's lies. But why had he said it? What harm could it have done for Libby to keep in touch?

She sighed. Were you fated to repeat the mistakes of your parents? Her mother's second marriage had been unhappy – but not, she thought, as unhappy as her own. Libby had married young, desperate to escape her stepfather and enjoy a proper family life. It had been all right at first, not perfect, but mostly happy.

The turning point came when she got pregnant. Steven hadn't planned for a child yet, so he grew angry when she suffered morning sickness and let the house get a little untidier than usual.

After Ned's birth, things had continued to deteriorate. Steven had taken charge of her life so slowly she hadn't understood for some time what he was doing to her. By then it was too late: she had no friends, little confidence in herself, no money of her own and a child dependent on her.

How to get away from him had been worrying Libby for some time. You couldn't escape without money and he made sure she had none to spare.

She turned back to reread the letter with a surge of hope,

bright and shiny as a new coin. This was the answer to her problem. She could now afford to leave him.

At six o'clock, Steven turned into the drive and Libby stiffened her spine. The small inheritance had given her the courage to act. Tonight she was going to tell him she wanted a divorce. She would try to do this openly first.

Steven didn't beat her, so she wasn't afraid of him physically, but she sometimes thought the way he treated her was worse than physical violence.

He sauntered into the kitchen from the garage, stopped to hang up his keys and then studied her face. 'What's wrong this time?'

So she blurted it out, couldn't hold it in any longer, not now she was filled with hope for the future. 'I want a divorce, Steven. I can't go on like this.'

His face went expressionless, something he'd perfected over the years. 'No.'

'I mean it.'

'I mean it, too. If you try to leave me, I'll take Ned from you. They'll give him to me, too, you know they will, because you don't have any way of supporting a child and I do.'

She didn't tell him she knew about the money. 'I can get a job.'

'Your skills are way out of date. You aren't even au fait with modern technology.'

'And whose fault is that? You won't buy a new home computer.'

He had the gall to smile. 'You don't need one. You'd only play around on it.'

'I could soon catch up with technology.'

'Oh, and who'll care for our dear little son while you're working *and* studying? I, on the other hand, can easily afford to employ a nanny, and I have a history of stable employment, not to mention a very successful career.'

She tried one last time to make him see sense. 'Steven, you know we've not been happy together for a while. Can't we just call it quits and arrange an amicable divorce?'

'There's no such thing. They always give far too big a share of the goods and chattels to the wife. I'm not handing my money over to you.'

'I won't ask for anything financially.' She gestured to the house. 'You can have all this. I just want Ned and my freedom.'

He moved closer, impaling her with those icy grey eyes. 'But I don't want *my* freedom. You're very useful to me – most of the time, anyway – a credit to me in public, if not always satisfactory in private, and an excellent housekeeper, for all your other failings. Besides, your timing is terrible, as usual. I'm in line for another promotion and, though the company may not specify it, given the stupid rules for political correctness people have to comply with these days, it's well known they prefer married men. Maybe we'll think about a divorce in a year or two, once I've reached the top echelons . . . *if* you do as I ask in the meantime.'

He'd said that last year when she hinted at a divorce. She'd thought he meant it, because he'd moved into a separate bedroom that very night, but he'd laughed in her face after he got the promotion.

'I mean it this time, Steven. I'm leaving you.'

There was the patter of footsteps and their son peeped into the kitchen, saw his father's scowl and ran away again.

She pointed her finger at the retreating child. 'See what you've done to him! Ned runs away from you.'

Steven flicked one hand in a carelessly dismissive gesture. 'He'll learn to obey me once I turn my attention to training him. He's getting old enough to understand what I want now. Maybe I'll start at the weekend.'

He pushed her roughly aside. 'End of discussion. Now, get the dinner on the table. I'm hungry.'

'Get it yourself.' She turned to leave the kitchen, knowing it would infuriate him to be directly disobeyed.

But what happened shocked her rigid.

Joss Atherton drove slowly home from the physiotherapist. Final session, thank goodness. They'd done as much as they could for him. He felt well again; better than he had for years. A crash during a car chase had put him and another police officer in hospital. The other guy had recovered fully, but Joss would always have a weakness in his left leg.

He'd been offered a desk job but couldn't stand the thought of spending his life in an office, so had opted for compensation. He could live on it for years, but he was bored and couldn't seem to settle on another direction in life.

He picked up the mail – one catalogue and two bills – and moved into the back room of the small terraced house he now owned outright. Ironic really. Fate had taken away with one hand and given with the other. His elderly neighbour, who had been his landlord for the past five years, ever since his divorce, had left him the little two-up two-down house when she died.

He'd rather have had her here still, because she'd been like a grandmother to him, but death was brutally final.

Just as he was making a cup of coffee, the phone rang. He picked it up and a voice he recognised instantly said, 'Leon here.'

He was surprised that this man would call him now that he'd left the force. Leon was in charge of a government unit whose name said nothing and whose true purpose wasn't known to most people, since it dealt with the practicalities of tidying up minor security problems. Even after working with him a couple of times, Joss had no idea what Leon's surname was.

'How are you feeling now, Joss?'

'I feel great, but I've been left with a slight weakness in my left leg.'

'Do you limp?'

'No. They just don't want me getting involved in hard physical work or sports that involve twisting and jumping. Why?'

'A genuine limp is rather hard to disguise.'

Joss frowned. Did this mean what he thought?

'Would you be interested in some contract work with my unit?'

'Very interested. What exactly did you have in mind?'

'We never have specific ongoing roles. It's whatever needs to be done at the time. A bit of this and that, escort duty and protection mainly. The work is only intermittent and we haven't got a job for you at the moment, but we'll get you down to London for a briefing soon and give you a few useful bits of gadgetry.'

'Great.'

'I'll be in touch soon.'

Joss beamed as he put down the phone. Who knew where this might lead? To something a damn sight more interesting than desk work, that was sure. He'd been right to take a settlement.

The following morning Libby stayed in bed, pretending to be asleep till Steven left for work. Thank goodness he had a long commute into London and had to set off at seven-thirty.

It was an effort to get out of bed and she winced as she stood upright. She suspected a cracked rib. He'd gone mad last night.

After one shocked look in the bathroom mirror, she avoided it, not wanting to see the huge bruise on her cheek and the puffy, black-rimmed eye. He'd always been able to use words to hurt, but he'd never hit her before or she would definitely have left him by now.

When she peeped into her son's bedroom, Ned was pretending to be asleep, his cheeks tear-stained, as if he'd rubbed them with dirty hands. His teddy was clasped tightly in one arm, as always. Boo-Bear was his constant companion.

Last night's quarrel had upset him and when Libby screamed involuntarily in pain, he'd tried to intervene, only to be shoved violently out of the way by his father.

'Daddy's gone to work. We can get up now,' she said softly and watched her son open his beautiful blue eyes.

Why had Steven beaten her last night? She'd been prepared for verbal tirades, for more restrictions on her comings and goings, but not this. All she could think was that something had upset him badly at work. Maybe . . . maybe he wasn't really in line for the next promotion. Or maybe a valuable account had gone to someone else. Who knew? He rarely told her any details of his working life.

But he was wrong about one thing: if she left him, she would have some money to start her off now, thanks to her grandmother. So surely the courts would look on her favourably when it came to custody?

This year Steven had installed a program on the elderly computer, which made sure she had only limited Internet and email access, and that he saw everything she wrote or viewed. It was a program for controlling children's use of computers.

'It's that or nothing,' he'd said when she protested.

Well, never mind looking backwards. She had to look forward now and leave here before the bruises faded and her ribs healed. She needed evidence against him and he'd certainly provided it. She'd have to see a doctor and get some photographs taken, however much she hated the thought of that.

In spite of the pain in her ribs, she smiled as she cuddled her son. *You made a bad mistake last night, Steven Pulford. You won't get custody of Ned now. And I will ask for my share of the house and family goods after all. I deserve it.*

From across the road, Mary Colby kept an eye on the house opposite. She hadn't seen any signs of movement this morning so far, not even after Mr Pulford left. She was worried about the young woman who lived there after the sheer violence of the quarrel the previous night.

The Pulfords had quarrelled before – often – but not like that. They must have forgotten to close the windows and the sound of Libby screaming had carried clearly in the still night air. The poor young woman didn't usually scream. Had he started thumping her?

She'd wondered whether to call the police, but the sounds had stopped abruptly, so she hadn't.

When the quarrel began, her husband had scowled and retreated to the conservatory at the rear, from where he couldn't hear the noise. He'd told her to stay out of it, but Mary couldn't do that any longer. Not after what had happened to their daughter.

In the end she went out and crossed the street, needing to make sure Libby was all right this morning. When the door opened, she was shocked at the sight of the bruises on the younger woman's face. 'Oh, my dear! What has he done to you now?'

'Hit me, as you can see.'

'I couldn't help overhearing the quarrel last night. Is there anything at all I can do to help?'

'I'm all right, thank you, Mrs Colby.'

'You're not all right, Libby, and you haven't been for quite a while. I can't help noticing things, and I really would like to help you. Why don't you come across and have a cup of tea with me? We could . . . talk.'

'I'm leaving him today, so I can't spare the time, but thank you for offering. I shall miss you.'

'I'm glad you're leaving him. Best thing you can do. Excuse me asking, but do you have enough money?'

'I'm going to pawn something to pay for the petrol.' She looked down at her hand. 'My wedding ring, perhaps. But I will have some money once I've claimed an inheritance. It couldn't have come at a better time. I just have to get up to Rochdale to do that. Look, why don't you come in for a moment? There is one thing you can do for me.'

'Anything.'

Libby picked up the letter and gave it to Mary. 'Read this first. Steven threw it away without telling me.'

Mary scanned the letter, surprised. 'Why would he not tell you about a bequest that large?'

'Because he wants to keep me dependent on him.'

Libby took the letter back. There was a phone number on it and an email address. She didn't dare email because Steven would find out what she'd said. She couldn't phone from home, either, because Steven had arranged for the phone only to be used for local calls, but perhaps . . .

'Would you let me phone the lawyer from your house, please? Or on your mobile? I can't phone long-distance, as you know, and anyway, I don't want my husband to know where I'm going. He won't know that I've seen this letter.'

'Of course you can use our phone. Use our landline. Our mobile phone's playing up a bit. Come across and do it now.'

'Ned's just finishing his breakfast. I'll have to bring him with me.'

'Why don't you go across to my house and phone? It's in the hall and my husband's out, so you won't be interrupted. I can keep an eye on Ned for you. And Libby . . . it doesn't matter that it's long distance or how many minutes you talk.'

As she went into Mary's house, Libby again caught sight of her face in the mirror and her anger burnt even higher. She'd never give Steven the chance to do that again.

She was on the phone for ten minutes and when she put it down, she swallowed hard. Here was her chance – if she dared to go through with it.

No, why was she thinking like that? Of course she'd dare do it.

When she got back, she told Mary about her call. 'I managed to contact the lawyer. I'm going to see him before I do anything else. He'll give me some money.'

'That's good.' Her neighbour glanced at her face, hesitated, then said, 'Look . . . tell me to mind my own business if you want, but would you like me to take some photos of the injuries? In case you need evidence.'

'You'd do that?'

'I don't tell many people this, but my daughter nearly died as a result of a physically abusive relationship. I learnt a lot about the things a woman needs to do to prove her case. And I'd be a good person to do this for you, because I overheard the quarrel and the screams, and I've heard quarrels before. I'm quite prepared to stand up and say that in court.'

Libby hugged Mary. 'Thank you. You've been a wonderful neighbour. Where is your daughter now? She doesn't visit you.'

'She's overseas. It's safer. Her ex is out of jail now,

released early for good conduct. Ha! He doesn't know the meaning of the word. Tess and I Skype one another regularly, and Don and I are going to Australia to see her next year. She's met a lovely man and has married again.'

'I'm glad for her.'

'I'm not just doing it because of Tess, but for your own sake as well, Libby. I help out at the local women's refuge and I hear a lot of stories. Now, I'll fetch my camera and in the meantime, you start packing. Presumably you're driving?'

'Yes. At least the car still belongs to me.'

'It's rather old.'

'It runs better than you might expect.'

'Never mind pawning your ring; let me lend you some money. You need to get on the road quickly.'

Libby hesitated. 'Thank you. Just enough to buy petrol. Forty pounds, maybe.'

'You'll need more than that. No, I insist.'

'All right. Thank you. It'll be a loan, though. I should be able to pay you back quite quickly once I get Grandma Rose's money.'

When Mary came back with her purse, Libby had dumped a pile of things she wanted to take on the kitchen table, including her albums of family photographs. She accepted the contents of Mary's purse, several notes and even the coins, then hugged her neighbour. 'Thank you.'

'I wish it were more. And now we need to take those photos.'

Shame filled Libby. 'Maybe we don't need to bother now that I have the inheritance.'

'And maybe we do need to bother. It will only take five minutes.'

Libby felt humiliated to have to display the marks on her body, was glad when she could put her clothes on again. Mary didn't comment, just asked her to move as necessary and took several photos.

'Shall I bath Ned for you while you pack?'

'Would you? You're an angel.'

She saw them into the bathroom, got out the suitcases and began packing their clothes at top speed.

'Libby, could you come here a minute?'

She went into the bathroom.

Mary pointed to Ned's leg. 'Did you know about this?'

There was a huge bruise on his thigh – no, two bruises. Libby stared at them in horror, shaking her head. She knelt by the bath. 'How did you hurt yourself, darling?'

'Daddy kicked me last night.'

Those twin bruises on Ned's leg, shockingly blue against his tender child's skin, stiffened Libby's resolve as nothing else could have done. 'We shall need a photo of that, too, Mary.'

'I'll go and get my camera from downstairs.'

She took the photo, then said briskly, 'Get on with your packing. I'll finish bathing Ned.'

'I'll put some clothes on the bed.'

When Mary came down with a sweet-smelling little boy, she hugged Libby. 'I'll get out of your hair now. Keep in touch. You know my email address and phone number. I'll email you copies of the photos when you get online again.'

'I can't thank you enough.'

'Get yourself and the child free of him. That'll be thanks enough.'

Ned followed Libby round while she finished packing, silent but clinging.

Everything seemed very unreal. Was she really going to escape from Steven at last? What would he do about that? She didn't let herself think about it. One thing at a time.

First, she had to get away and claim her inheritance.

As for the conditions attached to that, which the lawyer had summarised when she spoke to him, they suited her perfectly.

Libby left twenty minutes later, her car piled high with possessions thrown in anyhow.

She hadn't eaten because she couldn't face food, but she'd drunk two cups of strong coffee and that gave her plenty of energy as she wound through the country lanes till she got on to the M5 motorway.

No matter how she sat, though, her chest hurt. A cracked rib, she supposed. She tried to ignore it, telling herself: *This too shall pass.*

For Ned's sake, she stopped every hour and a half at a motorway services, buying some painkillers for herself the first time. She used the facilities and let him run about a little before they got into the car again.

I'm heading north, she told herself each time she set off again, *heading home to Lancashire*. The mere thought of that lifted her spirits. She'd been born there and spent the happiest years of her life there.

She wished she could have seen Grandma Rose again. If

she'd known Rose was still alive, she'd have got in touch once she was away from her stepfather. Walter was living in London now and she hoped she'd never see him again as long as she lived.

Of all the cruel things Steven had done, telling her that Grandma Rose was dead was one of his most unkind tricks. But this inheritance surely proved that her grandmother didn't blame her for their estrangement. That thought was a comfort.

Unless something went wrong, Libby would arrive in Rochdale by about four o'clock and be able to visit the lawyer to find out the details of where the house was because Rose had moved a few years ago. She'd have to live there for six months in order to gain her inheritance. She'd have a living allowance during that time, more than adequate, and best of all she'd have peace and quiet.

Libby didn't intend to tell Steven where she was and she hoped he'd give her up as a bad job. She didn't have much confidence in that happening, but you had to hope for the best, didn't you?

Her husband would contact the lawyer, she was sure, but he wouldn't know exactly where she was living, so maybe she had a chance of staying hidden there for the six months stipulated in the will.

Maybe.

Steven could be very determined when he wanted something and, with the Internet, it was much harder to stay hidden these days.

But, if necessary, she would go to the police for help. Or to a women's refuge.

She glanced at her watch. Steven didn't get home from work until six, often later, so he wouldn't know yet that she'd left. She and Ned were perfectly safe for the moment, and that felt so good.

She wished she could be a fly on the wall when Steven realised what had happened. She hadn't even left a note, just a house in chaos from her hasty packing.

He would hate that.

Chapter Two

It was a relief to see the first sign saying LANCASHIRE. Libby let out a tired sigh. Nearly there now.

Then Ned was sick without warning, and she had to stop at another services to clean him up, not to mention trying to clean up the car.

He began to cry miserably when she put him back into his seat, poor little love.

'Don't want to get in! Don't want to!'

She gave him a hug. 'Not long now, darling, then we'll be there.'

But there were bad hold-ups on the M62. She rotated her shoulders, trying to ease the ache as the line of cars stopped and started, moving forward only in frustratingly short bursts. She wasn't used to driving such long distances and felt exhausted. Only determination was keeping her going now – mixed with a hefty dose of desperation and another couple of painkillers.

When she got to Rochdale, it was almost six o'clock and though the office building was still open, the lawyer's rooms were closed, the blinds pulled down. She stood in the foyer, fighting tears, wondering what to do.

She didn't have enough money for a hotel room.

In spite of her efforts to remain calm, a sob escaped her.

She turned as someone spoke. 'Were you trying to see Mr Greaves?'

She nodded, managing only a strangled, 'Yes.'

'It must be urgent to upset you like that. Is there anything I can do to help?'

'My grandmother has died and left me somewhere to live. I need to see Mr Greaves about that.'

'He'll be in tomorrow.'

Libby couldn't prevent tears from rolling down her cheeks. 'I've just left my husband and I don't even have enough money to pay for a hotel till I've seen Mr Greaves.' She hugged Ned to her as he began to wail in sympathy.

'Ah. Well, look, I have Henry's home phone number. I'll give him a call. Your name is . . . ?'

'Libby Pulford. And this is Ned. Thank you.'

'Come and wait upstairs in my office while I phone. You'll be warmer there.'

There was the murmur of voices in another room, then the woman came back. 'Henry can't come and see you, but he thinks he can sort something out on the phone.' She held out the handset.

Libby took it from her. 'Hello? I'm afraid I got delayed. I've nowhere to stay and . . . very little money.'

'Why didn't you phone me when you got delayed? I'd have made arrangements.'

'I don't have a mobile phone. Mine got broken and my husband wouldn't buy me another.'

Ned insisted on getting down and wandering round the

room, so she tried to keep an eye on him as she listened to Mr Greaves.

'Now, Libby – it's all right if I call you Libby, isn't it? It's how I think of you because that's how your grandmother always referred to you.'

'My husband told me she died several years ago.'

'Far from it. She remained a redoubtable woman until the end. Rose King was one of my favourite clients. Actually, she's been keeping an eye on what you've been doing for the past few years.'

'She has?' Libby was startled.

'Yes. She paid a private investigator to track you down and find out if you were happy. He . . . um, didn't think you were. She knew you had a child, too, wished she could meet him. But she decided, regretfully, that getting in touch with you would probably only make matters worse between you and your husband.'

Humiliation seared through Libby. 'There was nothing to upset. My marriage was a mess. I'd not have stayed with Steven for so long, but it's hard to leave someone when you don't have any money, especially when you have a small child.'

'Yes. Rose guessed that was a problem for you and she understood. Sadly, she was too sick to face any upsets during the last year when the cancer began to spread. She's left you a letter, though. I'll give you that tomorrow.'

Someone spoke to him and he tsk-tsked under his breath. 'I'm sorry, my dear. Any other time I'd have cancelled my evening engagement and taken you out to Top o' the Hill myself, but I'm presenting some awards, so I can't miss tonight's ceremony. I'll tell you how to get there.'

She smiled. 'I've been to Top o' the Hill before. I know where it is. Grandma Rose grew up near there and sometimes she took me walking across the moors, showing me the places she'd loved as a child.'

'The house she grew up in has been knocked down, but she'd inherited money from a friend and was able to buy another property. She loved living up near the moors.'

'I'm sure I'll have no trouble finding the house. But what about a key?'

'The front-door key is on top of the lintel of the coal shed at the back. Do you have enough money to buy food and necessities for tonight and the morning?'

She could feel herself flushing again. 'I raided the fridge before I left, so Ned and I will be all right tonight as long as we have a roof over our heads.'

'Come in to see me tomorrow morning, then. I'm free at nine. Is that too early?'

'No. I'll look forward to it.'

She thanked the woman for her help and left.

Ned protested again about getting back into the car, throwing a tantrum, and Libby had to spend a few moments coaxing him. 'We're nearly there now. Just a little while longer, darling. We're going to . . . a friend's house.'

She lost her way almost immediately because they'd made a lot of changes to the road system in Rochdale since she was a child. But when she stopped to ask for directions, the northern accent of the woman who pointed out the way comforted her. Grandma Rose had talked like that, slowly and with flat vowels.

Libby smiled as she saw the sign, wincing as a movement made her ribs twinge again. Top o' the Hill was a strange name for a village, but a very accurate description of the position of this modest group of houses.

The road twisted up a cleft in the edge of the moors. It was only single lane for the most part, with occasional wider places where vehicles could pass one another. The village itself sat almost at the top, with a few houses straggling down the upper reaches of the cleft.

She'd wondered whether the village would have been developed into a dormitory for nearby Rochdale and Todmorden, with rows of dwellings thrown up at minimal cost, ready to become the slums of the future. To her relief it still looked much the same: a few older, stone-built weavers' cottages with huge third-floor windows to give the weavers light. There were a couple of short terraces of smaller houses, as well as bigger ones round a central paved area. There were one or two newer homes lower down the hill, but that was all.

Two smiling older men were walking into the Crown, the only pub, gesticulating as they chatted, and a little girl was skipping along the street, her lips moving as she earnestly counted something.

The little village shop was shutting, the cheerful, well-lit displays in its twin windows brightening the evening scene. Apart from the cars parked everywhere, it was as if Libby had stepped back into her childhood.

Slowing down, she muttered the directions Mr Greaves had given to get to her grandmother's new house. She had to turn up towards the tiny church.

For a moment her mind went blank as she tried to find the little lane that led up the final stretch of hillside to the church and graveyard. Surely it should be round here somewhere? She slowed down to a crawl, relieved there were no other cars impatient to overtake her.

She nearly passed the turn and braked so suddenly Ned jerked awake and cried out in protest. 'Sorry, darling.'

'First and only turn left,' she muttered. She missed that completely and had to turn round in the little car park outside the church and go back. Ah, there it was!

Other tyre marks in the curving dirt track showed clearly in the damp ground, but from here she couldn't see the four cottages she was looking for. Then they came into sight a hundred yards down the track. None of them was showing lights, even though the daylight was fading now. There was a car outside one house, though, so someone else lived here.

Stopping the car, she bowed her head over the steering wheel for a moment, so weary she could hardly move. She'd done it! She'd got here.

It was Ned who got her going again, calling anxiously, 'Wanta wee, Mummy. *Mummy!* Hafta go wee-wee.'

She helped him out and since he was clutching himself and no one seemed to be around, allowed him to wee on to the grass to the side of the car, which he thought great fun.

When he'd finished, she stayed where she was, studying the cottages. They were very similar to Grandma Rose's original home, with a third storey and with long mullioned windows across the whole frontage. Weavers' cottages. She liked the idea of living in one.

She shivered. What was she doing standing out here? It

was cold for May. Holding Ned's hand firmly, she walked along the short row of dwellings to the end one on the right: the one she'd be living in.

Please let the key be where Mr Greaves said it was, she prayed as she walked past the car and peered into 'her' cottage window.

This was such a chancy arrangement, but the lawyer had assured her the key would be where he'd left it.

As he was coming out of the bathroom, Joss heard a car turn into the lane, something so unusual he went to look out of the front bedroom window. A battered old Ford came to a stop in the common parking area and the driver switched off the engine.

He was the only one living in the group of cottages now. The others had been empty for several months and the only visitors had been people from the lawyer's office checking them out regularly. But they wouldn't be doing that at dusk.

He couldn't get a proper look at the face of the woman who got out of the car, but she was moving slowly and stiffly as if something hurt.

She reached into the rear seat then stepped back to let a little boy scramble out. Joss smiled as the child made jigging movements that showed an age-old need. After a quick glance round she helped him to pull down his pants and relieve himself.

When she'd set the little boy's clothing to rights, she took hold of his hand firmly, though he tried to pull away, before walking along the path to Rose's cottage, next to his. Intrigued, Joss continued to watch her.

She peered through the front window of the cottage, though he doubted whether she'd see much in the half-light of dusk.

He sighed as it occurred to him that if she was looking for Rose, he'd have to go and tell her she was too late by six months. He didn't enjoy being the bearer of sad news and hated it when women cried.

She vanished round the back of the houses and he wondered what she was doing there. He hurried into the back bedroom, fighting his way quickly into a sweater as he peered out again. She was fumbling on the lintel of the outhouse and as she stepped back her shoulders sagged and she pressed one hand to her mouth.

He hurried down the stairs and opened the front door, waiting for her to come round to this side of the houses again. 'Hi there. Are you looking for Rose King?'

She had been lost in thought and jerked in shock, looking at him warily.

'I'm afraid you're too late. She died six months ago.'

'Yes. I know that. I just . . .'

Even in the fading light Joss could see that her face was white with exhaustion. Suddenly she swayed and before he could get close enough to catch her, she'd crumpled to the ground. 'Damnation!'

The little boy started screaming in terror as Joss bent to pick her up, shouting, 'Don't hit her! Don't hit my mummy!'

He froze, surprised that such a small child would react like that. 'I'm not going to hit her, lad. I'm going to pick her up. She can't lie there in the mud.' He reached out to gather her into his arms just as she started to regain consciousness.

The minute he touched her, she began fighting like a wildcat.

In the end he had to yell, 'Stop it! I was only trying to help you up!'

She let out a muffled sob and sagged against him. At that moment he saw her face clearly for the first time, because her hair had fallen back. There was a huge new bruise on her cheekbone, just below a black eye. He knew the signs only too well. Someone had thumped her – hard.

Drops of moisture spattered his cheeks and he looked up at the dark clouds, which were piling up ominously. Well, the weather people had forecast storms for this evening and, for once, they were right. He couldn't leave these two out here. 'Come inside out of the rain. I'll make you a cup of tea and you can tell me what brought you here.'

She hesitated.

He spoke very gently. 'I was a friend of Rose's and I don't beat women. Or little boys.'

Her pallor was replaced by a flush and she looked ashamed now. It always upset him when victims of domestic abuse looked as if *they* had done something wrong.

It began to rain in earnest and he gestured towards his house again, not daring to touch her. 'Come inside, or you and the boy will be soaked.'

She followed him inside, staying near the door, looking nervous.

'I've got a fire in the back room. This way.'

Again there was a hesitation but the little boy ran forward, calling out, 'It's warm in here, Mummy.'

Joss followed the boy and she hurried after him. 'Yes, it is warm here,' he said to the child. 'Why don't you sit on that little stool in front of the fire? My nephew uses it when he comes to visit. He's five.'

'I'm four. I'm a big boy now.' He watched Joss move across to the cooker and put the kettle on, then turned his head to make sure his mother was still there.

'Tea or coffee?' Joss asked. She was leaning against the door frame as if her bones weren't strong enough to hold her up. He didn't try to touch her again. 'You might as well sit down. Look, if it makes you feel safer, I'm an ex-policeman.'

'Can you prove that?'

Outside his work, he'd rarely met anyone quite so suspicious. For answer, he reached up to the highest shelf of the dresser and took down the farewell photo, offering it to her.

She took it from him, staring at the line-up.

Too late, he remembered that he'd been in a wheelchair at the time, hated photos of himself in the damned thing.

'You were invalided out?'

He shrugged. 'Car accident. We were chasing a guy who'd shot a woman. It happens.'

'I hope you caught him.'

'Not then, but later on my colleagues did, yes.' By that time he was in hospital, starting the long journey back to full health and mobility – well, almost full mobility.

'Thank you.' She relaxed visibly, gave him back the photo and went to sit down near her son.

'I'm Joss Atherton, by the way.'

'Libby P—no, I won't use that name any longer. I only left my husband today and I'm not used to giving my maiden name yet.' She frowned, head on one side, mouthing something, as if trying it out. 'How does Libby King sound to you?'

'You must be Rose's granddaughter.'

'You knew my grandmother?'

'We were neighbours for years and she was my landlady.'

'I hadn't seen her since I was twelve.' Her voice thickened. 'I didn't know she was still alive. I was told she'd died a few years ago.'

'She kept an eye on you, though, even had photos of you and the boy. After she died, your stepfather told the lawyer you'd gone overseas and he didn't know where you were.'

She gaped at him. 'Walter knew perfectly well where I was.'

'He swore he didn't.'

'That was . . . even meaner than I'd have expected from him. We didn't part on the best of terms after my mother died, but to do that . . .'

'I long ago came to the conclusion that some people are born nasty. Tea or coffee? And how do you like it?'

'Coffee. White, no sugar, please.'

He sorted that out and handed her the mug. 'Milk all right for the lad?'

'Ned would love a drink of milk. Thank you.'

'And a biscuit?'

She nodded, cradling her mug in her hands for the warmth. She still looked pale and the bruises startled him every time he looked at her.

'I found a letter from the lawyer in the rubbish last night,' she volunteered suddenly. 'My husband – my *ex* now – had kept the information from me.'

'Why did you go round to the back of the cottage?'

'The lawyer said Gran's spare door key was there, hidden on the lintel.'

'Ah. We had some prowlers two days ago and I took it down. I've been a bit preoccupied with something and I forgot to let Henry know.' He walked across to the mantelpiece. 'Here.' He handed her a key.

Then he frowned. 'It'll probably be cold and feel a bit damp. Look, I'll nip next door and switch on the central heating for you. You don't want to take that lad in there till it's warmed up.' He surprised himself with that offer, because lately he hadn't wanted to get involved in other people's troubles. But she looked so vulnerable and that bruise really upset him. 'Won't be a moment.'

When he got back he asked, 'How about I open a tin of soup and make us some cheese and ham toasties to go with it?'

She hesitated, then her eyes went to the boy. 'Thank you. That'd be very kind.'

'Kind' wasn't the way people usually described him these days. 'Grumpy' was the word most commonly used. He wasn't sure he was fit for this Good Samaritan role, or that he even wanted it. Except that she'd fainted. And the boy was only four.

'No trouble.' He busied himself getting the food ready, which avoided the need to make meaningless small talk, at least. He'd never been good at small talk, except with children. They were so honest, so easy to chat with. Still, he couldn't stay completely silent.

He searched his mind for something to say. 'You'll be living next door for a while, will you?'

'Yes. It's a condition of the legacy.'

He knew that, because he was one of the trustees, but they hadn't been sure she'd comply. 'Rose told me.'

Libby let out a mirthless laugh. 'It's a godsend, that house is. I'm twenty-seven and I only have the money in my purse and the things I slung in the car this morning.'

'If I can do anything to help you settle in, don't hesitate to ask.'

Suspicion was back in her face, and her tone was harsh suddenly. 'Why should you help me?'

'Because I was very fond indeed of Rose and she worried about you. It's the last thing I can do for her.'

'Oh. She was . . . a lovely woman. I really missed her, but children are so helpless about where they live and who they see. When my mother remarried, my stepfather cut the connection because Rose had told my mother not to marry him. She was right, too. It wasn't a happy marriage and he got all of Mum's money when she died.'

He let the words sink into silence for a moment or two. 'I'd better tell you that I'm one of the executors for Rose's will. I probably ought to tell you as well that she left me this cottage. I hope you don't mind?'

'It was hers to leave as she pleased and it sounds like you were a good friend to her.'

'She was a good friend to me after the accident.' He hesitated again, wondering whether to get further involved, but he couldn't bear her to make a major mistake. 'You're going to need some help straight away about one thing.'

'What?'

'You need to contact the domestic violence unit and put that beating on record, with photographs.'

She shivered. 'My friend took some photos, but . . . I think Steven might murder me if I use them.'

'We can get you into a refuge if he pursues you and . . .' He broke off. 'No, we can't. There are conditions to your inheritance. You have to live in the house for six months. But I do think it's essential to put this on record.' He indicated her bruises.

She sighed. 'I'll think about it tomorrow.'

He let the matter drop. She was white with exhaustion and the bruises wouldn't go away overnight. He'd planted the seeds and could only hope they'd germinate. He didn't feel very hopeful. He'd seen it all too often. Women too frightened of their abusive husbands to do anything about reporting them to the authorities. He'd ring Henry first thing in the morning and get him on side about this.

He ate slowly and watched her eat, not saying anything else. She kept an eye on her son as she cleared her plate. He could see it was an effort and she was forcing the food down, but it showed she had some common sense and he didn't think it was his imagination that she was gradually getting a little more colour in her face.

The boy made a mess but he too cleared every bit of food put before him. When he spoke to his mother, her expression softened and she replied quietly, at one stage stroking his hair back with one hand and smiling down at him. It was a lovely smile, even from a battered face.

Afterwards, Joss helped Libby carry all the things she'd brought with her from the car into the house next door. He stacked most of them in the front room and took the two suitcases of clothes upstairs. Then he left.

'Don't hesitate to come and ask if you need help.'

'Thank you.'

'Lock the door carefully behind me. Slide the bolts as well, just to be sure.'

She nodded. He could see that she understood what he was saying.

He lay awake worrying about her. The husband could come after her and cause trouble.

He worried too that this woman stirred something inside him, something that had been missing for a while. *Oh, no, you don't!* he told his body. *You've got enough on your plate building a new life.*

He wasn't getting involved with any woman. Relationships didn't fit in with the sort of work Leon could offer him.

He was being stupid, letting his imagination run wild. He'd only met her this evening.

In the morning he felt even more stupid, because he'd dreamt about her, too – and it had been a lovely dream.

Steven Pulford was later than usual getting home from work. The last meeting had taken far longer than expected, after which the CEO had invited them to have a drink with him, to celebrate. You didn't turn down invitations like that, unless you were stupid.

His car sounded a bit rough, needed a service. He'd better get Libby to arrange that soon.

He sighed and wriggled his shoulders as he pulled up at

the house and clicked the remote to open the garage door. It had been a long, tiring day. He hoped Libby wouldn't be awkward tonight. He hadn't meant to hit her so hard, but she'd forced him to chastise her, talking about divorce. No, surely she'd have learnt her lesson.

It wasn't till he was driving into the garage that he realised her car wasn't there. He stiffened. Where was she? She knew he liked her to be ready with his meal when he got back from work. Anyway, she *never* went out on her own in the evenings. He didn't allow it.

The kitchen was in chaos, with cupboard doors open and a packet of sugar spilt on the floor.

He guessed at once what had happened. She'd run away.

Well, she wouldn't get far. You needed money for that and he'd made sure she had very little. Unless she'd gone into a women's refuge, and even if she had, he'd find her.

He walked slowly through the house, checking every room. She'd taken a lot of her clothes, and most of Ned's, too.

'You will definitely regret this, Libby,' he muttered.

He swept up the sugar first, annoyed by the crunching sound it made underfoot and the stickiness it left behind. When he started to get his own meal, he found the fridge nearly empty of fresh things. She'd taken those too. No thought of how he'd cope, the selfish cow.

He didn't start thinking clearly until he'd eaten and poured himself a glass of wine. He was never at his best on an empty stomach.

Where would she go that required her to take food with her? Not a refuge, he reasoned.

She had no close family left. He got up to stare down

the street, wondering if any of the neighbours had seen her leave. But he wasn't going to ask them. He'd never encouraged neighbours to poke their noses into his business and he wasn't going to start now.

In the end, he phoned her stepfather. 'Walter, keep this to yourself, but Libby's gone AWOL. She hasn't come to you, has she?'

'No. I'd have sent her straight back if she had. She hasn't stayed in touch since her mother died, not even a Christmas card, and after all I did for her, too. When did she leave?'

'Earlier today.'

'Ungrateful bitch. She should have counted herself lucky to marry a strong man like you.'

'Thank you. Er . . . you can't think of anywhere else she'd go?'

'Not really. That nosey grandmother isn't still alive, or I'd say Rochdale. Was it this year or last that she died?'

'She died at the end of last year.'

'Good riddance to her.'

Walter's voice was slurred and Steven realised he was half-cut. He'd wondered once or twice whether Walter had a drink problem.

Steven would never allow himself to rely on drink, or on anything but himself. He realised the other man was speaking and paid careful attention again.

'It's so long since Joanna and Libby left Rochdale, I doubt she knows anyone there now.'

'Hmm. Well, I'll find her, I promise you.'

'Good luck. If you want her back, that is.'

'Oh, I do. She married me, made promises, and she's

damned well going to stick to them. Besides, she's an excellent housekeeper and I have a son to raise.'

Where to start, Steven wondered as he put the phone down. He didn't want word to get out at work that Libby had left him. He'd have to set about this quietly.

He paused, wine glass raised to his lips. His son. Maybe Ned was the key. Maybe he should consult his lawyer about getting custody. If he got his son back, Libby would follow. He smiled and drank a delicate mouthful of wine, then set to work cleaning up the house.

He could not and would not live in a pigsty.

But he'd find Libby. Oh, yes. And his son.

Chapter Three

In the morning Libby woke early, unable to figure out for a moment where she was. She glanced sideways to see Ned fast asleep beside her, looking utterly angelic, the only time he ever did. She smiled at him, then stared round the bedroom. They were at Grandma Rose's.

Her son didn't usually share her bed, but the poor little love had been nervous of the strange house, so she'd made an exception last night.

'Mummy!' Ned sat up, beaming at her, and she quickly took him to the bathroom.

'You can come here to wee-wee on your own from now on,' she told him. 'Look, I've put your special seat here.'

He nodded, seeming relieved by the sight of the familiar object. He looked round the bathroom, which was old-fashioned. 'Where's the shower?'

'There isn't one. There's only a bath in this house.'

'I like baths. Where's my ducky?'

Oh, damn! She hadn't thought to bring his duck and bath toys. 'He's still in his old home. We'll buy you a new ducky for this house.' As Ned's mouth began to wobble and shift into a square shape, the forerunner to tears, she said hastily, 'Come on. We'll get our breakfast first then have our baths.'

That distracted him. He was always hungry in the mornings. She had completely lost her appetite, but knew she had to keep up her strength, so forced down a bowl of cereal.

She kept an eye on the clock and by half past eight, she was dressing Ned in his outdoor clothes, ready to go and see the lawyer. The sooner the better.

As soon as she went outside, Joss came out to greet her, which suggested he'd been watching out for her. He looked casual and relaxed this morning in jeans, a plain grey top over a blue checked shirt and sneakers. She thought the lock of hair standing upright at the back of his head looked cute.

'Everything all right?' he asked.

'Yes, thank you. I'm just off to see Mr Greaves.'

'And the domestic violence squad? You will go and make a complaint to them, won't you? I've written down their address.' He held out a slip of paper.

She took it reluctantly. 'I'm . . . not sure.' She hated the thought of exposing her body and her troubles to strangers. Besides, she already had some photos and a witness. 'Must go.'

She strapped Ned into his seat, got in and turned the key in the ignition. It clicked and there was a faint ticking noise, then nothing. 'Oh, no!' She tried again but it was no use. Either the battery was dead or something else had gone wrong. She'd been lucky to get here in a twelve-year-old car, really.

But what was she going to do now? Unless things had changed greatly in the village, she couldn't get into Rochdale without a car.

There was a tapping on the side window and she wound it down.

'Pop open the bonnet and I'll see if I can find out what's wrong.'

She did as Joss asked and waited, tapping her fingers on the steering wheel, praying that it was just a loose connection.

He came back, wiping his fingers on a tissue. 'I think your battery has died. It's not as ancient as the car, but it's pretty old.'

For all her efforts to stay calm, tears welled in her eyes and she couldn't think what to do. 'I'm not . . . in the RAC, or anything like that. Steven wouldn't . . . pay for it.'

His voice was gentle. 'What time are you seeing Henry?'

'Nine o'clock.'

He glanced at his watch. 'Why don't I take you into Rochdale and, after you've seen him, we can go and buy you another battery?'

She heard her voice wobble, was ashamed of what a struggle it was not to weep. 'Thank you. I hate to keep bothering you. Only, unless Mr Greaves can advance me some money, I don't have enough to buy a new battery.'

'I'm sure Henry will give you what you need. You are an heiress, after all.'

She managed a watery smile. 'You must think I'm a fool, crying like this.' She blew her nose, determined to stop.

'No. Just a woman driven to desperation. And I'm happy

to help. It's a poor show if neighbours can't look after one another. Oh, and if you need to buy some groceries afterwards, it'll suit me to do the same.'

'Thank you. That'd be great. I'll have to change Ned's booster seat over to your car.'

'I know how to sort that out. I have a five-year-old nephew.' He opened the back door, reached in to unfasten the straps and lifted the little boy out.

To her surprise, Ned went to him willingly and stood beside him watching as he fitted the car seat. When Joss offered to lift him in, Ned smiled and held up his arms.

Libby realised she was sitting there staring at her neighbour like an idiot. But she felt exhausted this morning. She didn't have time to rest, so gave her eyes a final wipe and got out of the car, fumbling to put the key in to lock the doors. No fancy remotes to lock and unlock her old car.

'Just a minute.' Joss turned to her. 'I need to get your battery out. We have to make sure we get the right sort of replacement.'

His car wasn't a luxury model like Steven's Mercedes, but the seat was comfortable and she leant back against it gratefully, happy to let someone else do the driving.

The journey into Rochdale went smoothly. Once again Joss didn't say much, and she didn't feel like making conversation, either. She listened to Ned chatting to Boo-Bear about what they were passing and that happy little sound soothed something inside her. Her son was coping with the changes more easily than she'd expected. It was she who was struggling to keep her emotions under control.

She'd married expecting to stay married for life. Divorce was such an admission of failure.

She felt as if she'd reached rock bottom. Surely things would improve from now on. She had to believe that.

When they stopped in the parking area beside the lawyer's rooms, which were in a large old house that had been converted, Joss said abruptly, 'As a trustee of your grandmother's will, I need to have a quick word with Henry about something. Do you mind if I nip in to see him first? It won't take more than a couple of minutes. Then I can go to the bank while you're speaking to him.'

'Fine by me.'

He opened the door to the lawyer's rooms with a cheerful, 'Hi, Mrs Hockton. This is Rose's granddaughter, Libby.'

The receptionist gaped at Libby's bruised face, but quickly summoned up a professional smile. 'Welcome to Rochdale, Mrs Pulford.'

'Thank you. I'll be using my maiden name again from now onwards, though. Ms King.'

'I'll remember in future. Your grandmother would have liked that.'

'I need to see Henry first, Mrs H,' Joss said.

'I'll check if he's ready.' She vanished for a minute, then came back smiling. 'Go straight through.'

As he walked along to Henry's office, Joss smiled as he heard her speak to Libby about finding some toys for Ned to play with. Very capable woman, Helen Hockton. He tapped on the door. 'I need a quick word about Rose's granddaughter before you speak to her.'

'Is there a problem?'

'*She* has problems. Mostly to do with her husband, who's beaten her quite badly. She has a bruised face and I think probably a cracked rib or two from the way she's wincing when she moves. She also has no money whatsoever and a very elderly car that wouldn't start this morning. It needs a new battery. There are provisions in the will for advancing her extra money for necessities. I think we should exercise them.'

Henry studied him for a moment and Joss stared back, puzzled. 'What's the matter? Have I got oil from her car on my nose or something?'

'No. It's just that you sound like the old Joss, the one I knew before the accident, the one who used to care about other people's problems. Welcome back.'

That was the trouble with people who'd known you as a boy, Joss thought. They felt they could say anything they liked to you. 'This isn't about me, Henry; it's about Libby. There's one other thing to sort out, but it's probably the most important of all, and that's to persuade her to go to the domestic violence unit *today*. I'll take her after she's finished with you.'

'Is it that bad?'

'Yes. They need to document her injuries and claims while the bruising still shows. The boy has some bruises too. Apparently the father kicked him out of the way. She's reluctant and embarrassed. I do understand that it's a hard thing to do, but nonetheless . . .'

Henry scowled. 'I can't stand men who beat women.

As for kicking a small child, well, there aren't words bad enough for that.'

'I agree. Libby says her neighbour overheard the quarrel and took some photos the next day, but she needs evidence that's incontrovertible. Neighbours can be got at by abusive men; the people in the local unit can't.'

'Ask Mrs H to ring up and make an appointment. You can drive Libby there after you've been to the bank. I'll make sure she agrees to do it. As your fellow trustee, I'll countersign a release form for the money.' He swung round and opened a drawer in his filing cabinet to take out some papers. 'Oh, and we'd better get her a debit card. With limits, of course.'

'I can get all that started.'

'I'll leave the practical details of settling her at the cottage in your hands, but keep me up to date with where you're at. I trust your judgement absolutely.'

Joss left the office feeling satisfied that between them he and Henry would do what was necessary. But after he'd got Libby settled, he'd get on with his own life. He wasn't getting involved in her everyday life long-term.

He sighed. His divorce had been bitter and he'd decided not to get too deeply involved with anyone from now on. It hurt to see your marriage going down the tube and he'd hated the quarrels.

From now on, he wasn't looking for anything permanent, because he couldn't face all the legal hassles you got if things went wrong.

Anyway, apart from the fact that he respected Libby too much to offer her a casual fling, she was still married.

Even when she got her divorce, her violent husband had probably put her off men for life, or at least for a few years.

No, he'd keep things simple and friendly, be a good neighbour but nothing more.

She was sitting in the waiting room, leaning against the back of the chair with her eyes closed, as she had done in the car. She looked exhausted even after a night's sleep. The bruising stood out starkly, a livid stain across her fair skin. He exchanged quick, concerned glances with Mrs Hockton.

'Libby.' When she didn't move, he knelt beside her and repeated her name more loudly, putting one hand gently on her arm.

She jerked in shock. 'What? Oh, sorry. I must have drifted off. That's so unlike me.'

'Long drives are tiring for everyone, and it's been a very stressful time for you. Look, I'll go and attend to my business then come back and collect you. And please . . . do what Henry advises. He's a very astute man.'

She watched Joss leave before turning to the receptionist.

Mrs Hockton smiled across at her. 'Shall I take you through to Mr Greaves now, Ms King?'

'Yes, please. Come on, Ned. Bring Boo-Bear with you.'

Mr Greaves wasn't the fatherly figure she'd expected. He might have silver hair, but he was tall and as elegant as his receptionist. That well-tailored suit must have cost a fortune. Had her down-to-earth grandma really had a lawyer like this?

He came across to her, smiling warmly and offering his hand. 'Libby, I'm so pleased to meet you at last. You don't mind if I call you Libby? Only it's how I think of you from talking to your grandmother.'

She shook his hand and he kept hold of hers for a minute, studying her bruised face openly.

She tried to distract him. 'This is my son, Ned.'

'Hello, Ned.' He gave the little boy a quick glance, turned back to Libby and asked bluntly, 'How did you get those bruises?'

She thought of lying, then told herself not to be stupid. 'My husband hit me.'

'Has he done that often?'

'No, but . . .' She hesitated.

'But?' he prompted.

'But he's been abusive in other ways, verbally and in restricting my life. I'm never going back to him.'

'Do you want my help getting a divorce? Or is it too soon to think of that?'

'Not too soon at all. Please make a start. I should have left him years ago.'

'We'll need another meeting to discuss the details of the divorce.'

'Yes, please. I shall want custody of my son and I think it'd be fair for me to get a share of the family property, don't you? I won't be greedy.'

'Of course. That's all straightforward enough. I can set things in motion and tell your husband formally that you're divorcing him. I'll ask him to stay away from you and, if necessary, we can take out an injunction to make sure he does so.' He indicated her bruises. 'Photos of those will make it pretty obvious why it's essential, if he objects.'

'He'll find a way round it. Steven can be very tenacious when it comes to getting his own way. The trouble is, if you write to him formally, he'll know where I am. Could we wait a little to start things off, do you think, till I've got settled in here?'

'Very well. But there are other things that need doing straight away. Have you seen a doctor about your injuries?'

'No.' She explained about Mary and the photographs.

'Good thing to do, but we need more than that.'

'Why? Mary's prepared to act as a witness.'

'Men like your husband can . . . upset witnesses. We need to be very careful how we gather evidence if you're to keep custody of your son.'

The mere thought of handing Ned over to his father made her feel physically sick.

'Joss mentioned the domestic violence unit to you, I believe.'

'Yes, but . . . well, that seems rather extreme, don't you think?'

'It's what they're there for. Let him take you to see them. You really can't afford to miss a trick.'

She felt humiliated by the mere thought of facing strangers with her injuries when she was still trying to come to terms with the fact that Steven had beaten her, but she wasn't stupid. 'I suppose I'd better see them. I'll do anything to stop Steven getting custody of my son. He hit Ned as well as me, you know.'

'Yes. Joss told me. It's despicable to hit a little child. Would you mind showing me?'

She called her son over and ignored his outraged

squirming to pull down his trousers and show the bruises on his thigh and buttock.

'I have a grandson of a similar age. If anyone hurt him like that, I'd not be responsible for my actions.' Mr Greaves' expression was grim as he added, 'Joss has offered to take you to the unit after you leave here. He used to work there, so he can help you through the various procedures. I'd go with you myself, but I have another appointment.'

She sighed. 'I have so much else to do today. Couldn't we go tomorrow?'

'Sorry, but it's rather important that you do this immediately.'

'I couldn't ask Joss to do that. I hardly know him.'

Mr Greaves lowered his voice. 'Let him help you. That'll help him, too. He misses his job still. He was injured and took early retirement.'

'Yes, he told me.'

'There's just one other thing we need to attend to today. Do you have formal proof of your identity? You look very like your mother as a young woman, so *I* don't doubt who you are, but this has to be done properly. A passport would be best.'

'Do I really look so much like my mother?'

'Yes. I was madly in love with her at one time, but she never even looked at me.' He smiled reminiscently.

'I don't have access to my passport. I do have one, because we went on holiday to Ibiza last year, but Steven keeps it in his safe at work.' Libby fumbled in her bag. It took her a couple of goes to find her driving licence in the general chaos. She'd stuffed things into the bag willy-nilly yesterday.

'We'll get the passport back for you later.' Mr Greaves took the driving licence from her, made a note of its number and handed it back. 'I've authorised Joss to withdraw some money for you and help you open a bank account. You should apply for a debit card while you're at it. Money will be paid into the account every month for your keep, and if you have any other problems like needing a new battery, the trust will pay extra for that.'

Relief washed through her in a great tidal wave. 'Thank you.'

'We're doing what Rose asked. She knew exactly how she wanted to manage this.'

'I wish I'd seen her again.'

'At least she left you a letter.' He picked up a large, bulky envelope. 'She asked that you read it when you're on your own.'

Libby fingered the letter, which had only her first name on it. She remembered that handwriting, jagged strokes, leaning to the right and always black ink. She wanted to hold it to her cheek, because it was as near as she could get to cuddling her grandmother again.

Mr Greaves waited till she looked up. 'Rose loved receiving your Christmas letters. She was thinking about contacting you directly when she fell ill. She was ill for several months, went downhill very rapidly and didn't want you to see her like that. Cancer can be a cruel way to go.'

'I could have helped her if I'd known.'

'You were still with your husband and, as far as we could tell, were making no attempt to leave him.'

'I was afraid they'd take Ned away from me, and I

thought I could cope, because Steven worked very long hours so I didn't have to spend a lot of time with him. But when he hit me, I reached my absolute limit.'

He nodded, then glanced quickly at his wristwatch. 'I'm afraid I have to see my next client shortly. You'll be all right with Joss. You can trust him with anything.'

'Yes, of course. Thank you for seeing me so quickly. Come along, Ned. Say goodbye to Mr Greaves.'

The two of them walked back to Reception, but Joss wasn't there, and she immediately felt nervous. Steven had had time to follow them now and he did know the lawyer's address. But there was nothing she could do. She didn't even have a car that worked.

She took Ned to the toilet then sat down to wait, annoyed with herself for being such a wimp. Once all this was sorted out, she mustn't become dependent on anyone else.

Not even a kind neighbour like Joss.

Emily Mattison walked round the front area of the old pub on the edge of the moors. When she'd inherited The Drover's Hope the previous year, it had been in a tumbledown condition, but she and her partner Chad had decided to convert it into an antiques centre.

Before his accident, Chad had run a prestigious antiques gallery in London, and antiques had always been her hobby, so they'd both enjoyed setting up the antiques centre.

This place would be very different from Chad's London gallery. They weren't intending to cater to the rich so much as to people who loved beautiful old things. They hoped the centre would attract visitors to the district, bringing a few more much-needed jobs to a depressed area. Of course, they'd offer things online as well. And buy things as well as selling them.

They were both in their later middle age, comfortable, and they wanted to do something they found enjoyable.

The rear room, a former barn with parts of the structure dating back to medieval times, was now a hall in which they would rent out space to other dealers.

They were putting a small coffee shop in the wide corridor that led to the barn, using an old storeroom with a wall knocked out for the prep and cooking area. Surely anyone driving past would stay longer if refreshments were on offer? The café would be run by one of Emily's friends.

Now they were almost ready to open the centre. Most of the stalls in the Old Barn had been rented quickly and it was looking very attractive. It was almost as if the complex of old buildings had been designed to fit their needs.

It had been a long time since Emily had felt so positive about life. She'd thought herself too old to find love again, but she and Chad had settled in happily together.

Hearing footsteps behind her, she turned, happy to see him come out of the office. 'I'm thrilled with the way it's all coming together. Aren't you?'

He came to lace his fingers in hers. 'Delighted. The stall holders understand that we're not dealing in tat or modern stuff, however pretty, only quality items that are at least fifty years old. This isn't a car boot sale.'

She hid a smile. He'd told her this several times already. He had very high standards. 'Did I hear the phone ring?'

'Yes. It was the removalists. The last of my stock will

arrive from London tomorrow, after which my London gallery can be handed over to the new owner.'

'Has Toby got back?'

'Not yet.'

Emily looked at her watch. 'It's the first time he's been so far on his own. I so hope he's all right.'

'He wanted to try going into Rochdale independently. He's perfectly capable of asking people for help, and he also has his mobile phone, so he can ring us if necessary. He's surprisingly good with that gadget.'

'I know, but still . . .'

'You're over-mothering him again. He may have Down syndrome, but he's at the higher achiever end of the scale. There's enough routine here for him to feel safe and yet he can learn new things. The people at Community Services are over the moon with the accommodation we've provided. They were on the phone earlier. They're bringing a young woman to see us tomorrow as a possible tenant for the second flat.'

'It'll be good for Toby to have someone to fill Nicky's empty flat. He misses her. The two of them were good friends.

'We knew that heart condition meant she could die at any time. At least she had the pleasure of a few months living here.'

They'd converted the old stables at the rear of what had once been the oldest part of the inn, setting up a trio of studio flats for intellectually challenged young men and women. It had a communal socialising area, and was only for people who were capable of living on their own with some regular help and supervision from a social worker.

This was Emily and Chad's way of saying thank you to fate for letting them escape from a difficult situation.

When they heard a bus chug up the hill and stop outside, Emily hurried across to the front window. 'Toby's back. Thank goodness.'

'I told you he'd be all right.' Chad came to put his arm round her and they waited for their tenant to come inside and report his return.

'Everything go all right?' Chad asked him casually.

Toby beamed at them. 'Yes. I walked round the market on my own and bought this.' He held out a carved wooden figure of a woman.

It was a fairly crude carving, but when Chad took it from him, he whistled softly. 'It's probably seventeenth century. How did you know it would be a good thing to buy, Toby?'

The young man shrugged. 'She felt old and . . . lonely. I like her.'

When he'd gone round to his flat at the back, Chad looked at Emily. 'I'm beginning to think that young man is an idiot savant about antiques. When he bought that little painting last month, he said something similar: he thought it looked old and he liked it. At this rate, his flat is going to be full of valuable antiques.'

'How valuable are they?'

'That little painting would sell for a couple of thousand pounds.'

'Wow!'

'And the figure . . . several hundred, I think, but I'd need to do some research about recent sales to be sure.'

'Either this place or the people living here seem to provide us with surprises at regular intervals.'

'I've had a lot of surprises since I met you, not least what your job used to be. You don't look at all like someone working in the security field. It must have made for an interesting life.'

He put his arm round her waist and they went upstairs to the spacious new flat they'd had built out of the former inn's bedrooms. They'd also put in a pair of guest bedrooms. The previous owners' flat downstairs was now the office suite and contained a strong room for the centre's more valuable acquisitions.

It was all so normal and peaceful these days. She hoped it would stay that way.

Chapter Four

Libby didn't open her grandmother's letter as she sat waiting, but she did take the big envelope out, just to touch it. It was quite bulky and must contain more than just a letter.

When Joss came back to the lawyer's rooms, Libby felt better as soon as she saw him. He seemed to bring in with him a swirl of cool air, freshened up by last night's rain. He looked rosy-cheeked, sane and ready to take on the world.

Now, where did the emphasis on 'sane' come from, she wondered. Steven wasn't insane, just . . . a bit warped. No, a lot warped. Why did she keep denying that in her own mind? Because he was Ned's father? Probably. She hated to think her son might grow up like that.

'All finished?' Joss asked.

She realised she'd been staring into space and nodded quickly.

'I thought I'd take you to the Domestic Violence Unit first, get it over with. Then we'll do our shopping.'

'I suppose so.'

'I know it's embarrassing, but it's to keep you and Ned safe.'

'Embarrassing! It's totally *humiliating*.' She snapped her mouth shut before she said something worse. After all, he was only trying to help her.

Without a word, he set off, making no more attempts to start up a conversation. She should have apologised, but she couldn't think about anything except what was going to happen to her at this unit.

A few minutes later he pulled up in front of a detached house in the suburbs. 'This is it.'

Libby was surprised at how normal the place looked. She didn't know what to say, so she made a non-committal noise and unbuckled her seat belt. By the time she got out, Joss was releasing Ned.

She stood back, waiting as he locked the car. To her surprise Joss put his arm round her shoulders and gave her a quick hug. She'd thought he was annoyed with her for being ungrateful, and hadn't expected this unspoken gesture of support. Tears came into her eyes. 'Sorry for being . . . grumpy.'

He fumbled in his pocket and shoved a bunch of tissues into her hand. 'You're bound to be emotional, but they're really good people here and they do understand what you're going through and feeling.'

She blew her nose hard and straightened her spine, determined not to weep on him again. She couldn't help wincing, though, as pain stabbed through her, but she ignored that and managed to speak fairly normally. 'Mr Greaves said you used to work here.'

'For a time. Some cops don't like it, but I considered it a very worthwhile experience. Frustrating, though, when a woman refuses to press charges against her husband and goes back to him. You know she'll meet with further abuse. A leopard doesn't change his spots easily.' He held the front door open for them.

'I won't do that.'

He stopped to look at her. 'No. I don't think you will.'

The hall had a reception desk to one side, with a young woman sitting behind it. 'Hi, Joss. Haven't seen you for ages. How's the leg?'

'A lot better, thanks.'

'We were sorry you had to leave the force.'

'I'm not a desk person.'

She grinned. 'No. We figured that out when you worked here.' She turned to Libby. 'Welcome to Rossholme. You must be Ms King.'

'Yes, I am.'

'And who's this?' She waved to Ned.

'My son, Ned.'

'All right if I offer him a S-W-E-E-T-I-E?'

'Yes.'

Ned took the little orange sweet and popped it in his mouth, but stayed pressed against his mother. He seemed overwhelmed by his surroundings and perhaps he'd picked up on his mother's tension.

'Ms King, why don't I take you through to Carina, who'll be looking after you? Joss, do you want to come back later?'

'I'll hang around, as long as I'm not in the way. If Ned gets restless after the doctor's checked him out, I can take him for a walk round the garden or we can play with the toys. Would that be all right with you, Libby?'

'If he'll go with you.'

'Kids usually do.'

The receptionist watched him go with a wistful look on her face, as if she fancied him. 'Joss is brilliant with kids, you know. He loves them and they love him.'

Carina was a slim, elegant woman, with coffee-coloured skin, lightly silvered hair and the most beautiful dark eyes. Libby felt instantly at ease with her.

Talking about what had happened upset her, though, especially when she had to show them Ned's bruises and he played up, so that she had to hold him still for the photos.

She tried to accept the doctor's examination of her own body stoically. It was necessary; she knew it was. But she hated being exposed and photographed, couldn't hold back the tears of utter humiliation, which upset Ned again.

She thought that would be it, but Carina took her back to the cosy little sitting room, dropping Ned off with Joss on the way. 'Just a few more minutes then you're clear for today, Libby.'

She gestured to a chair, sitting sideways to it. 'You'd really benefit from counselling about this.'

She had enough on her plate. 'I'll be fine now that I'm away from Steven.'

'You'd probably recover more quickly if you came here for counselling, and since you're new in the town, if you joined a group, you might also make some friends.' She held up one hand to stop Libby's protest. 'Could you trust me enough to give it a try? Just one visit? Oh, and we have childcare here, so Ned will make friends too.'

That made another refusal die on Libby's lips. Steven hadn't wanted Ned to go to playgroups or anywhere with other children, who were, he insisted, walking germ carriers.

Libby hadn't had any experience of counselling, but she didn't like the idea of someone poking around in her emotions. Her words came out more sharply than she'd intended. 'Why do I feel as if I'm being steamrollered?'

'Oh, dear, I didn't mean to make you feel like that. I do apologise. But you've been steamrollered for a few years, from what you tell me, and that sort of conditioning doesn't just go away. Please try one session, Libby.'

'Who does the counselling?'

'I do, if you're comfy with me. Or we have others we can call in. Your choice.'

There was something about the warmth in those dark eyes that pushed Libby the rest of the way into changing her mind. 'Oh, very well. I'll try it once, but I'm not promising anything after that, mind.'

'I'm so pleased.'

When they went out, Libby made an appointment for the following week, before walking along to the play room. Joss and Ned both looked to be enjoying themselves, so she waited in the doorway, not interrupting.

When Joss turned round, he studied her face, nodding. 'Carina's great, isn't she?'

'Yes.'

He turned to Ned. 'Remember I said we had to pick up the toys afterwards?'

Ned nodded, helping to throw them into baskets, before running across to grab his mother's hand. 'I built a tower with wooden bricks. It was so high.' He held up one hand above his head. 'But it all fell down.'

'You can build another tower next time you come here.' Joss tossed the last wooden brick into the basket and joined them. 'Ready to go?'

'Yes.' Libby fell in beside him. 'Where to now?'

'Lunch, I think.'

'I'm not really hungry. Couldn't we just get the shopping done?'

'I'm afraid I'm ravenous. You can watch me eat, if you don't want anything, or I can treat you and Ned to a sandwich. Last of the big spenders, me.'

'Oh. All right.'

'I know a great little café near a big supermarket. We'll go to the bank after we've eaten, or we can go tomorrow, if you prefer. We have to buy our groceries and get your new battery, after which you can go home and settle in.'

She was tired now. She'd be wiped out by the time they'd finished. But she'd be financially independent and have a car that worked, in case she had to flee again. She'd be stupid not to make the effort. 'We'll go to the bank as well today, if you don't mind.'

People were still steamrollering her, she thought as she got into the car. But not in a bad way. She was suddenly hungry, for the first time in days, and had no doubt Ned was too.

She glanced sideways at Joss. He was better looking than she'd realised last night, and very attractive to women to judge by the receptionist's reaction to him. At the moment he was favouring one leg slightly, as if it was aching.

How must it be to be fit and healthy, then suddenly be injured and left with a permanent weakness?

As bad as it felt to have your willpower stripped bit by bit, and the bars of an invisible prison erected around you before you'd fully realised what was going on?

At least Joss had known that what had happened was by accident, though that didn't mean his enforced change in lifestyle would have been easy.

But she hadn't understood till too late what Steven was doing. It had been a carefully calculated way of controlling her. And he'd succeeded for more years than she cared to think.

She was going to get over it, though. She was. Whatever it took.

Steven took out the bag of rubbish from the kitchen, even though it was only half-full, because it was beginning to smell. He dumped it in the bin and turned to go back into the house, but something wasn't right, so he turned back.

He lifted the new bag of rubbish out of the bin again, and stared at the crumpled, empty bin liner lying on top of a full bag of rubbish.

Why would Libby throw away an empty bin liner? She wasn't a wasteful woman.

He went back into the kitchen, put on a pair of rubber gloves and a face mask from the box he kept for dirty jobs. Picking up the empty rubbish bag, he shook it out.

Ah. It had split. He must not have taken it out before he went off to work yesterday morning. Well, it had been a hell of a week, and he'd been angry at the second letter from the lawyer in Rochdale.

He was about to throw the bin liner away again when he remembered that he'd thrown the letter from the lawyer into the rubbish that last evening. Had she seen it? Had that been the trigger for her leaving? It couldn't have been the beating, because he hadn't laid a finger on her before. And he wouldn't again.

He was angry at himself for losing control. That hadn't happened for years. Wouldn't again. His father had helped him overcome early problems with his temper, and he was grateful for that, even though it had been a painful series of lessons at the time.

What was the damned lawyer's name? He racked his brain, but couldn't remember. How stupid he'd been to throw away those letters. Only they'd made him angry, because they had the potential to disrupt his carefully planned life. He should have kept them at work, or in his safe at home. Just in case.

Had Libby seen the letter?

He stared down at the open dustbin, his nose wrinkling in disgust at the smell. But it was no use.

He had to find out whether the letter was still there. Because if it wasn't, she'd definitely seen it and that was probably why she'd run away. The grandmother hadn't left her a lot of money, but it was enough to help her get away.

She could be anywhere by now. In a women's refuge, as had been his original guess, or in Rochdale, where her grandmother had lived and where this lawyer was. She'd have to go there first, wouldn't she, to claim the inheritance?

He smiled. The pieces were coming together, as they always did.

The dustmen were due tomorrow, so he had to check the rubbish tonight. Almost itching with disgust, he methodically spread other bin liners on the garage floor and tipped out the rubbish.

Item by item he picked through the stinking heap. The smell of it after only two or three days made him retch, but he persevered, because he had to know.

He found the other letter he'd thrown away at the same time and set it aside. But he didn't find the one from the lawyer, not even the envelope.

He stood up, staring down at the stinking mess. The letter should be here, with the other one. Only it wasn't. Which meant she'd definitely found it.

He picked up the other letter. She hadn't found this one, though, had she? How stupid not to have checked everything! Well, she was stupid, compared to him. Women just didn't think logically. Which was why they needed a man to look after them.

The letter was from the adoption agency. He recognised

their acronym. They'd written once before, asking if Mrs Elizabeth Pulford was the former Elizabeth King from Rochdale. He'd tossed that one away. No need to stir up Libby's past.

Methodically he packed the rubbish back into the bin liner and set the dustbin ready to take out in the morning for the weekly rubbish collection. Then he picked up the other letter, stained and dirty though it was.

When he went inside, he sprayed it with disinfectant. He kept the rubber gloves on, though, until he'd brought a document protector from his study and slipped the letter inside. Only then did he take off the gloves and mask, and wash his hands thoroughly.

He read the letter. They wanted to know if she had received their previous letter. Would she kindly reply to this one so that they could set their records straight? If she refused all contact with her birth mother, she would hear nothing more from the agency, but they would be grateful if she'd make her wishes known.

Irresponsible fools, upsetting families. He'd had good parents who'd given him a sound education and brought him up to recognise the importance of tidiness and doing things the *right* way. His parents were dead now and he hadn't kept in touch with any of his relatives. Well, they'd never liked him and he thought them fools.

He was grateful to his parents for the careful upbringing and sound education, though. Always would be. He intended to do the same for his own son.

He left the letter in its transparent cover lying on the

draining board. He'd think about it carefully. No use rushing to act.

And he'd need to remember the lawyer's name. It wasn't like him to forget. If he didn't remember, he'd phone every lawyer in Rochdale, if necessary, till he found the one who'd contacted his wife.

He went to bed at his usual time, not having taken in what had been playing on the TV, because he had a lot to think about. The TV was just a noise, something to fill the silent house.

He did not, he decided, like living alone. Not that he wanted to live in a tribe. No way. One wife and one child suited him perfectly. He'd had a vasectomy so that he couldn't have any more children. Hadn't told Libby. That was his decision, not hers.

He'd get her back, however long it took. Oh, yes.

Ned sat in the café, wide-eyed, taking it all in.

Joss watched him, then looked at Libby. 'Hasn't he eaten out before?'

'Not during the past year. Steven preferred to eat at home and I couldn't afford to eat lunch in cafés when we were out shopping.'

'I thought your husband had a good job.'

'He has. A very good job. He has a luxury car, expensive suits, anything he wants.'

Joss shook his head very slightly, disapproval etched on his face, but he made no further comment. When he turned back to the little boy, his expression changed completely, becoming warm and caring.

The receptionist was right. He really loves children, Libby thought. For all his cat-that-walks-alone act with adults, Joss could win children's confidence easily. She'd never seen Ned take to a stranger like this before. He usually stayed close to her when they were out.

Joss showed him the menu. 'This tells you what there is to eat, Ned. You can choose what you want. Shall I read it to you?'

Ned nodded, listened intently as Joss read out the three items that were specifically for children.

'Tell Joss which you want, darling,' she prompted.

'Cheesy chips, please.'

Joss gave her a wry glance. 'Not the most healthy option. Do you mind?'

'No. I give him healthy food the rest of the time. If he wants chips and melted cheese once in a while, he can have them.'

'Does he know what they are?'

'Yes. I've made them for him at home once or twice.' When she'd needed comfort food, needed to rebel against Steven's ferociously healthy meals. Childish, but it had made her feel a bit better. And Ned had learnt not to tell his father anything which she said was a secret.

'What would you like to eat, Libby?'

She realised Joss wasn't the only one who was ravenous. 'A burger, chips and a garden salad, please.'

'That's what I'm having. Pot of tea for us and an orange juice for Ned?' At her nod, he went to put in the order.

When he came back, he pulled an envelope out of his

pocket, opening it to show a wad of notes, but shielding that from the other customers. 'Henry asked me to get some money out of the bank for you, and when we go to the bank to sign the papers, you can put in an application for a debit card.'

'Thank you.' She put the envelope into her handbag, feeling so much better for having it.

'Are you sure it's not too much to do after yesterday? This is a pretty full-on day. We could go to the bank tomorrow.'

'I'll be fine. Oh, I forgot to bring Ned's pushchair.'

'I can carry him if he gets tired.'

She didn't protest, because at the moment her chest hurt too much to carry her son. 'Thanks. I'm very keen to get my *own* finances sorted out.' It was such a strong need, she almost ached with it.

'Um . . . I forgot to ask Mr Greaves, but maybe you know. Do the payments I get during the six months I have to live in the house come out of the bequest money?'

'No. The living allowance is extra. And there may be a little more than the £20,000 at the end. It depends how things go with the rest of the bequests.'

'Did Grandma Rose leave many bequests?'

'I'm not at liberty to talk about the others, just as they know nothing about you.'

'OK.'

When the food came, her mouth watered, and apart from keeping an eye on Ned and offering him a few mouthfuls of her salad, she ate steadily. It felt as if she was filling up a huge empty hole. 'Paint me a cavernous waste,' she murmured without thinking.

'T. S. Eliot.'

She was surprised. 'Do you like poetry?'

'Some of it. What made you quote that one?'

'I was thinking of how hungry I was, so I left out the last word of that line and it seemed to describe how I felt.' She concentrated on the pleasure of eating, finishing before he did. She pushed her plate back a little and sighed with pleasure. 'That was absolutely delicious.'

'Abs'lookly d'licious,' Ned echoed, eating the last three chips covered in melted cheese and licking his fingers before drinking the rest of the orange juice.

She took him to the toilet before they left, teasing him as she wiped grease off his chin and fingers. She could see them both in the mirror above the washbasins. They looked like a normal mother and son. Happy, even. Except for her bruises.

Since she'd checked the tinned and dry goods at her grandmother's house, she knew exactly what she wanted from the supermarket, so that didn't take too long. Afterwards they went to the bank, then to get a car battery.

By the time they returned to Top o' the Hill, it was nearly teatime. The skies had cleared and the view from the road up the cleft was stunning.

She stared out of the car window in delight. 'The scenery is like something from *Last of the Summer Wine*. I love that programme.'

'So do I. The villages where it was filmed aren't far away from here.'

'Really? I must go and visit them once we've settled in.'

'It's playing on TV again. They often repeat it. I'm especially fond of Nora Batty.'

Libby chuckled. 'She has some brilliant lines, doesn't she?'

And they were off, comparing favourite incidents from the series as he negotiated the final bends and the narrow streets of the village.

Joss helped her carry in the bags of shopping. 'If you give me your car key, I'll put your new battery in.'

'I could do it myself. Though probably not as quickly as you.'

'I don't mind doing it.'

So she found the keys and went out to watch him, Ned trailing along behind her. She had to learn to look after herself, so she watched carefully. Yes, she could have done it. 'Thank you.'

Joss sat in the driving seat and turned on the ignition. The car started first time, at which he let out a crow of triumph. 'Want me to check your oil and tyres in the morning?'

'Thanks, but I can do that myself. Steven wouldn't have anything to do with my car, nor would he pay for a service, so I did what I could myself.'

'Mean sod.'

'Yes. Very.'

'OK. Then I'll see you tomorrow.'

Ned watched Joss go into his house, the corners of his

mouth turning down. 'I want Joss to stay with us.'

'He can't. He lives next door. You'll see him again tomorrow.'

She diverted his attention by unpacking some of his toys and settling him at one end of the table in the back room. He began to play with them as she unpacked her groceries, telling his trio of tiny stuffed animals that they were in a new house now and had to be very good and not make a mess.

Libby had already examined the fridge. It had been cleaned out and the door left partly open, so it didn't need anything but a quick wipe of the shelves. The fridge was elderly, but it seemed to function well enough and soon grew cold.

There was a small freezer in the scullery, more than big enough to hold the few packets of frozen food she'd bought.

When she'd finished unpacking, she looked round in satisfaction. This terraced cottage might be no more than twelve feet wide, but it felt like a palace to her.

She hadn't gone upstairs to the third floor yet. Joss had told her there was only a jumble of old furniture up there, but she wanted to check it out before dusk fell. Check it out and gaze out at the view. She felt she could never have enough of the big spaces. Even the sky seemed higher up here at the top of the moors.

'Come on, Ned. We haven't seen the rest of the house. Let's go and have a look.'

Docile as always, he put down his toys and came across to join her.

He was too docile, too afraid of upsetting people. She was looking forward to a few rebellions and tantrums. She'd discuss that with Carina. Helping her son was a better reason for getting counselling than indulging herself.

Chapter Five

Mrs Barley from Social Services turned up at the antiques centre the following day, as agreed, to introduce them to another candidate for the units. She was accompanied by a young woman who looked stiff and nervous.

Emily had asked Toby to meet the newcomer with her, hoping this would put her more at ease.

Mrs Barley shook her hand, then Toby's. 'This is Ashley Statham. Ashley, I told you about Toby and Emily.'

The young woman nodded, not offering to shake hands but staring at them as if memorising every detail of their appearance.

Toby smiled at her with his usual open friendliness. 'Shall I show you your flat?'

Ashley took a step backwards, looking at Mrs Barley in panic.

'We'll all go to see the flat,' the social worker said. 'This place looks so different these days, Emily. Perhaps you'd tell Ashley what you've done to the old inn?'

Emily explained briefly about the antiques centre, while Ashley stood near the door and stared round. Then something caught her eye and she moved a little closer to a display.

'This one needs dusting.'

'Ashley likes things to be kept clean, just as Nicky did,' Mrs Barley said. 'That worked so well, and Nicky was so happy here, I wondered if it might happen again if we chose the right person.'

Something made Emily say, 'Perhaps you can help me dust sometimes, Ashley?'

The young woman's face brightened a little. 'I like dusting. I'm very careful. Mummy taught me not to break things. I have her ornaments now and I won't let them get dusty.'

Emily knew Ashley's mother had died recently and there were no other close relatives, which was why the poor young woman had been handed over to Social Services. She had inherited some money, but wasn't thought fit to continue on her own in her old home.

They walked past the coffee shop and through the huge old barn, where a stallholder was setting out her wares. That led them round the back of the inn to the oldest part, which was parallel to the front. Here the flats had been made from converted outhouses.

They went into a new passage which had big windows on the right, looking out towards the moors, and three doors on the left. There was a door with frosted-glass panels across the far end.

'This is my home,' Toby said proudly, opening the first door with a key hanging on a chain round his neck.

'There are two other flats.' Emily moved forward to unlock both doors. 'If you think you'd like to live here, the middle one would be yours, Ashley.' She pushed the door open.

Slowly, watching them carefully, as if afraid they'd jump on her, Ashley walked inside. The two women stood near the door, letting her go round at her own pace, but Toby went in after her and started explaining about the facilities. In such a small flat, this wasn't really necessary, but Ashley didn't seem to mind.

Emily smiled. Toby was so friendly and assumed others would be the same, and they usually were with him.

Ashley went round opening every single drawer and cupboard to look inside, then she stood by the window and looked out at the internal courtyard. 'Flowers!'

Emily had put a few pots of flowers out to soften the courtyard, which was about twenty yards by thirty and was now paved by square grey setts. 'Do you like flowers?'

'We had flowers at home. I helped Mummy with the garden.'

'You could help me and Toby look after these, if you liked. I'm sure he won't mind.'

Ashley looked at her, then around the flat again, opening every cupboard and drawer for a second time.

After that, she turned to Toby. 'Is your flat clean and tidy?'

'She's a bit obsessive about keeping things clean,' Mrs Barley murmured to Emily. 'Her mother must have spent untold hours training her to look after a house. A good fault for a tenant, don't you think?'

'Indeed, yes.'

'Come and see my home.' Toby led the way next door and again the two women stayed by the entrance.

'It's quite tidy,' Ashley said. 'I'll help you keep it better than this, though.'

'That'd be good,' Toby agreed.

Bless him, Emily thought. He'd do anything for anybody.

'Ashley's brilliant at housework,' Mrs Barley said. 'Oh, and she has her own furniture. Would she be able to bring it?'

'Of course. We can move these things out.'

'We'll send someone to check up on her a couple of times a week at first, and of course someone will take the two of them shopping every week.'

Ashley came out of Toby's flat and he took her into the courtyard. She stood with her head on one side, as if listening, then turned to Mrs Barley. 'This is a good place. I can come and live next to Toby. I can keep everything very clean.'

Mrs Barley turned to look questioningly at Emily.

'I'd be very happy to have you here, Ashley,' she said at once.

The young woman nodded, as if expecting that answer.

'We'll go and choose the things you'll need and arrange for them to be brought over tomorrow, Ashley,' Mrs Barley said.

'I'll have this furniture taken out,' Emily said.

'And I'll help you set up your new home, Ashley,' Mrs Barley said.

'No. I'll arrange everything. I know where things go.'

'Your furniture might not fit in here the same way as it did at home.'

'Mummy and I rearranged things sometimes. I can rearrange things here.'

'I can help you lift the heavy things,' Toby offered.

'If you do it carefully. We mustn't scratch the furniture.'

He beamed at her. 'I'll be careful. I'll be happy to have a friend next door. Come and look at this.'

He took Ashley along to the communal room at the end. 'This is where we can all meet and watch television together.'

She looked round it, eyes narrowing. 'This room needs rearranging. You can help me do that, too, Toby.'

He nodded cheerfully.

'What exactly is Ashley's diagnosis?' Emily asked in a low voice.

'A form of autism. Her mother gave her a lot of attention, so she learnt to interact with people, but she's very rigid about keeping things tidy and arranging them just so. Obsessive even. We don't want her to upset Toby. If you want to employ her in the antiques centre, she'd probably be brilliant at dusting everything.'

'A job that bores me.'

Mrs Barley nodded. 'It's a wonderful thing you're doing, not even charging them rent.'

'Chad and I were both trapped in poor care after accidents, and we know how bad the experience can be,' Emily explained. 'We have enough money to do this as long as the tenants' social benefits cover their living expenses.'

* * *

Libby went up to explore the third floor of her new home. These stairs were slightly narrower than those below, and the stairwell was enclosed in panelling, with a door at the bottom. She opened the door and found herself facing a dark space with six steps then a bend from which some daylight showed. The treads were of bare wood with the stain worn off in the middle, where countless feet must have trodden their way up.

As she and Ned walked up, their footsteps echoed in the stairwell and he laughed, stamping his feet to make more noise.

It was brighter in the big room at the top than anywhere else in the cottage, because of the long walls of windows, from waist to ceiling height, on either side. They had stone uprights between each panel of glass. Mullioned windows, she thought they were called. She'd have to look that up online.

She went to gaze out of the front windows at a view you would have paid millions for elsewhere: rolling moors, with the occasional clump of trees surrounding old-fashioned stone farmhouses, or short rows of workers' cottages. Not many red bricks up here.

She'd explore the area around the village gradually, taking Ned on little outings, she decided. The weather was getting warmer and they were both due to have some fun.

She stood him on a chair, so that he could look out properly, but held him carefully as she pointed out of the window. 'See the cows in that field, Ned? And the white things over there are sheep.'

He soon tired of staring out and got down to explore the big room. As he walked round, he began to look more and more worried. 'It's not tidy. Daddy will shout. We have to clear up quickly.'

Only four and he knew that already.

'Daddy doesn't live here. He won't see it.'

Ned stared at her, as if he couldn't take this in.

'Come on, darling. We need to have our tea, then unpack more of our things.'

On the floor below, she stopped at the doorway of the back bedroom. 'This is your room. We'll make up the bed and you can sleep in here tonight.'

He looked round the room and inched closer to her. 'Don't want to.'

'You'll like it when Boo-Bear is here with you.'

Looking dubious, Ned followed her down the stairs and without telling began to put his things away.

'No need to put them away. Daddy doesn't live with us now.' She wondered how many times she'd have to say that before he believed it. 'We can do what *we* want here.'

But such a big change was a lot for a child of four to understand and Ned still kept listening as if waiting for his father to come home from work.

Not until Ned had fallen asleep in his new bedroom, clutching his bear, did Libby open the letter from her grandmother. She wanted desperately to see what was inside, and yet she was almost afraid to read it.

She opened the envelope to find many sheets of letter

paper, all filled with that angular black handwriting.

The covering note alone had her in tears.

Darling Libby,

I'm writing to say goodbye. It won't be long now before I die and I'll be glad to go. What do people say? Old age isn't for the faint hearted. Neither is cancer, however caring the doctors and nurses.

I do understand you'd have come to see me if you could. And I thank you for the annual letters. They meant a great deal to me and I still reread them occasionally.

I don't know why you stopped writing a few years ago, but no doubt you had a good reason. Perhaps it was to do with your husband.

I confess that when a second Christmas went by without a letter, I paid a private investigator to check what you were doing, to make sure you were well. And I sent him every year to do another check.

It didn't sound as if your husband was making you happy, but at least he gave you a son. I've seen photos of Ned. What a darling!

I hope my legacy helps you with whatever you want for yourself in life and please forgive me for making conditions. Only I didn't want the money to go to your husband.

Last year my private investigator thought you were looking very strained, so I took a chance that you might want to leave Steven if you could.

If you're reading this, then perhaps I was right.

*Whatever you decide to do in the future, I hope
you have a happy life and that your son grows into a
fine young man.*
Much love,
Rose

By the time she finished reading the cover letter, Libby
was in tears. She read it again, sobbing helplessly. Why
hadn't she been braver and left Steven before? She could
have found help. She could have seen Grandma Rose again
before she died.

She didn't start to read her grandmother's unsent replies
to her annual letters, couldn't face them yet.

She'd had so much stress during the past few days
that all she wanted was to curl up in bed and sleep for a
long time.

He had to act, get Libby back, Steven decided the following
evening as he opened the door to a cold, silent house and
realised he'd not thought about what he was going to have
for tea.

Anger rose in him. He could manage perfectly well for
himself, of course he could, but he didn't see why he should
have to. He was a business executive, not a housewife.

He went to the freezer and found a freezer bag neatly
labelled 'Spaghetti Bolognese'. He pulled it out, put it on a
plate and stuck it in the microwave.

How long, he wondered. Shrugging, he put it on for five
minutes.

When the microwave pinged and he pulled it out, half

the cling film cover had melted and yet the food was still frozen in places. Gingerly he pulled off the pieces of cling film and stuck the plate in the microwave again, this time for three minutes.

When he pulled it out, the edges of the food were overcooked and hard in places, but at least it had thawed. He wanted to hurl it at the window, smash everything in sight . . . He stopped and took a deep breath. Of course he wouldn't do that. He mustn't lose control.

He sat down at the kitchen table, unable to face setting the dining-room table, though he despised eating in here. Gingerly he picked his way through the mess on his plate, discarding bits that seemed too hard, eating the rest stoically.

He'd prepare in advance for tomorrow. In the freezer he found a 'roast beef dinner' and put it in the fridge to thaw out overnight.

After he'd cleared up the kitchen, he went into his study and typed a reply to the agency which facilitated reunions of adopted children with their birth parents. He took pleasure in saying Libby never wanted to hear from 'her' birth mother again. He signed it with an indecipherable scrawl and wrote the address on an envelope, trying for the same nearly illegible scrawl.

He knew Libby would have loved to meet her birth mother, because she'd spoken of it wistfully after her adoptive mother died, so doing this made him feel very satisfied. She might not know this woman was trying to find her, but *he* would and one day he'd tell her; one day when she needed pulling into line.

The idea of watching television didn't appeal, so he checked various things online, impatient to put together a plan. He always made a rough plan before beginning a new project, and this was no different. After that, he'd work on a detailed plan.

By chance he came across a website for a divorced fathers' coalition and read avidly. Men were complaining about how unfairly they were treated by the law these days, how everything they'd worked for went to the wife, how hard it was to get custody of or even see their own children. Dozens of maudlin emails on the message boards. Why didn't the fools *do* something about it? He intended to.

But reading the posts on the website had made him more aware of how careful he would need to be. He didn't want to be caught breaking the law. She wasn't worth that.

When he felt thirsty, he glanced at his watch. Nearly bedtime. He bookmarked the site and jotted down some of the ideas it had given him, before switching off the computer.

As he made a final cup of tea, he wondered if he should go to the police and complain about his wife abducting his son.

Yes, he'd certainly consider doing that.

And he still hadn't remembered the name of the lawyer in Rochdale. That situation had to be factored into his plans.

He was looking forward to confronting Libby and bringing her home. He'd teach her not to do such a thing again. Not hit her. No. That was too risky, given the stupid laws they had these days. He shouldn't have allowed himself to lose control the night before she left. As his father had taught him, there was always another way to reach your goal.

A thought occurred to him. He'd probably bruised her – well, he was bound to have done – so he'd be best waiting for the bruises to fade before he took action. A couple of weeks, maybe.

What if she'd made a formal complaint? No, she'd never do that. Even if she considered it, she'd never dare, because she knew he'd punish her.

He went to bed and slept soundly. No child crying in the night, no footsteps going down to the kitchen, just a peaceful house. He did enjoy sleeping alone.

That was the best thing about this whole mess: the peace and quiet in the house.

That evening as they sat chatting about their day, Chad waited for Emily to confide in him and, when she didn't, he raised the matter himself. She'd grieved for long enough. They had to solve the mystery.

'We need to find out about your birth daughter.'

She hesitated, giving him a wry smile. 'You're not the only one nagging me. Leon keeps prodding me too.'

'He still looks out for you, doesn't he?' And she still talked to Leon sometimes when she wouldn't talk to anyone else.

'Yes. But with him, there's often an ulterior motive. I think he might want to use this place occasionally when he has to spirit someone away.'

'I don't mind that, Emily. Leon seems to be as much a friend to you as a former boss, and he helped us when we were in trouble.'

She shuddered at the memory of how she and Chad had both been locked up in a secure facility for dementia patients with the sister in charge taking money to keep them there. Such a strange way to meet a man and fall in love.

She'd no desire to go back to working in national security, though she was proud of having helped prevent some nasty incidents. She saw that Chad was waiting patiently for her to give him her full attention. 'Sorry. My mind wandered just then. Where were we up to?'

'We were discussing looking for your daughter.'

'Yes. It's time, isn't it?'

'So . . . what's the next step?' The daughter who had been stolen from her as a baby was the one darkness in her life and he would do anything to remove this unhappiness, even if it meant pushing her into action.

'The people at Adoption Reunions let me know they'd sent a letter to the one they're pretty sure is my daughter, but there was no reply, so they've written to her again.'

She'd fallen pregnant by mistake and the affair had fizzled out. When she found she was pregnant she'd been glad, but the father hadn't wanted to know.

Her baby had been born nearly a month early in a central European country. The birth hadn't gone well and Emily had been too ill to be fully aware of what was going on. They'd told her the baby had died and shown her a grave.

And that was that. She'd moved on as best she could.

Only it had been a lie. The child had been stolen and sold to an English couple. She'd never have known if Leon hadn't found out about her involvement when he was dealing with another similar case in this scam.

'That's good that they're writing again, isn't it?'

'I don't know. If she doesn't want to be contacted, that's her prerogative, surely?'

When her voice broke on the last word, Chad pulled her into his arms. 'We'll find her for you one way or another, my darling. And we won't stop looking until someone hears from her own lips that she doesn't want to meet you.'

Emily sighed. She didn't dare hope for success, and yet she ached to know that her daughter was all right.

'If AR doesn't get a reply this time, I know a private investigator who's an absolute whiz. He maybe bends a few rules – I never ask for the details of how he obtains his information – but he gets results where no one else can. He's our next step if the regular processes fail. He'll find out where she is.'

She cried then, sobbing in his arms.

'You'll let me do this, won't you, Emily?'

'Yes. I shouldn't, but if I could just know she's all right, even see a photo of her, I'd feel better. I know I would.'

Joss was woken early by the bedside phone ringing. Who the hell was calling at six o'clock in the morning? He picked it up. 'Yeah?'

'Leon here. Is there any chance of you coming down to London for a briefing today? We're starting at noon.'

'I'll come if I can get a flight.'

Leon laughed. 'I guessed you'd say yes, so we've already booked you on the nine o'clock flight from Manchester to Heathrow. Have some photo identification ready to pick up your ticket. A car will meet you at Heathrow and we have a room for you. You can return tomorrow. See you.' He put the phone down without waiting for an answer.

Excitement filled Joss. It was happening. It really was. Something to fill his empty days.

Then he remembered his new neighbour and little Ned. No, they'd be all right now. He'd enjoyed helping them and would continue to do so, but he needed some real purpose in life.

So did Libby, he supposed. Or she would once she'd sorted matters out with that damned husband. He still felt angry at the way the bastard had knocked her around.

And what was he doing standing around thinking of Libby when he needed to get ready?

He was on the road to the airport in half an hour and it wasn't till he was waiting to board his plane that he realised he hadn't left a message for her, as he'd meant to do. Damn!

Henry had kept Rose's phone connected, so after a moment's hesitation, Joss phoned Libby. He didn't want her worrying about whether she'd upset him.

The phone rang five times and he was wondering if she'd gone out, and if so, where she would be at this hour of the morning, when it was picked up.

'Hello?' Her voice was breathless as if she'd run to answer it.

'Joss here. Look, I'm calling to let you know I have to go down to London on business. I'm at Manchester Airport now and I should be back tomorrow.'

'Oh. Well, thanks for letting me know.'

He didn't know what else to say, so trotted out the phrase an American friend was always using. 'Have a great day.' He couldn't help adding, 'And don't overdo things.'

He was annoyed with himself for that. She'd think he was poking his nose in where he shouldn't. She wasn't his responsibility. Only . . . he felt concerned about her. That bruise and the cracked ribs were the mark of a violent man. Her husband might not have hit her before, but he'd certainly not held back this time.

If Pulford came after her . . . Well, Joss would be around most of the time and he'd not let anyone hurt her, or Ned.

He wondered if there was anyone in the village who'd help her if he had to go away again. He should have arranged that straight away, knowing Leon might have work for him.

Maybe Terry at the pub or Pete at the village shop. He'd have a quiet word with them once he got back.

They began calling for people to board the plane, so he picked up his backpack and followed the crowd, excitement rising in him.

Libby was woken by the phone and felt only half-awake as she spoke to Joss. She was pleased that he'd bothered to let her know he'd been called away. She would have worried if she hadn't seen him around for two days.

When she put the phone down, she stretched luxuriantly,

then got up, drawn yet again to the window and the view over the moors. The light held the pink glow of dawn still, something she loved to see.

She wondered if Ned was awake yet. He might be. He'd learnt to stay quietly in bed till she fetched him.

She tiptoed into his room and found him just stirring, rubbing his eyes sleepily and smiling when he saw her.

'Come to the bathroom, darling.'

'Has Daddy gone to work?'

So she said it again, like an affirmation. 'Daddy doesn't live here.'

'But when he comes—'

'He won't come here. There's just you and me living here.'

'And Joss.'

She was surprised by that. 'Yes. But Joss lives next door, not in our house. Do you want to go to the bathroom now?'

'Yes. I'm a big boy. I can go by myself.'

But big boy or not, he took Boo-Bear with him, chattering away to the nearly threadbare furry object he'd loved since he was tiny.

When he'd finished in the bathroom, she supervised the washing of hands. In the kitchen, she gave him a drink of milk while she made a mug of tea. While she waited for the tea to brew, she started to go through the nearest cupboard, putting the things she didn't want or was uncertain about on the table.

She didn't realise what the sound was for a while, then it dawned on her that she was humming, that she felt *happy*.

'Sing "Twinkle", Mummy,' Ned begged.

So for about the millionth time, she sang 'Twinkle, twinkle, little star' and he joined in. He loved singing and had a very tuneful voice for one so young, but Steven hadn't encouraged him to sing. Steven never whistled or hummed. She'd asked him once why not, and he'd said he wasn't a performing monkey, thank you very much, and didn't want to listen to other performing monkeys, either.

When she and Ned went upstairs to wash and get dressed, she decided to clear out the drawers and cupboards in the front bedroom, so that she could put her own things away. She winced when her rib hurt, but didn't let it stop her, because suddenly she was eager to claim the bedroom for herself.

There weren't a lot of drawers, but they were crammed full, as was the wardrobe, and the bed was soon piled with clothes. Had her grandmother never thrown anything away? She hated to go through someone else's clothes, but had no choice, so muttered, 'Sorry, Grandma Rose!' and set to work.

When she came to a bundle of letters tied up with a fancy Christmas ribbon, she realised they were the ones she'd written and couldn't hold back tears. She put them with the letters from her grandmother. To think Rose had kept all the letters and Christmas cards she'd ever sent! They looked rubbed and worn, as if they'd been read many times.

She went back to clearing things out. Some of the clothes weren't worn or dirty, but they were very grandmotherly. She might keep a couple of cardigans and a coat for the cooler weather, but as for the rest, she'd offer them to a charity shop if they were in decent condition, or throw them away otherwise. She went to get rubbish bags and bundled everything that was no use into two of them, stacking the bags on the landing. The decent items she took up to the top floor.

Then she unpacked her own clothes, sighing once she'd hung them up to see so few. She hadn't brought the smart going-out clothes she wore for Steven's work functions, didn't want anything to do with those. He had chosen them and told her which to wear each time. They wouldn't bring back any happy memories.

She stared at her reflection in the wall mirror. Her everyday clothes were cheap and cheerful, hardwearing but definitely not fashion statements. Not particularly flattering, either. Cost had been the main criterion.

She turned her head from one side to the other. She might grow her hair again. She'd always preferred it shoulder length, but Steven had considered short hair smarter and more hygienic.

Maybe she could find a few pieces of clothing for herself in the charity shops – something with a younger look. It might be fun searching.

By late morning she felt ready for a break, so decided to walk into the village with Ned and renew her acquaintance with the village shop. There was still a lot to buy before she'd consider her pantry adequately stocked. They might not have everything she needed, but it was good to support local businesses.

She took the buggy along to bring the shopping back, as

she'd done many times before to save petrol. Ned could ride in the buggy too, if he got tired. It was old-fashioned and bigger than the ones they used today. Steven had refused to spend the money on a fancy new one. He'd hated how much it cost to outfit a new baby. Not as much as even one of his fine suits, she'd guess.

Why had she put up with it?

The village shop was far more modern inside than it used to be when she was a child. It had been extended right to the back of the building and was now a miniature supermarket, which stocked all the basics. Oh, good! She could shop here most of the time.

She started to smile at the woman behind the till, then frowned, recognising her and searching for a name. 'Allie?'

At the same time the woman exclaimed, 'Libby! It *is* you, isn't it? Someone saw a light in Rose's house and we wondered if they'd found the heir.' She came out from behind the counter and gave Libby a hug. 'You haven't changed a bit!'

'I think I've changed a lot. You have too. Wow, you look so capable and efficient.'

Allie grinned. 'I've grown up. Pete and I took over this place from his mum and dad, who've retired to St Anne's. Strange that we've both wound up in Top o' the Hill, isn't it?'

'Amazing.' She glanced round, wondering if Allie's husband was there too.

'Pete's just gone to get supplies. I'll introduce you next time.' She stared at Libby's hand, minus its wedding ring now, but with a band of paler skin where it had been.

Then she looked at Libby's face. 'What happened to you?'

'I . . . tangled with my ex.' It was the best she could manage. 'I've just left him. If a guy comes looking for me, balding and wearing his hair short all over, quite tall, with icy grey eyes, well, you haven't seen me.'

'That bad?'

She nodded. 'But at least I got Ned out of it all. He's four and a half.' She smiled down at her son.

'He's about the same age as my Gabbi. She's at the local playgroup. You must enrol Ned.'

'I'm not sure he'll leave me yet. He's been through some difficult times as well.'

'I'm sorry.' Allie laid one hand on Libby's shoulder, reminding her that her friend had always been a toucher.

Someone came in and stood nearby, obviously waiting for attention.

'Got to go. Fresh fruit and veg down that side, frozen things at the far end. See you when you've finished your shopping.' Allie turned to the newcomer. 'Your special biscuits have arrived, Denise. How many packets do you want today?'

Libby filled her basket and went back to the checkout. 'Look, it's a bit hard for me to get out in the evenings, because I don't have a babysitter, but if you'd like to come round one evening and have a chat over a glass of wine, it'd be nice to catch up.'

'Love it. Early next week, perhaps? A girls' night is exactly what I need.'

Libby turned to leave.

'Just a minute.' Allie came round the counter and pressed

a business card into her hand. 'If you need help, *any* sort of help, my husband's a big guy. You've only to phone. We won't let your ex beat you up again.'

Libby had to swallow hard, and she was so touched by this that tears welled in her eyes.

Allie gave her a wry smile. 'You befriended me when I was a rebellious idiot child. You were such a good friend to me. And this village is still old-fashioned enough that people help one another if there's need. I'll spread the word about your ex.'

Libby could only nod and sniff back a tear. She was so used to managing on her own. 'I've got Joss next door as well. He's been a great help to me.'

'He's a bit reserved, our Mr Atherton, isn't he? He occasionally goes for a drink in the pub with Pete and his friends, but he doesn't say much about himself.'

'He's been very kind to me and Ned. He's really good with kids.'

'Perhaps he's been getting over the accident. He used to limp really badly.' She looked back at the checkout. 'Have to get on.' She turned to her next customer. 'Sorry to keep you waiting. Libby's an old friend who's just moved back to the village. She's Rose King's granddaughter.'

The woman turned to beam and say, 'I hope you'll be happy here.'

The last thing Libby had expected was to see Allie running the shop. She looked so capable . . . and happy. Her voice had softened when she spoke about her husband.

What must it be like to . . . ? Libby cut off that thought.

No use pining over the past. It couldn't be changed. She had to look to the future and build a happy new life for herself and Ned.

If Steven would let her. She couldn't shake the thought that he'd come after them, if only out of spite. He certainly didn't love either of them.

Chapter Six

At Heathrow several people were standing in the big space where passengers were released back into the world. They were carrying big pieces of card with people's names on them.

One, who didn't have a card, stepped forward when he saw Joss. 'Nice to see you again, Cousin Tom.'

Joss wondered if this was taking caution too far, but played along with it. 'Nice to see you too, er, Frank. How's the family?'

'Great. Everyone's looking forward to seeing you again.' He led the way out at a fast pace, and unlocked an old hatchback in great need of a repaint.

Joss tossed his backpack on to the rear seat and got into the front. 'Why the false names?'

'Why not? It's a game we play, though we usually choose names we detest to make a joke of it. Think yourself lucky I didn't call you Aloysius.'

They were soon out of the airport car park and driving along the road.

'Where are we going?' Joss asked.

'A small place near Amersham. You'll get a thorough

briefing and see if the work appeals, and we'll see how you get on with the rest of the team.'

'Sounds like a fun day. What's your real name?'

'You can call me Robert, if you like. I prefer it to Frank.'

Joss didn't challenge him on that. Robert was clearly not his companion's name, either.

The 'small place' was a huge detached house in the country, the sort usually inhabited by millionaires or sports stars. They approached it along a rear service road and parked round the back. Robert led the way inside, keying a number into a hooded pad by the door.

A woman looked up from cooking, a sharp knife in her hand.

Was that knife intentional or accidental? Joss wondered, noting the way she was holding it.

This all seemed rather like a spy movie, except that neither he nor Robert was good looking, and the woman was decidedly middle-aged.

Robert led the way to the front of the house, knocked on a door and, when invited to enter, gestured to Joss to go in. 'See you later.'

Leon was waiting inside the room, looking as immaculately neat as always. The Police Superintendent who had been his own former boss had had enormous respect for Leon. As did Joss.

'Sit down, Joss. Nice to see you walking properly again. How was the flight?'

'Short and sweet.'

'It didn't trouble you to leave home at short notice?'

'No. Though I have a new neighbour and I'm a bit concerned about her safety.'

'Oh? Is that relationship likely to stop you working for us?'

'It's not a relationship. Libby's recently run away from an abusive husband and has only been in the house for a couple of days. I'd better set up a support system for her in the village, so that she has someone to turn to for help if I'm not there.'

'How did you come to know her?'

'She's the granddaughter of my former landlady and I'm a trustee for the legacy the old lady left her.'

'The woman who left you the house?'

'Yeah.' He looked at Leon in puzzlement. Why this interest in his neighbour?

'We like to know how our casual staff fit into their local communities, in case we have to ask them to take someone home for a day or two. Would that be a problem for you?'

'No. I'd been intending to renovate the top floor and put in an en-suite bathroom. This'll give me the impetus to do it.'

'Took you a while to get over the accident, didn't it? Not just physically.'

Joss shrugged. 'I was due for a change anyway, I think. That seems obvious now. I was getting stale.'

They chatted for a long time, a seemingly innocuous conversation, the sort any friends might hold when they hadn't seen one another for a while. But by the time an hour had passed, and they were on their second cups of coffee, Joss realised how much Leon had found out about him from his answers.

'You're good at it,' he said.

'What?'

'Chatting to people and finding out about them. What else do you need to know about me? Just ask openly.'

Leon grinned. 'Nothing much. I need to see you with some of my team, though, before we take the next step. Come and have lunch, then you can sit in on a briefing. We'll get drunk together tonight and—'

'I don't get drunk. A couple of drinks is fine, but that's as far as I go.'

'That's the right answer. I hope it's true.'

'It is.'

By the end of the evening, Joss felt wrung out. But he also felt sure that he could work with these men and women. It still wasn't quite clear what the scope of the unit's duties was. When he'd asked, Leon had just shrugged and said, 'We do whatever's needed to tidy up the messes other people make, sometimes people on our own side, sometimes those of our so-called allies.'

A couple of people excused themselves to go to bed and Joss couldn't prevent a yawn.

Leon pushed his chair back. 'I'm tired now. Robert's booked you on the 6 p.m. plane tomorrow, Joss. He'll spend the day equipping you with various . . . bits and pieces of technology.'

'Technology?'

'Surveillance gadgets, our own mobile phone, a few little things we find useful. Can you get those renovations to your house done quickly? If it's all right with you, we'll use your place as a staging post for people escaping from trouble. Just at first. We'll see where we go from there.'

'Fine by me.'

'Oh, and keep your fitness level up. You never know when you'll be needing it. Night, everyone.'

Joss nodded. He'd have kept fit anyway. He enjoyed exercise and feeling in control of his own body, even with the limitations he now had. He sighed happily as he went to bed in a cell-like room in the attic. He didn't care what he did, as long as he had some purpose in life.

To his surprise, though, he amended that mentally a short time later. He was glad he'd be working for his country. As a uniformed police officer and later as a detective, he'd spent his working years so far in service to various local communities. He'd never been drawn to money-making as a *raison d'être*.

On the Friday, the postman came into the antiques centre with a bundle of letters and a couple of packages, dumping them as usual on the reception counter near the door. 'There's more mail every day.'

Emily grimaced. 'Yes. And most of this will be junk mail we didn't ask for. People are getting really cheeky about sending brochures and catalogues.'

'We've all got to earn a bob or two.' He turned and ambled out.

'I'm not sure sending out advertising bumf is the best way,' she muttered. 'Just think of all the trees that are wasted to make brochures and catalogues that get chucked out straight away.' She tossed a couple into the wastepaper basket which proved her point.

She sorted through the letters, stopping at one which

had a logo she recognised on the envelope. The AR was very tastefully embossed but the sight of it always filled her with apprehension.

Dumping the other letters on the counter, she went through to the Old Barn, the big room at the back, glad no one was around today. She always felt better in here. Taking a deep breath, she tore the letter open, hoping desperately that it would bring good news.

But no, the letter was a formulaic message, saying simply that the adopted child had declined to meet her, now or in the future. There were no names, nothing to personalise the message. It might as well have been a damned circular.

She bent her head, fighting against tears.

When arms she recognised went round her, she turned and burrowed into Chad's chest.

'What is it?'

She thrust the crumpled letter into his hand. 'What do you think?'

'Oh, my darling.'

'Why can't she even give me a chance? I didn't give her up for adoption, after all. She was stolen from me. When Leon told me she was still alive, I tried to persuade myself she'd be fine, that someone must have wanted her desperately to go to those lengths. But since then I need to see her. I just . . . need to.'

Still keeping an arm round her shoulders, he read the brief message from AR. 'That settles it. All this working through faceless organisations is highly unsatisfactory. And you can't ask Leon for help with a private matter, not one which would take up his scarce resources anyway.'

He frowned, thinking it through. 'How do we know they even told her she was taken from you by a trick? Come to that, how do we know it's she who replied? It could just as easily have been a husband or adoptive parent who'd intercepted the letter from AR, and was trying to keep you apart.'

His words echoed in the big room and suddenly light glowed in one corner of the high ceiling, a corner which sometimes felt as if it had a friendly spirit living here.

Toby's voice sounded from the side of the room. 'The light's shining. She's come to see you.'

Chad asked without turning his head, 'Who's come, Toby?'

'The lady. I see her sometimes. She used to live here. She likes to help people.'

He'd spoken of this ghost before and everyone who lived at the old inn accepted the fact that something happened occasionally in this room, something beyond people's normal experience, whether it was a giving of comfort or a reinforcement of a decision.

'She thinks you should find the lost person.' Toby's voice echoed slightly. 'She says the person wants to be found.'

Chad and Emily exchanged startled glances. How could he know that?

The light began to fade and Toby's voice lost its echo. 'Can I look round in here, please?'

'Of course you can.' Chad shook his head in bafflement. 'You know, I didn't really believe in ghosts till I came here. But I can't deny there's something, especially here or in the secret room. Besides, I don't think Toby is capable of making up something like that.'

'I've always believed in ghosts, or spirits, or whatever you like to call them. I see them sometimes. I hardly dare believe that Toby's right about this, though, but . . . what if he is? What if someone really is trying to stop me meeting my daughter?'

'I'll get in touch with my friend Des and see if he can investigate for us. We'll see what he can find out and then decide what to do. Now, let's go and find something to eat. I'm hungry.'

She stopped him moving, standing on tiptoe to kiss his cheek. 'Thank you, Chad.'

'I didn't do much.'

'You were there for me.'

He hugged her close. 'I always will be. I love you. We'll find your daughter.'

And dammit if his voice didn't echo too.

Libby was annoyed at herself for missing Joss, when he hadn't even been gone for a full day. But this little enclave of houses was so quiet without him that she felt lonely . . . and vulnerable. No one would even know if Steven came back and attacked her again.

Just before lunch she went out for a breath of fresh air and let Ned run around. She looked at the two empty houses and wondered why no one was living there. When she looked at Joss's house, she wondered when he'd be back.

How stupid could you get? Missing a man you barely knew.

Only he was so solid and reassuring she felt safer with him next door. And . . . she liked him.

Even Ned kept asking about him.

That afternoon she took her son for a short drive to Hollingworth Lake, a place she'd loved to visit as a child. It had been created to supply water to the local canals, but now it was a leisure area.

As they walked along the promenade, she watched some people in canoes, who looked to be enjoying themselves hugely.

But although the lake was only about two and a half miles in circumference, Ned wasn't old enough to walk round it. After a while he grew bored and fretful, clinging to her hand. She wondered if he'd had too many new experiences lately, if what he needed for a time was a quiet life getting used to his new home.

She didn't trust the car enough to go further afield, so turned back towards the village, taking a winding side road and enjoying the beautiful scenery.

On the Friday morning she took Ned for a walk up to the little church. He wasn't interested in it, or the graveyard that lay up a slight slope above it, but she wished she could take more time looking round. She knew some of Grandma Rose's ancestors were buried here, but many of the graves were overgrown.

She didn't know anything about her own ancestors – the blood relatives, that is – not a single thing, because of being adopted. Her mother had always vehemently refused to consider contacting her birth mother to find out; she wouldn't say why.

In the evening, Libby decided to go to bed early and read a book she'd picked out of Grandma Rose's huge collection of romance novels. Not that she believed in that sort of romance, not any more. But you could enjoy a fairy tale without believing it was true, couldn't you?

Outside, a car turned into their close and pulled up. It was likely to be Joss, but her heart began to thump in apprehension in case it was Steven. It'd be so like her ex to turn up at night.

In the front room she peered carefully out of the window, letting out a huge sigh of relief when she saw it was indeed Joss's car. He was back.

A heavy burden seemed to fall off her shoulders and it took her only a few seconds to work out what it was: the burden of trying to keep her son and herself safe, trying to make sure Steven couldn't ill-treat either of them again.

He'd been violent once. Very. Her rib still hurt when she moved carelessly. Maybe he'd got a taste for violence now. She'd never forget the savage triumph on his face as he punched and thumped her. Or how afraid she'd felt that he was going to kill her.

As Joss got out of the car, he looked towards her house, she wasn't imagining that. Then he moved towards his own home, turning to lock his car with the remote before taking his backpack inside.

She went back into the kitchen, but a couple of minutes later there was a knock on her door. It didn't have a peephole in it, and though it wasn't likely to be anyone but her neighbour, she still called out, 'Who is it?'

'It's me, Joss.'

She'd opened the door before she remembered she was wearing a rather flimsy nightdress and dressing gown which she'd found in a drawer, neatly covered in gift wrap. She didn't know who Grandma Rose had meant it for, because there was no name on it, but she hadn't been able to resist trying it on. It had been so long since she'd owned something frivolous and pretty.

Joss stared at her in surprise and she could feel herself blushing, even though her outfit was perfectly decent, being suggestive rather than revealing.

'I didn't mean to disturb you, Libby. I saw your light and just wanted to let you know I'm back, so that you don't worry if you hear noises from next door.'

'Thank you.'

He turned to leave and she remembered something. 'The postman left a parcel for you this afternoon. Please come in while I get it.'

He moved into the hall and followed her into the back room. 'I suppose Ned's in bed?'

'Yes, and sound asleep. We went for a walk up to the church and the graveyard this morning and played ball this afternoon. That tired him out nicely.'

Joss nodded. 'It's like *Wuthering Heights* come to life, isn't it, up there? A walled graveyard on the edge of the moors, with the wind howling round the tombstones.'

'That's what I thought. I'd like to think I have ancestors buried there, but I have no idea what my birth mother's connections were. The graves are all overgrown but I do wonder if some of Grandma Rose's ancestors are buried there.'

'Rose investigated it and found out where her ancestors were just before she fell ill. She wanted me to show you once you'd settled in. She would have liked to be buried in the churchyard near them, but they don't allow burials there any more, so she had a cremation and we scattered her ashes near her grandmother's grave.'

'You must show me where. I'll take some flowers. Um, have you eaten recently?'

He grimaced, 'An airline snack.'

'I baked a cake. Would you like a piece? And . . . I bought a bottle of wine. To celebrate coming to live here. Only it doesn't feel like a celebration when you drink a toast on your own.' She gestured towards an almost full glass on the table.

'I'd love both the cake and the wine, if I'm not keeping you up. I'm still too wired from travelling to fall asleep.'

'Do sit down. We'll stay in here because the front room feels damp and unused. I'm going to light a fire in there tomorrow.'

'Rose didn't use it much.'

Libby got out the chocolate cake and the bottle of white wine. 'Did your business go well?'

'Very well. It'll give me some intermittent work, but I'm not quite sure what my role will be yet.'

'You must miss having a career. You were doing quite well before the accident, weren't you?'

'I suppose so. Detective Inspector. I miss being busy, but I don't miss being fitted into the straightjacket of rules and regulations, and the higher I rose, the more paperwork there was. Thank you.' He took a bite of cake and chewed it slowly, murmuring in appreciation. 'That's absolutely delicious.'

'I like baking better than any other sort of cooking. My ex didn't eat cake. He insisted on a very healthy diet, which was fine by me. But never to have cake or biscuits seemed a bit too much, so I sometimes made it anyway and hid it.' She clapped one hand to her mouth. 'Sorry!'

'Whatever for?'

'There's nothing as boring as someone who goes on and on about their ex.'

'I'll swap tales with you one day.'

She looked at him in surprise. 'You were married?'

'For a couple of years. It wasn't the best time of my life.'

'What was?'

And they were off swapping stories of their childhoods until suddenly she realised they'd been doing this for an hour, it was nearly midnight and he was yawning.

'You look exhausted, Joss. I shouldn't have kept you so long.'

'I've enjoyed your company. Thank you for inviting me in. I've . . . been a bit reclusive since the accident.'

She walked with him to the door.

'Lock up carefully,' he warned.

'Oh, I will.'

She went to bed marvelling at how easy Joss was to chat to, how he didn't seem to judge her or put her down. It made the contrast with Steven even more vivid. Why had she put up with that for so long?

She walked slowly up the stairs. She'd sleep better knowing Joss was next door.

It was only as she got into bed that she realised she hadn't changed out of the negligee while they chatted. That was because he hadn't stared or done anything to make her feel underdressed. In fact, she'd felt totally comfortable with him.

But still, she ought to have put on something more . . . more . . . No, her dressing gown was so dowdy. She was glad she'd been wearing the lovely negligee.

Steven wasn't enjoying living on his own. Even after a few days, the house needed thorough cleaning, a task he'd never undertaken before. And he didn't intend to do it now, either.

He went online and found a cleaning agency, but when he tried to ring them, a mechanical voice referred him to office opening hours. Which would mean ringing from work. He hadn't told his team leader that Libby had left him. His home life was no one else's business.

He decided to do something he'd never done before: take a day off sick. He'd plead a gastric upset, which seemed to be the most common excuse offered.

He rang the cleaning agency as soon as office hours started, but they only dealt with commercial properties. He had to try three places before he found one that grudgingly agreed to do a residential house – though the price they were going to charge for this made him furious.

After that, he went shopping to a big centre where he hoped no one from work would see him. He needed to buy fresh food, healthy stuff. Since he wasn't used to shopping, it took him two hours to go round the supermarket and pick out what he needed, including some frozen dinners and pieces of meat he could cook quickly, like steaks or chicken breasts.

There were cookery books in the house. He'd find some recipes. If Libby could manage to cook, then he was damned sure he could too. He could do anything if he set his mind to it, as his mother had always assured him.

On his way home he saw an office building whose discreet sign announced a legal practice. On an impulse he turned into the car park and went inside.

'I'm looking for a lawyer specialising in marital problems,' he told the woman at reception.

'That'll be Ms Whorton.'

'I'd prefer to consult a male lawyer.'

Her expression suddenly became chilling. 'We don't distinguish our lawyers by gender. In fact, I believe that's illegal.'

'Fine. I'll go elsewhere.'

He heard her say, 'Good riddance!' as he left and turned to glare at her.

When he got home, he put the frozen food away, made himself a healthy salad and sat down to eat.

As he was clearing up, he suddenly remembered Libby's lawyer's name: Greaves, Henry Greaves. Pleased with himself, he went online to find out more about the fellow, only to discover that his firm didn't have a web presence.

So he looked Greaves up in the online telephone directory and found an address and phone number for Greaves and Hallibourne. That had to be the one. He copied the details down.

But he wouldn't get in touch until the bruises on Libby's face had had time to fade, and anyway, he was still gathering information, planning his strategies.

Once he set out after her, he had no doubt that he'd find her. No doubt at all. He'd take some leave – he had plenty owing – and bring her back where she belonged.

And Ned, of course.

What's more, he'd take an interest in his son's upbringing from now on. It was time to set some standards for behaviour, to inculcate the child with the right attitudes and beliefs.

As his own father had done.

Chapter Seven

Two days later, Libby tried to start her car, but the motor only coughed and refused to do anything.

Not again! She covered her face with her hands, feeling like bursting into tears. She'd planned to go into Rochdale to wander round the markets and perhaps a few charity shops, to buy toys for Ned and a few more clothes for herself.

She'd hoped the new battery would have sorted out the car's problems, but clearly not. She'd better join a motoring organisation, in case she ever broke down while she was out and about. In the meantime she didn't know what to do about this car. If it cost too much to repair, she wouldn't be able to afford to have it seen to.

Once again, Joss came out to help her.

'I'm so sorry to trouble you again.'

'It's no trouble, because I'm not a mechanic. That car of yours seems terminally ill to me. Mind if I fetch someone up from the village to have a quick look at it? Giff's semi-retired but he still repairs and services cars for people, as long as they're not major jobs.'

'Would you?'

'I'll stroll down to see him now. I could do with a brisk walk.'

'I could too, but that's impossible with a small child.' She glanced down at her son, smiling involuntarily. 'But Ned's worth it.'

'I'll just lock up then I'll be off.'

Like her, he was always careful about locking up. She watched him stride down the track that connected the group of four houses with the rest of the world, before going back inside. She was going through the contents of the front room today.

A quarter of an hour later a van turned into the parking area, and Joss got out, followed by a rather large man in stained overalls.

'We have to go outside,' she told Ned.

'Don't want to. Want to draw.'

'You can draw after we come back. Joss is outside.'

Ned immediately got down from his chair and ran towards the front door, fumbling at it, but not able to turn the key.

She opened it for him, holding his hand firmly, even though he squirmed, then went out to meet the mechanic.

'Giff, this is Libby, Rose's granddaughter.'

'Pleased to meet you. I won't shake hands, love, because mine are filthy.'

'And this is Ned.'

Giff beamed at the child. 'Fine young fellow. Rose would have loved him. Now, let's have a look at this car of yours.'

She handed over the keys and he bent over the motor.

Joss moved closer and whispered, 'I took your name in vain and promised him a piece of chocolate cake and a big mug of strong tea. His wife died last year and he misses her greatly. She was an excellent cook.'

'I'll get a snack ready. I'm no use out here. You'll call me if he finds anything?'

'Of course.'

She went inside and put the kettle on, hunting out the biggest mug in Rose's collection and setting the chocolate cake on a plate, ready to offer Giff a piece or two.

She let Ned stand in the doorway to watch the men, telling him not to move from there. Sadly, she knew he'd do as he was told, for fear of his father coming to shout at him.

It was about fifteen minutes before she heard voices and Ned came running to say, 'Joss is here. And a man.'

'Come in!' she yelled, switching on the kettle.

Ned stood beside her, eyeing the stranger suspiciously.

'Now that looks like a home-made cake,' Giff boomed.

'Yes. I love baking. I thought you might like a piece with your cup of tea.'

His beaming smile was answer enough.

She waited till they were all sitting round the table to ask, 'Well, how's my car?'

Giff shook his head. 'Not good, Libby, not good at all. It's well past retirement date. I can repair it but I can't make it reliable and it's sure to let you down again. And the bodywork isn't so good, either. One thing always leads to another when they're in this condition. You didn't have it serviced very often, did you?'

'No. I couldn't afford it. I did manage to change the oil.' Mary's husband had shown her how to do it. She saw Joss look at her sharply and guessed he'd figured out that Steven had refused to pay for her car to be serviced.

'Can you get her anything for it as a trade-in, Giff?'

'Couple of hundred, maybe a little more. Someone might want a cheap fixer-upper. You've kept the upholstery nice, and it's an easy model to put a new engine in, so someone wanting a cheapie might do up the bodywork.'

She bit her lip. She couldn't afford to buy another engine, let alone a new car.

Giff drank the rest of his tea with every appearance of enjoyment, and popped the last mouthful of cake into his mouth. 'I'll leave you two to discuss this. If I can help, get back to me. Nice meeting you, Libby. See you, Joss.'

He was gone before she could gather her wits together. 'Do I owe him some money?'

'No. But if you were to bake him a cake, he'd appreciate that.'

'I can do that easily.' She stared down at her plate. She'd been crumbling her cake without realising it and there was quite a big pile of crumbs there now. 'If I haven't got a car, and if Steven comes after me, I have no way of escaping.'

'We'll do our best to keep him away from you.'

She shook her head. 'It's only a matter of time. I've been thinking about it . . . about him. He never gives up when he wants something. It'll be a matter of pride for him to drag me back.'

'Are you sure he'll still want you?'

'Oh, yes. Not me specifically but a housewife and someone to raise his child . . . someone to bully. We haven't, you know, shared a bedroom for a couple of years.'

Joss took her hand. 'If he's that bad, we must make sure you do have a means of escape and somewhere to go.'

'How?'

'There's a contingency fund in the trust for emergencies.'

'You mean I can draw on the inheritance money now?'

'No. I mean we can supply you with a car as an extra. Not a new one, but a reliable one. It'll be in Henry's name, not yours, so no one can take it away from you. Giff will find you a vehicle, if you like. He has friends still working in the trade. Well, Giff has friends everywhere. He's a universal uncle.'

She looked at Joss uncertainly. 'Are you sure you're not just making this up, being kind to me?'

'You mean, would I be supplying the money?'

'Yes.'

'I'm not a rich man and there really is a contingency fund, Libby.'

She sighed in relief so deep it came out as more of a groan. 'You always seem to be there when I need something.'

'From now on, my job will take me away from time to time. But I'll make sure there's someone else you can call on for help. Not Giff. His fighting days are over. But Rose was well liked in the village. She helped a lot of people and they in turn will be happy to help her granddaughter, I'm sure. Now, where did you want to go today?'

'It's not important.'

'I have nothing to do, so I can easily take you, as long as

you don't mind waiting while I nip into Henry's rooms to discuss the question of a car.'

'I don't mind waiting at all. Are you sure? I was going to stroll round the markets in Rochdale and look in a few charity shops. Ned needs some more toys and I need some clothes.'

'From charity shops?'

She flushed at the surprise in his tone, but wasn't going to lie to him. 'I've bought everyday clothes from charity shops for years. You can pick up some real bargains.'

'I've never even been inside one. It might be fun. How soon can you be ready to leave?'

'A few minutes.' It was kind of Joss, she thought, as she got Ned ready to go out. If Henry hadn't said Joss needed something to do, she might have been less ready to accept his offer to take her, because she didn't want to impose.

But there again, she enjoyed her neighbour's company and so did Ned. Could it do any harm to spend time with him occasionally? You could never have too many friends, and she'd lost touch with most of hers. Which reminded her, she must email Mary to say she was all right, and arrange to have Allie round for a drink.

They left the car in a town-centre car park and Joss led the way down a maze of stairs and passageways into the markets. The indoor area didn't seem to have changed all that much, and Libby stood for a moment listening to the familiar Lancashire accent issuing just as happily from people of a variety of races.

She smiled. It was lovely to hear that slow, gentle way

of speaking. It took her back to the happy days when her father had been alive and they'd all lived in Rochdale.

When her mother had remarried and moved near to London, Libby's stepfather had forced her to speak 'properly' so she'd lost her own accent, except for what he'd called 'that damned northern twang of yours'. And now she was back where she'd started from.

Joss's voice pulled her out of her memories. 'What do you want to look at first?'

'I usually compare the food prices, so I know which is the best value. I won't buy straight away, if you don't mind me taking my time. Afterwards, if you're not in too much of a hurry, we'll go and look round a few charity shops in the same way. Checking things out first.'

She waited for him to say something, but he didn't, because he'd suddenly lunged sideways. Grabbing Ned's arm, he pulled the little boy out of the way of a large woman who was so busy talking to her friend that she didn't seem to have noticed the child and would have bowled him over.

'Thanks for protecting him.' She took Ned's hand more firmly.

'My pleasure,' Joss said.

As they explored the market, he became thoughtful. 'Some of the food looks super-fresh and it's really good value.'

'You probably don't need to count pennies.' She eyed some strawberries regretfully.

'No, but it's good to support the smaller sellers sometimes, even though the big supermarkets are very convenient. I've no need to rush in and out after work these days, after all. Do you want to look at the charity shops before you buy your food? Then we won't have to carry bags of vegetables around.'

'Yes, please.'

They wandered out into Yorkshire Street, heading uphill. Libby investigated several shops and also a store whose windows bore garish posters screaming about its low prices.

When they got to the top of the shopping area, she turned back. 'I'm ready to start buying now, but if there's something else you need to attend to, just say.'

'We'll do your shopping first. I'll pick up some things from the market too. After that I need to see Henry about releasing the money for a car.'

The words escaped before she could stop them. 'What would I have done without you?'

'Hey. Not only am I a trustee, so it's my duty to help you, I'm a normal human being and I *like* to help my friends.'

'Friends? Can you make friends with someone this quickly?'

'Sometimes.' He stopped moving to look at her solemnly. 'As I think you and I have done. Or don't you feel that?'

She flushed, but could be no less honest. 'Yes, I do feel we've become friends.'

'Good. Now, if you just let me phone Henry to check when he'll be available, I'll hold on to this young scamp while you go back into whichever shops you need to visit to try on your clothes.'

He got through to Mrs Hockton and arranged to see

Henry just after lunch. As he closed up his mobile phone and slipped it in his pocket, he said, 'That means I've got time to buy us lunch. I know a place which makes the very best pizzas, sold by the piece.'

'You can't keep feeding me,' she protested.

He grinned. 'Oh, it's Ned and me who need feeding. You don't seem to eat much at all.'

She gave in to temptation. 'I've been too worried to eat properly, but I'd love some pizza. I'll pay my share, though.'

'I'd rather you kept feeding me home-made cake in return.'

That made her feel better, less of a charity case. He had definitely enjoyed her cake.

'Now, let's get on with this shopping, Libby.'

She always bought carefully, but she was particularly lucky today and found several garments she liked, as well as a few clothes and toys for Ned.

In the markets she stocked up on fresh fruit and vegetables, as well as a range of spices.

'You enjoy curries?' Joss asked.

'I used to. Steven didn't. He preferred what he called *real* English food. Oh, damn! I'm doing it again, talking about him.'

'You're bound to. You've only been away from him for a few days. It doesn't worry me. As well as making cakes, could you show me how to make a curry or two? I love them but it takes too long to go into Rochdale or Todmorden to buy a takeaway. The food is cold before I get home again.'

'I'd be happy to teach you.'

* * *

After lunch, they parked outside Henry's rooms and Joss went inside, not expecting to be more than a minute or two.

'Go straight through,' Mrs Hockton said. 'He's expecting you. Everything all right?'

'More or less. There's been no contact from her husband, at least.'

'No.' She lowered her voice. 'And if he comes in here I shall be hard put to speak civilly to him. That was a bad bruise on her face.'

'I'm first in line for a confrontation. Did you know he'd hit the boy as well?'

The fury on her face was similar to his own feelings every time he saw the bruises on her face, and on Ned's leg.

He went down the corridor to find Henry scowling at a desk covered in piles of paper.

'What's so urgent, Joss?'

'Libby's car has died. We need to buy her a new one.'

'Fine by me, as long as we keep the car in the name of the trust, so that *he* can't take it if he drags her back.'

'She's not going back to him.'

'You can't be sure about that.'

'I am. Very sure.' He wouldn't let her. As a police officer, he'd failed to prevent some women going back. As a friend, he was going to make sure Libby didn't get forced back.

'What if he gets custody of the boy? On the face of it, he's a respectable executive and she doesn't even have a job. Courts have done stupid things before. She might feel obliged to go back to him for her son's sake.'

Joss groaned. 'Thanks, Henry. You've just given me

something to have nightmares about. *You* have to make sure he doesn't get to her through the law.'

'And you have to keep an eye on her safety. You've nothing else to do, after all.'

'It's bad timing because I've just found myself a part-time job, one that'll take me away sometimes. I thought we'd give her your address, and I know a couple of guys in the village who'd protect her, too.'

'What's the job?'

'Security.'

'And that means . . . ?'

'Oh, this and that.'

'I see. Something hush-hush.'

'That's one way of putting it.'

'Well, let me know whenever you go away. Emma and I would be happy to give her shelter at our house any time.'

'I knew that already. You're one of the good guys, Henry.'

His old friend rolled his eyes. 'My work usually involves house sales and contracts. This goes way beyond my normal brief. Only for Rose would I have done any of this.'

'I know. You like a quiet, elegant life: concerts, art galleries, cultural holidays. You don't usually do divorces, even. Are you going to help her with that?'

'I've made arrangements for a good divorce lawyer to get involved once Libby starts proceedings. I know my limitations. We have to tread very carefully with this.'

'Anyone I know?'

'Annie Bainborough.'

'She's the best around here. She does pro bono work for the abuse unit.'

'I know. About this car. You'll have to choose it, Joss. I'm no expert on second-hand cars.'

'I've already got Giff Marshall looking into it. He's a mechanic who lives in Top o' the Hill and is semi-retired. How much can we spend? I don't want her driving around in another old rattle-trap. It's a miracle that one even got her here.'

'Miracles do sometimes happen. And spend whatever it takes to get a decent second-hand vehicle with all the necessary safety features – two or three years old maybe.'

Joss was smiling as he went outside again. He was enjoying today's outing and things were going really well.

Then he stiffened. Libby and Ned weren't in the car. He could feel himself going on what he'd always thought of as 'full alert'. He stared up and down the street, while getting out his mobile, in case he had to call for help quickly, his mind skipping from one possibility to another.

Where could she have gone? She'd assured him she'd stay in the car. He'd only given her the spare car key in case she wanted to listen to the radio.

Could her husband have come after her already?

Before he could dial for assistance, Libby appeared at the corner, with Ned walking beside her. She speeded up when she saw him.

'Sorry to keep you waiting, Joss. Ned was getting a bit fidgety. I locked up the car, so it wasn't in any danger of being stolen.'

'It's you I was worried about, not the bloody car.' It surprised him how upset he'd felt.

'I'm really sorry to have worried you. I don't know what I was thinking to walk off like that.'

'I was afraid your husband might have turned up.'

'You think he could snatch us off the street without me screaming my head off?'

'Could happen. Do you think he'd try that?'

She bent her head, then looked up and nodded. 'Yes, after the way he beat me, I do think he would. It was probably stupid of me to go for a walk in such a quiet area. And I was out of earshot, so you couldn't have helped me.'

'Not your wisest move . . . Don't do it again, or you'll turn my hair white.'

'If I manage to last the six months and get the money, I should probably move on, change my name and never, ever let him know where we are. Only he'll go for access, I know he will.'

'We have the photos of what he did to Ned.'

'Will a judge consider that enough to separate him permanently from his son?'

'Not necessarily. Even if it's supervised access, they usually try to keep parents and children connected.' Joss sighed. Everyone involved in family law did their best, but sometimes a bad 'un got through the safety nets, and then innocent people suffered.

Libby echoed his sigh. 'I wonder if it'll ever end, if I'll ever be really free.'

He wondered that, too. He knew of a case where an abusive husband had tracked down and killed an ex-wife years after she'd left him, but he didn't say that. He was still trying to come to terms with the realisation that he cared enough about Libby to get upset as quickly as he had a few moments ago at the thought she might be in danger.

She put her hand on his arm, tentatively, as if afraid he might shake her off. 'I won't do it again. I'm sorry to have worried you.'

He took her hand in his. 'Don't keep apologising. I'm not angry with *you*; I'm angry with the situation. You shouldn't have to hide and worry like this. No one should have to do that.'

When they got home, she thanked him for his help and went to put her purchases away. It gave her great pleasure to unpack her new clothes. She held them in front of her as she stood before the full-length mirror. She'd also bought a couple of pairs of new jeans from the market.

As she went downstairs again to prepare tea, she realised that the house was beginning to feel like home. It really was.

That evening she phoned Allie and invited her round one evening for a drink and a natter.

'Not tomorrow, but the day after!' Allie said at once. 'Pete's going out for a drink with the lads tomorrow. His Sunday treat.'

A voice called out from a distance. 'He said to say hi. He may never have met you, but he's heard about you.'

'Say hi back to him. I'll see you on Monday. About seven-thirty all right?'

'Great. I'll walk up so we can have a drink or two.'

'But you'll have to walk back on your own after dark.'

'I never feel afraid up here. Anyway, once I get to the end of your little lane, I'm never out of screaming distance of someone, if I need help.'

Libby couldn't have done that, walked back in the dark. Not with Steven on the loose.

It made her angry that she felt that way; that she was so afraid of him.

Chapter Eight

On Sunday, Joss worked on clearing things out of his attic. He caught glimpses of Libby and Ned, but didn't go out to chat with them.

By evening, he'd had enough of housework and decided to take Pete up on his standing invitation to join a few of the lads for drinks. He'd gone out with them a few times before, but wasn't a regular.

He had an ulterior motive: he wanted to find other guys who'd be ready to help Libby if her ex turned up.

But that wasn't his only reason for going out. He was feeling more sociable these days, didn't know why he'd been so determined to live a solitary life. The Crown was a nice little pub, genuinely old, needing no fake beams or pretend inglenook fireplaces to make you feel at home there. And Pete's friends were a pleasant lot, men of all ages from the village and neighbouring farms.

He might even get a game of darts. It had been ages since he'd played.

On the Monday, various tradesmen turned up to see Joss, the first at eight o'clock. Libby couldn't resist peeping out of the front-room window each time. Their vans said they were bathroom specialists, plumbers, electricians. She was intrigued. Was he planning some major renovations?

She'd made a good start clearing out the front room yesterday, but wanted to finish it today so that she and Allie could sit there in comfort for their girls' evening.

The main problem now was Grandma Rose's ornaments. There were dozens of them, none of which Libby liked. They were not only lined up along the mantelpiece and windowsills, but jostled one another in an old-fashioned display cabinet. She wasn't into fussy decor and these were the kind of pieces her grandmother's generation had liked – no, her great-grandmother's generation or even earlier. Some of them looked really old.

Picking them up one by one, she studied the marks underneath. She'd watched enough antique shows on television to recognise some of the makers and had to wonder if any of the ornaments were valuable enough to sell. She might not have the right to do that, though, not if she had to run away to escape from Steven before the six months' condition of her inheritance was fulfilled.

Should she go and ask Joss about the ornaments?

No, she couldn't keep pestering him.

But who else was there to ask? And he *was* a trustee.

Oh, don't be such a coward, she told herself. *It'll only take a couple of minutes to nip next door and ask.* She checked that there were no vans outside Joss's house, then called for Ned to come with her.

He came running, an eager look on his face. 'Are we going to see Joss?'

'Yes. Let's look at your hands. Ooh, I think we'd better wash those before we go.'

When her neighbour opened the door, he looked happy and relaxed. For a moment, the breath caught in her throat at how attractive he was in an understated way. Well, *she* found him attractive. Very.

How long was it since she'd even looked at a man in that way, let alone reacted to one? She wasn't free, though, shouldn't be doing this. Pulling herself together, she asked as calmly as she could, 'Have you got a minute, Joss? I need to ask you something about the trust.'

'Of course I've got a minute. Two, even. Come in. Would you like a coffee?'

'I didn't mean to disturb you. You've been so busy all morning.'

He beamed at her. 'I'm putting in an en-suite bathroom on the top floor and making that the master bedroom. I've been meaning to do it for ages and I suddenly decided the time had come.'

He led the way into the kitchen, which seemed a lot more cheerful by daylight than it had the night she arrived.

'Milk for Ned?' he asked.

'Just a glass of water, if you don't mind.'

'I've got fruit juice.'

'No, water will be fine. I don't want to encourage a taste for sugary drinks.' Nor did she want to spend money on expensive drinks when tap water was free.

'Do sit down. Remind me how you like your coffee.'

'Milk, no sugar.' She sat down at the end of the table and looked round. Joss must have been making a drink for himself because the jar of coffee was already out, and a mug stood next to the kettle with a spoon handle showing and steam rising from it.

The coffee smelt good. Steven sneered at the mere idea of instant coffee and had bought himself an elaborate coffee-making gadget, which she hadn't been allowed to touch. She didn't think it was worth all the fuss, but of course she hadn't said that.

Her ex would have scorned all sorts of things about her new life, but she was enjoying the peace she'd found here, even if it was only temporary.

Just as Joss was putting a mug down in front of her, the phone rang. He got up to look at the caller ID. 'Ah. Would you mind me taking this call? It could be important.'

He took her agreement for granted and walked out into the front room, closing the door behind him.

She looked round, seeing a room that was untidy but not dirty, filled with the paraphernalia of daily life. There was a pile of brochures on the table and she leant over to look at them. Renovations and bathrooms. She would have loved to do what he was doing. Perhaps one day.

That made her smile. A few days ago, she'd run away on borrowed money, unsure of whether she'd have a roof over her head that night. Now she was getting grandiose ideas about modernising her grandmother's old house. *Get real, Libby!*

The door to the front room opened and Joss came back into the kitchen. 'Sorry to leave you like that. It was about my new job. How can I help you?'

He hadn't told her any details about the job, so she

didn't like to ask him. 'Um, I'm trying to clear out the front room and I wondered what I'm supposed to do with Grandma Rose's ornaments. There are an awful lot of them and they're not at all to my taste. Some of them seem quite old, though, and I've watched enough antiques shows to know they might be valuable, so I don't want to just give them to a charity shop.'

She hesitated, then finished in a rush, 'Only, if I'm living here, I'd rather not be surrounded by little statuettes and ornate vases. Especially with a child of Ned's age running round. If I sell them, do I give the money to the trust?'

Joss stared at her in such a strange way that she tried to think what she might have said to upset him. 'What?' she asked.

'When coincidence smacks you in the eye, you have to wonder if someone up there' – he glanced towards the ceiling – 'is pulling your strings.'

She still couldn't work out what he was on about.

'Sorry. It's just that I've been planning to visit a new antiques centre on the edge of the moors. I really enjoy looking at antiques. That place buys things as well as selling them.'

He hesitated, wishing he could tell her more but knew he mustn't. The centre was going to be one of a chain of temporary refuges for the people Leon's unit sometimes had to protect at short notice. Joss's brief at the moment was to make himself familiar with the place without betraying who he was, in case he ever had to take someone there.

Libby's antiques would give him an ideal excuse for going there. He had planned to buy something small, pretending it was for a present, but asking for a valuation of Rose's antiques would be much better.

His new colleagues seemed absolutely paranoid about anyone suspecting that their unit even existed, and about keeping the various refuges secret. Maybe that was why they had such a good track record for dealing with particularly sensitive problems, as Joss had found out when he worked with them before he left the police force.

He realised she was still waiting for his answer. 'I could take you with me, if you like, and we could get the ornaments valued, but not till later in the week if you want to enjoy looking round as well as selling, because it's a new place and isn't open yet. There's a grand opening on Wednesday.'

Libby frowned. 'Are you being kind to me again? You don't have to drive me around.'

'I'm not being kind in that way. I really was going to visit the centre. I'm not a collector of anything, but I've always wanted a piece of cranberry glass, a decanter with a silver top. I love the colour.'

'Then I accept. I'll have to see if Allie has any spare boxes from the shop to pack the ornaments in. She's coming round for a drink and gossip tonight and I want to get the front room cleared up a bit and aired. That's when I decided the ornaments must go, even if they're only banished up to the third floor. Um . . . so what do I do with the money?'

'I'll ask Henry.'

She drained her coffee. 'Right. Come on, Ned. We have to go now. Say thank you for your drink.'

'Just a minute.' Joss went to get the list from the

mantelpiece. 'These guys will come and help you if your ex turns up when I'm away.'

She stared at it in surprise.

He thrust it into her hand. 'Pete is your friend Allie's husband, and Max has a little farm nearby. Tom comes and goes because he has a smallholding and also contracts himself and his van to a freight service. One of them is bound to be home and they'll come running. We'll get you a mobile phone and put their numbers in on fast dial.'

'Thank you.'

'We're all neighbours here. We look out for one another.'

She nodded, her eyes bright with tears.

Joss watched her go, then rang his contact at the unit to explain what he was setting up as an excuse for visiting the antiques centre.

'Good idea.'

'Will the people at the centre know who I am?'

'No. We just want *you* to know your way there at this stage.'

'Is it going to be one of your major staging posts?'

'Not sure yet. We'll see how things pan out. No other worries?'

'No. I'm just looking forward to some action.'

The contact laughed. 'It'll happen out of the blue; it always does. You'll get called into play soon enough.'

Emily's former neighbour Rachel came back from a trip down south, where she'd been making arrangements for renting out her former home. It had seemed silly to keep the house standing there empty when she had now moved in permanently with Oliver in the hamlet of Minkybridge, just down the hill from the antiques centre. She was determined to go and visit her son and his family in Australia and she needed more money for that.

Oliver had offered to pay her fare, but she didn't intend to let him, even though as a retired lawyer he was very comfortable financially. She might allow him to join her if things continued to go well, though, because she didn't intend to spend a whole month living with her son. Apart from the fact that it was an imposition to stay with anyone for so long, and guaranteed to cause tension after a few days, if she was going all the way to Australia she wanted to see something of the country.

Emily and Rachel sat down with mugs of coffee to catch up on the latest news. Things were happening every day now that the centre was so near to opening. They were as close as sisters, probably closer than Emily was to her half-sister Liz, who had said she'd move to live nearer to Emily, but hadn't yet done anything about it.

Emily had, of course, sent an invitation to Liz to attend the opening and stay for a few days, but she hadn't heard back. She forced her thoughts away from her nephew and back to her friend. 'How's my house looking, Rach? They haven't been able to sell it yet.'

'I saw the real estate salesman showing someone round the other day. You'll never guess who it was.'

'Oh?'

'Your nephew.'

'What? He has a cheek. And I thought he went to Australia.'

'He was probably just saying that. I think he really liked living in our former street. It *is* an extremely convenient location if you need to get into London regularly. And since you're never going back there, does it matter whether you sell to him or not?'

'It's not like you to plead George's cause. He wasn't a good neighbour to you.'

'His wife came to see me and apologised for the time he slashed my tyres. She gave me a cheque for the money, and I accepted it too. It's only fair, after all.'

'Why would she do that?'

'She wanted me to intercede with you. She said they're going to make an offer because it'd be easy to extend the house to suit their needs, and they'd already made friends in the area.'

Chad came in and they had to explain what was making Emily scowl so darkly. He laughed. 'You have to give it to your nephew. George doesn't let anything stop him when he wants something.'

'It'd have served him right if I'd pressed charges against him for the way he kept me shut up in hospital for all those weeks. I only let him off because of my sister. But I'll never forgive him for how he treated me.'

He grinned. 'Then tell the salesman you'll only sell to George at twenty thousand pounds over the asking price.'

She stared at him, mouth open.

Beside her, Rachel chuckled. 'Oh, yes! I really like that idea!'

Emily couldn't help smiling, then she laughed out loud. 'I suppose it might be poetic justice.'

Rachel's smiled faded. 'On the other hand, if you do that, I shan't want to go back to live next door to him, whatever his wife says.'

'Are you likely to go back at all?' Emily asked. 'You and Oliver have been all lovey-dovey for months now.'

Rachel blushed. 'I'm not sure. I can't quite believe it'll last. And I don't think my son approves of the idea of me finding someone else, though his father's been dead for years now.'

'O ye of little faith. Of course it will last with Oliver. And since your son really is in Australia, unlike my nephew, he should just mind his own business. But I won't tease you any more. And if you don't want me to sell the house to George, I won't. Think about it. Your call.'

'OK. I'll do that; maybe talk to Oliver about it.'

'Good. Now, the café is finished and looking great. It might be small but it's perfectly formed. Come and see it. You need to check that everything's been done as you wanted.'

'I think that's the post,' Chad said. 'I'll get it.'

The two women walked through to the rear of the building, stopping in the café area. Rachel checked the small kitchen, the serving area and the display cabinets, something she'd done several times already, then pulled down a couple of chairs from where they were stacked and set them at a table to get the effect.

'Oh, yes! It only needs the food and drink supplies bringing in now,' she said happily. 'Oliver's going to help me with that today. We aren't offering anything fancy or cooked.'

'He's enjoyed helping you.'

'Poor lamb, he was bored silly with retirement and living on his own. How are the plans for the grand opening going, Emily? How many people are coming?'

'I'm not sure yet, but a lot. Replies are still trickling in. I'm amazed at how many people are coming from London specially to attend.'

'Chad's a very likeable guy, as well as knowing his stuff about antiques.'

Emily's voice went soft. 'Yes, he is. It's a good thing you suggested we bring in some caterers and bar staff. There definitely wouldn't be room for you to prepare enough food in your small kitchen, let alone store it.'

'I know my limitations.'

Chad came back to join them, waving some letters. 'More acceptances. Even Leon's coming.'

'Wow, is he really? I'd have thought he'd be far too busy for that.' Emily's former boss was usually furiously busy. He must be doing something in this part of the country, she decided, and was using the opening as an excuse to head north. She doubted he'd be coming all this way just to see their centre.

'So . . . two more days to go.' She took Chad's hand. 'I'm getting nervous now.'

'Don't be. Just wear that dress we bought you and smile at everyone, whether you know them or not. You have a beautiful smile.'

Ashley moved into her flat that afternoon, looking quite fierce as she told the removalists exactly where to put her furniture.

Emily went round to the unit to welcome her, but could see that her new tenant wasn't interested in talking at the moment. All Ashley wanted was to keep an eye on what was happening to her possessions.

Even Toby got short shrift when he came to offer Ashley a cup of tea.

'Not now! Not now! Go away.'

Mrs Barley, who was also there, patted him on the shoulder. 'She's too busy to chat to us at the moment, Toby. You can talk to her once she's settled in.'

He turned to Emily. 'Can I go and look at the antiques?'

'Of course. Don't touch anything.'

'I never touch things unless Chad or you say I can.'

'He's a good lad, that one,' Mrs Barley said. 'He's coping really well with independence.'

'He loves the old house. I hope Ashley will settle in quickly.'

'I think she'll be all right. She needs an ordered life that doesn't change much. It's human emotions and strange places that flummox her.' Mrs Barley chuckled. 'And Toby will help her whether she wants him to or not. That young man has a very kind heart.'

Libby was getting ready for the evening with her friend Allie when Joss came round to see her.

'Got a minute?'

'Of course.'

'Henry says if you sell the ornaments, you can keep twenty per cent of what you receive, to pay for your trouble, plus any expenses you incur, and the rest should go into the trust.'

Her face lit up. 'That's even more incentive to drive hard bargains. Oh, I wish I had a computer! I could find out so much online.'

'I should have thought of that. I've got an old computer you're welcome to use, if you like, and I'm sure the trust would pay the cost of getting you online. It won't be fast, but it's always been very reliable.'

'That'd be wonderful. You're so kind to me.'

'It's my pleasure.' Joss touched the bruised area of her face very gently. 'It's starting to fade now.'

She grimaced at the sight of herself in a mirror. 'Yellow and purple aren't my favourite colours. There's no way of hiding this.'

'You're going to see Carina tomorrow, aren't you? I'll take you in if you like.'

'There's a bus.'

'Which goes all round the houses. No, let me take you, because one of Gift's friends has a car for sale. We can call and see it on the way back.'

'How wonderful! It's years since I've had a new car.'

'Well, this one's not new, but it's only three years old and hasn't had a lot of use. Giff assures me his friend wouldn't lie to him. We'll set off at nine-thirty. OK?'

She gave in and nodded. After seeing Joss to the door, she went to give Ned his tea. She had taken him for a walk into the village to tire him out and, to her delight, he went to bed without a murmur of protest.

Allie arrived on time, driven by her husband. She was brandishing a bottle of wine. 'As I said, I'm going to walk back, so we can have a couple of drinks.'

Libby still didn't like the idea of this.

Allie grinned. 'Stop pulling a prune face. I'll be perfectly all right. This is Top o' the Hill, not central London. Anyway, I've arranged to give Pete a call before I leave. You can stand at your door and watch me to the end of the lane, and he will stand at the bedroom window and watch me come down the hill.'

'That's all right, then.' She still wouldn't walk out at night herself; she had to remain alert for Steven. Top o' the Hill would be such a nice place to live. If only she could stay here!

When Steven arrived at work, his team leader's secretary rang. 'Can you pop up to see Bruce?'

'Yes, of course. Something wrong?'

'He just said he wanted to see you.'

Steven walked up the stairs instead of taking the lift, something more of his colleagues ought to do.

He was waved into Bruce's office.

'Ah, Steven. Thanks for coming so quickly. Look, the Human Resources people have been on to me about your leave. You've several years' worth owing.'

'I enjoy my work.'

'Well, they want you to clear some of the leave. About eight weeks. This project will be finishing soon. That'd make a good time to start your holidays. All right with you?'

'It'd suit me very well. I was going to ask for some leave anyway. Though eight weeks is too long.'

'The HR Director is adamant. So . . . are you taking the family away?'

'I'm not sure. We might do that.'

'Good.'

The silence meant Bruce had finished, so Steven smiled and edged backwards. 'I'll get back to work again. We're nearly there.'

'Yes. You've done well.'

They keep saying that, but they haven't offered me a promotion, have they? Steven thought as he walked back down the stairs. And they had offered one to Sam Cohen, who hadn't been here as long as him. What the hell else did he have to do to get a promotion?

He sat at his desk and did some calculations. He'd give the bruising another few days to fade, then he'd set off. He downloaded an application for leave, sighing as he filled it in. Eight weeks. What the hell was he supposed to do with himself for eight weeks? It surely wouldn't take that long to find Libby and bring her back.

He did have to teach her a lesson once he got her here, but even that wouldn't take more than a week or two. He wouldn't hit her, though. Not again. It left traces.

'You look as if you just lost your best client, Pulford,' someone joked as he finished filling in the form and left his office to take it to the HR section.

'What is it? Surely not your resignation.' Johnson twitched the paper out of his hand.

Steven stood still. They were off again, joking they called it; annoying him, he called it.

Carter looked over Johnson's shoulder. 'An application for leave? I thought you lived here twenty-four/seven, Pulford.' She grinned at the others, more one of the boys than he was, damn her. Why her husband put up with the long hours she worked, Steven couldn't understand.

He waited as they passed his form from one to the other. It never did any good to try to get back whatever they were teasing him about. He fixed a slight smile to his face, one he'd practised in the mirror.

'We'll miss you,' Johnson said as he handed the paper back. He let out an affected sigh and placed his hand mockingly on his chest. 'I shall be counting the days till you come back.'

'Not!' someone said loudly.

Steven couldn't quite figure out who that was, so he ignored it and kept the smile on his face till he'd left the room. They were fools – childish, prank-playing idiots. But you had to pretend to get on with your colleagues.

He wished he could find another job, but so far he hadn't been successful in his applications. He didn't understand why.

Chapter Nine

The day of the grand opening dawned bright and sunny, for once doing what the weather forecast said. Emily was up by five o'clock, unable to stay in bed when there was so much to check.

Chad turned over and growled at her when she asked if he was awake. She envied him his ability to sleep at will and to go back to sleep in the morning after she got up.

With a fond look at the lump under the bedcovers, she went for her shower, then left the flat and switched off the security system.

The big suite of showrooms was full of delicate dawn light and the displays looked mysterious, some of them even magical. Then she heard a footstep and stopped enjoying the antiques to investigate.

Ashley was standing in the rear showroom, not touching anything, just looking round with intense concentration, much as Emily herself had been doing.

She deliberately made more noise than she needed to as she approached.

The new tenant turned round. 'Is it all right if I look at the . . .' She frowned. 'What do you call these?'

'Displays.'

'Yes.' Ashley repeated it two or three times under her breath.

'Of course it's all right to look, but please don't touch anything.'

'No. I won't. Mummy taught me not to touch. I like dusting things, though. Can I help with the dusting?'

'Not today, but next week you and I will go through everything and we'll see how good you are at dusting.'

Ashley nodded.

'Do you know anything about antiques?'

'Mummy had some antiques. They belonged to her family. I've got them in my flat. I like to dust them. They're very old so you have to be extra careful.'

'Toby has some old things too. He finds beautiful pieces at the markets sometimes and buys them. You should go into town with him. He knows his way round.'

That won her a frown and silence, then: 'Mummy didn't like me to go out alone, except to the shops for food after she got sick.'

'You wouldn't be alone if you went with Toby.'

'Mmm. He thinks very slowly, doesn't he?'

'Yes, he does. But once he learns something he doesn't forget. He's kind and good-natured and will help you any time you ask, if he can.'

'Mmm. I'll sort out my flat first.'

A short pause. Ashley paused quite often, as if to bring to mind some rule. Her mother had certainly prepared her as well as she could, in many ways before her time when it came to treating autism. They were dealing with the condition in new and more effective ways now, but it involved giving the affected children a lot of attention. This young woman had obviously had that from her mother.

Ashley prefaced her next statement with a soft 'Hmm' as she often did. 'I'll go into town with Toby later. That's the best order to do things. You have to work out the right *order* before you start something.'

That sounded like another of Mummy's excellent rules. 'Good thinking. I'd better get my breakfast now. Chad and I have to give everything a final dusting before the opening starts.'

'Can I watch you?'

The young woman was tenacious, to say the least. But why not? 'Yes, of course.'

Ashley nodded and walked away, just as Chad ran lightly down the stairs, moving so differently from how he'd been after his accident, when he could hardly walk and had to use a wheelchair.

He stood with her to watch Ashley disappear by the rear way into her flat, which was through the Old Barn. 'Does she wander about a lot? Is that going to be a problem?'

'She was only looking at the displays, not touching anything. She says she likes to dust. We might even offer her a job. Nicky did the dusting really well. The new woman from the town isn't as thorough and doesn't seem at all interested in the antiques.'

'As long as I don't have to do the dusting. It makes me

sneeze. I couldn't get back to sleep. I was too excited. So I've got a pot of tea brewing up in the flat. Interested in a cup?'

'Oh, yes.' She reached out for his hand automatically and they went upstairs together. How wonderful to have found a soul mate when she was nearly sixty and had resigned herself to living alone.

How wonderful to have all this.

The younger generation talked about 'paying things forward'. A strange phrase. Emily preferred the image that if you wanted a garden full of flowers, you had to plant a lot of seeds.

By midday the caterers had finished setting up and the stall holders had all arrived to take the covers off their goods and make final adjustments.

As far as Emily could tell, everything was ready for the opening party to begin by one o'clock. It would start at two. She felt nervous, but Chad seemed quite relaxed about it all.

A journalist arrived from the local newspaper, and took photos of her and Chad with a group of fine china exhibits, then asked them a few questions about what he referred to as 'your little event', a phrase which set Emily's teeth on edge.

The journo had only just finished with them when guests started arriving. She smoothed her new dress, took a deep breath and went forward to greet them.

She missed her sister's arrival in the crush, which was just as well, because Liz was accompanied by her son, George. If Emily had seen her nephew, she'd have told the security guy at the door to keep him out. Boiling with fury, she began to make her way across the room.

Someone grabbed her arm and she found herself facing Leon.

'Not a good time to make a scene. I'll keep an eye on your nephew for you.'

'Of all the cheek!'

'Yes. I wonder why he can't keep away from you.'

'Because he's controlling and arrogant, not to mention a nosey-parker, and hasn't given up hope of getting his hands on my money. Well, I've changed my will, so he'll get nothing from me when I die. I do wish my sister wasn't such a soft touch.'

Leon grinned and patted her arm. 'Calm down. I won't let him cause any trouble.' As she turned to move away, he added in that soft, innocent tone which always meant he was up to something, 'After the guests leave, I'd like to have a little chat, if you don't mind?' He raised one eyebrow.

She wasn't going to play word games. 'You want something from me.' It wasn't a question.

'Yes.'

'I knew you would.'

'Just because you no longer work for me, it doesn't mean that we can't still help one another out from time to time. We agreed on that.'

'Leon, in the nicest possible way, you use everyone you know. And this is a busy time for me.'

'I admit that I use people – "in the nicest possible way", as you say. But it's in our country's service. And I do pay rather well.'

'I don't need the money. What I need at the moment is more time to get this started.' She gestured round them to the centre. 'But OK, if I can help . . . You've hit me on the patriotic nerve.'

She smiled wryly as she walked across the room to greet the tutor from the antiques course she'd attended early last year. She'd known very well Leon wouldn't come here just to look at the gallery.

'What are you smiling at?' Chad asked.

'Leon. He's after something.' She shrugged. 'I don't mind helping him. Do you?'

'Not at all. Though I can't imagine what we have here that he would want.'

Emily could, but this wasn't the time to explain because a large woman was bearing down on them. The words 'stately as a galleon' came to mind, which she thought came from a comic song about a large lady.

Chad stepped forward. 'Ah, Mrs Gerringson. How nice that you could come! Have you met my partner, Emily? Emily, this is one of my oldest customers and one of my favourites. She buys the things I'd love to own myself. You should see her house. It's a gallery in itself.'

Clearly this customer enjoyed being flattered, so Emily added her piece. 'You must have excellent taste, then.'

Mrs Gerringson laughed. 'Flattery will get you everywhere, Chad. And Emily, nice to meet you.'

But she wasn't paying attention to Emily; she was staring round, eyes darting from one piece to another. 'Anything I should look at?'

'Item twenty-seven. I thought of you.'

'Which is . . . ?'

'Go and find out.' He handed her a programme. 'And have a look round the stalls in the Old Barn, too. Not as expensive, but we've been a bit picky about who and what we've let sell there, so there are some very nice pieces.'

And so it went on: introductions, a glass of champagne that went warm and flat in Emily's hand before she could drink it, women wrapped in perfume and silk, expensive jewellery dazzling the beholder from wrists and necks and fingers. It amazed her that so many people had come long distances to see Chad's new gallery. It amazed her that many of them actually *looked* rich.

At one point, she managed to slip through to the Old Barn to see how things were going there and found it as crowded as Chad's front display area. To her delight, she saw several people buying from the stallholders. They called them 'stalls' but they were more like booths, one of them velvet-lined, literally, to show off exquisite costume jewellery.

In fact, if today was anything to go by, Chadderley Antiques was going to be a roaring success. Just as Chad had predicted. His name plus the range of goods offered for sale were a sure-fire recipe for success, she was sure.

It was well into the evening by the time all the outsiders left. People had lingered, as Chad had predicted. The food had had to be supplemented by some of Rachel's stocks of refreshments, and the champagne had given way to bottles of wine from Chad's personal wine stores, which were now safely racked in the cellars underneath the old inn.

Liz was among those still there, clearly waiting to speak to her sister. George was standing protectively beside her – but who was protecting whom? Emily wondered.

'Shall I tell Pilby to get the hell out of here, or will you?' Chad asked.

'I will.' Emily marched across the room. 'Nice to see you, Liz, but I don't remember inviting your son.'

'We thought . . . you wouldn't mind . . . you might be prepared to . . . to . . .' She looked helplessly at George.

'I can't apologise enough, Auntie dear, for my behaviour. But I thought I was acting in your best interests and—'

'No, you didn't, and you'll never convince me otherwise,' Emily said crisply. 'I don't want you coming here again, George. Not ever. If you do, I might change my mind and complain to the police about your behaviour. I didn't lay a complaint for my sister's sake, but there's still time to do it. And plenty of proof available about what you did to me.'

He drew himself up, glaring at her now. Had he thought she was so gullible? Emily was glad he was from her half-sister's mother's side, and not fully related to her.

Tears welled in Liz's eyes, but Emily wasn't going to be swayed by that. Some things were unforgivable and keeping her drugged and locked in a dementia facility was one of them, as far as she was concerned. If her sister's health hadn't been so fragile, she would have tried to get him prosecuted.

Chad came up beside her and simply stood, looking

angry, his body language showing clearly that he was waiting for Pilby to leave.

'We should go now, George,' Liz murmured when her son still didn't move. 'I'm sorry, Emily. I just . . . don't like the family to be at odds.'

'*You* are welcome here any time, Liz. George is not, and never will be.'

'Let me show you to the door, Pilby,' Chad said. 'Or do you need help getting out of here?'

The threat had George's breath whistling into his mouth. He glared at them both and drew himself up. 'Let's go, Mother. At least *we* tried.'

Liz gave Emily a reproachful look and let him lead her out. Chad followed them and had a word with the security officer at the door, who would be working for them from now on, about not letting that man inside again.

He went back and pulled Emily into his arms for a quick hug. 'It leaves a nasty taste to have to do that, doesn't it?'

She blinked away tears. 'Yes, it does. I don't like to hurt Liz, but she's a fool to let George into her life once more, son or not. What do you bet that he'll manage to take over her finances again and restrict her spending, so that she leaves more to him?'

'No bet. It's a certainty.'

She looked across the room to where Leon was sitting on one of the elegant chairs scattered in small groups around the place. He was waiting for them, patient and implacable as ever.

Rachel came across to join them, yawning. 'Oliver and I will be off, then. What about your two watchers?' She gestured towards the back of the room.

Emily smiled. Toby and Ashley had spent most of the time watching everything with great interest. She'd told the caterers to serve them food and non-alcoholic drinks; Chad had provided them with a table and chairs from the café, and there they'd stayed. She went across to them now.

'Did you enjoy our opening?'

'There were a lot of people,' Toby said.

'It's very dirty and untidy now.' Ashley looked around disapprovingly.

'Don't worry. There are cleaners coming in tomorrow morning to clean everything from top to bottom. By tomorrow teatime it'll all be perfectly clean and tidy again.' She could see that the young woman didn't like this delay, so said quietly, 'This isn't a home, so no one will be here after we close up. If it were a home, we'd tidy it tonight.'

Ashley stood frowning, taking this in, but she still didn't look happy about the mess, even though the caterers had cleared all the food and dirty utensils away.

'It's time for you two to go back to your units now, so that we can close up. See you tomorrow.'

Which left Leon still sitting there, perfectly relaxed and even a little amused.

On his last day before the enforced holiday, Steven left work early. He wasn't going to attend the usual Friday night drinks and chat session. Why should he?

It no longer felt strange to go back to an empty house, but he didn't like it and never would. If he didn't have plans for the next few weeks, he'd be very upset about not going into work on Monday, not having work to do over the weekend.

But he did have plans. He smiled grimly, adding mentally: *as Libby would find out.*

After he'd eaten, he cleared up the kitchen and switched on his computer, and began working on what he should do about his errant wife. It might be good to try a direct approach first, because if it did nothing else, it would upset her. She deserved to be upset.

She'd probably be spoiling the child and living in some seedy room. How was she managing to live anyway? She'd have rent to pay and food to buy. Had she found a job? Was she getting social benefits? Or had she gained access to that damned inheritance? How irresponsible of the old lady to leave Libby money. As if she knew how to manage it.

He'd take it off her and put it to better use . . . if there was any left by the time he brought her back.

The child was going to be the key to controlling her from now on. He knew that. She'd do anything to protect Edward. And he'd insist on giving the child his full name at all times from now on, as well as imposing more discipline.

He wrote down a series of points, large and small. He was just brainstorming at the moment. He'd pull together a proper plan only after he'd considered every aspect, every detail, every tactic he might employ.

The week passed quietly but happily for Libby. She saw her son relax and even make a mess when he played. She didn't want him to go to the other extreme and make a habit of creating chaos, so made a game of them tidying up his toys together every night.

He was always ready to play, so she wondered if she dare send him to the local playgroup. It'd be so good for him. And as long as Steven didn't appear, he should be safe there.

Allie agreed to mention Ned to Trisha when she dropped Gabbi off. She'd told Libby there was a vacancy at the playgroup, but there wouldn't be for long. Trisha sent word back that she should come and have a chat, bringing Ned with her. Around 11.45 would be a good time.

So Libby went to the playgroup just before the children left after their morning session. Ned clung to her, wide-eyed, watching the other little ones play in the sandpit or with the piles of brightly coloured toys.

Trisha waved to them when they arrived but made no attempt to coax Ned into joining in.

When the session ended, the children started to clear away.

Ned nodded and seemed reassured by this. 'They have to clear the toys away.'

'Just like you do, darling.'

The other children ran to greet their parents and soon the big room with its conservatory and outside play area was empty of all but Trisha and the two of them.

Libby bent down. 'The children had fun, didn't they, Ned? Would you like to come here to play?'

He looked at her solemnly, saying nothing, almost as

if he didn't understand the question. She felt her heart would break at how unused he was to other children. Guilt flooded through her, as it kept doing. Why had she let this happen to him?

Trisha came over to join them. 'Hi, Libby.' She bent down. 'You must be Ned. Would you like to come and look at the toys?' She began walking towards a big box of toys, taking his agreement for granted, and when his mother set off after her, Ned trotted along between them.

Trisha took a brightly coloured box of shapes out. 'This is a good game.' She showed him how to do it.

He looked at his mother.

'Have a go with it, Ned. It's all right. I'll stay near you.'

Hesitantly he reached out, taking the pieces, quickly learning how to thread them on to the correct plastic spokes.

When he'd finished, Trisha clapped. 'Well done! Try another toy.'

This time he chose on his own, and didn't even notice when the two women took a couple of steps backwards and began speaking in low voices.

'He's never been allowed to play with other children,' Libby said. 'I should have left my husband years ago. Do you think it's too late for Ned to learn to be a normal little boy?'

'Not too late at all. If you decide to send him here, we won't push him into anything, but just let him find his own feet.'

'I'd love him to come here.'

'You'll need to fill in a form. I'll go and get you one.'

That worried Libby. Would the information she supplied be something anyone could access?

When Trisha brought back the form, she said bluntly, 'I've left his father, who was abusive.' She touched the remains of her bruise. 'On no account must anyone except me be allowed to take Ned away from here. And no information must be given out about him.'

Trisha laid one hand on her shoulder. 'I understand. It may comfort you to know that we keep the outer doors and windows locked at all times, and if the kids are playing in the garden, there are high fences, which you must have seen. Besides that, either I or my helper will be with them at all times outside. As a final resort we have a panic button which sets off a siren and some of the people in the village will come running if they hear it. In today's world, you have to do this sort of thing, even up here at Top o' the Hill.'

'Good. I'll fill in the form and pay you in advance for the first two weeks.'

Ned kept an eye on her but continued to take out toys and examine them one at a time, putting them carefully back.

'When should I bring him?'

Trisha smiled. 'Why not tomorrow? Though I think you should stay the first time, maybe nipping out for a few minutes, then coming back, just till he gets used to being away from you.'

She turned to Ned. 'You can come here tomorrow and play with the toys again. You can play with the other children, too.'

He gave her a long considering look. 'Mummy too?'

'Mummy too,' she confirmed.

You're not getting your hands on him again, Steven Pulford, Libby vowed as they visited the shop then walked slowly back home, talking about the playgroup. *Never, ever.*

Chapter Ten

Chad arranged an Internet video call to Des Monahan, so that Emily could judge whether she would like to put the search for her daughter into his hands.

She studied the private investigator's face on the screen. Nondescript with perhaps a hint of Irish ancestry. He was studying her just as carefully.

'Chad's told me what happened, Ms Mattison.'

'Yes. The reunion people found her and were pretty sure it was her, but we got a message back that she had no desire to contact me. Which is strange, when she had instituted a search as well.'

'They were sure it was she who replied?'

'They wouldn't discuss it with me beyond giving me that information. So I don't really know how sure they are.'

He nodded three times, slowly and thoughtfully, before looking her straight in the eyes. 'Will you trust me to do this for you? It's a delicate matter, finding a lost child. On both sides.'

She gave him an equally searching look. 'Yes. I will trust you.'

'Good. Actually, I prefer this sort of case to messy divorces,

I must admit. It can be very rewarding if it's successful.'

'You'll pull out all the stops?' Chad said.

'You're in a hurry?'

'I think Emily has waited long enough, and it's the only cloud on our joint horizon at present, so I'd like it to go away. Do whatever it takes, don't count the cost. After that, perhaps we can settle down to planning our wedding.'

When the connection was broken, Emily dug Chad in the ribs with her elbow. 'I did not give you permission to discuss our wedding with all and sundry. I'm still not sure we need to marry.'

He leant forward to give her a lingering kiss. 'I'd go and get married next week, if it was up to me, Emily.'

She felt flustered. 'I'm still getting used to the idea. I was so very sure I'd never marry, and after all, there isn't the same pressure to do so in today's world.'

'I want our commitment to one another to be made in public in the traditional way – and celebrated in style!'

'Even if we do marry, I am *not* having an elaborate wedding. I'm too old for all that fuss.' She sniffed. 'You'll be asking me to wear a long white dress next!'

'You're never too old to celebrate a pairing like ours. But white wouldn't suit you. And to hell with tradition; *I* will help you choose the dress. I know a fashion designer in London and I know that you don't maximise your attractions.'

She spread her arms out in a gesture of helplessness. Chad had an unexpected romantic streak, which had surprised her. And he kept insisting she was beautiful, which she knew she wasn't.

But it was rather nice that he wanted so much to marry her, she had to admit, though she wasn't telling him that . . . yet.

The following week, Mrs Hockton picked up the phone. 'Greaves and Hallibourne, Solicitors.'

A rather harsh voice said, 'I'd like to speak to Mr Greaves, please.'

'May I have your name, sir?'

'Bainton.'

'I don't think Mr Greaves has a client called Bainton.' She heard a little growl of anger at the other end.

'Obviously I'm hoping to become his client.'

His patronising tone annoyed the hell out of her. 'Perhaps you'd like to make an appointment to see him? He's not free at the moment.'

'I'd rather speak to him first. What time should I ring back?'

She could hardly refuse to deal with a potential client, but she wanted to. 'I'll mention you to him. Perhaps you could ring back about one-thirty this afternoon.'

'Thank you. I will.'

She checked the client files then went through to Henry. 'A Mr Bainton just rang up, insisting on speaking to you. He isn't a client. I've checked.'

'I don't recognise the name.'

'No. I've told him to ring back at one-thirty.'

He looked at her quizzically. 'You don't like him, do you?'

'No, I don't. I've never even met him, but he spoke to me so patronisingly it set my teeth on edge.'

His smile broadened. 'He's risking his life if he speaks to you like that face to face.' Then he became more serious. 'As always, I trust your judgement absolutely, Mrs H. When this Bainton fellow rings back, tell him I'm too busy to take on any new clients.'

'Good. And thank you for your confidence in me.'

'It's been proved over the years that you're worth your weight in gold when it comes to assessing people.'

At one-thirty precisely the phone rang and she picked it up. 'Greaves and Ha—'

'Bainton here. You suggested I call back at one-thirty to speak to Mr Greaves.'

'I mentioned your call to him and he asked me to tell you he's too busy to take on any new clients at present.'

Silence. Then: 'If I tell you my name is Steven Pulford, I think he may change his mind.'

She gasped. Libby's husband! Then she said coldly, 'I think he'd be even more reluctant to speak to you, Mr Pulford.'

'Mind your own business, woman. Your job is to pass my message to him, not comment on clients. But don't forget to tell him I shall keep ringing until he does speak to me.'

'Please call back in ten minutes.'

'That's more like it.' He put the phone down without a word of thanks or farewell.

She put down her phone and went to find Henry.

'From your expression, that didn't go well,' he said before she'd even spoken.

'No. Bainton was a false name, but now he's admitted he's Libby's husband, Steven Pulford.'

'Oh, damn! I was hoping he wouldn't pursue her.'

'He says he'll keep calling until you do speak to him. And he was extremely rude to me.' She repeated the phone conversation almost verbatim.

There was dead silence, then Henry said in his usual quiet way, 'In that case, I shall have to speak to him. Would you ask Reg if he'll listen in on the call? I'm doing nothing without witnesses.'

She didn't offer to listen in. She knew another lawyer would be a more valuable witness than a mere secretary if anything went to court, so she went to see the other partner.

Exactly ten minutes after the call ended, the phone rang again. Henry nodded to Reg and picked up the handset, setting it on loudspeaker.

'Greaves here.'

'Pulford here. I need to contact my wife. Can you give me her phone number and address, please?'

'You can do any business that's necessary through me. I'm representing your wife from now on.'

'I don't wish to discuss *business*. I wish to speak to her about personal matters.'

'That won't be possible.'

After a rumble of anger and a pause, Pulford said, 'If I send you an email, can you forward it to her?'

'I'd rather you wrote a letter to me, and I must warn you that I'll still be the one dealing with it. She has no desire to see you or speak to you, and *I* have no desire to see her beaten and hurt so badly again.'

'She was only slightly bruised. It was an accident. And she has no right to keep my son from me.'

'Her injuries were not caused by any accident. I also saw the bruises on the boy's leg. She wasn't the only one who'd been hurt.'

Another silence. 'Children fall over all the time. I'd never touch Edward.'

'We both know that wasn't from a fall. Now, I'm a busy man and I have nothing more to say to you. Please write from now on if you need to get in touch. I shan't take any more phone calls from you.'

He put the phone down and looked at Reg. 'I don't like this. She said he'd come after her, and I'm sure he will.'

'He sounds . . . obsessed. Be very careful, Henry. Better let her know what's happened. She needs to be on her guard.'

'She's on her guard already. What I'm afraid of is that she'll run away and he'll catch her in a place where she has no protectors. I'd better ring both her and Joss to warn them.'

But though the phones rang again and again at both their houses, no one answered.

On Thursday morning, Joss came out of the village shop just as Libby was leaving the playgroup. He waved to her, so she waited for him to cross the road and catch up.

'Fancy going to the antiques centre tomorrow?'

'It'd have to be in the afternoon.' She slowed down for a moment, looking back towards the playgroup. It made her feel insecure every time she left Ned, but from now on he must learn to interact with other people and not be totally dependent on her.

'Hard to leave him?' Joss's smile was sympathetic. 'My sister cried all the way home when she left her eldest at school the first time.'

'This is the first time Ned will be staying all morning without me popping in. He said he'd be all right. He insists he's a big boy now.' Her lips quivered. No one had asked whether she'd be all right, and she wasn't. She was worrying about her son already.

Joss smiled. 'He *will* be all right, though. Trish loves children and she'll look after him carefully. You were lucky to get him a place there.'

'I know.' But her voice wobbled.

He put an arm round her shoulders. 'From what you've said, your husband didn't do any of the daily caring for a child. I bet *you* haven't been without Ned since he was born.'

She nodded. 'Not for a single day. Stupid, isn't it? As if I wasn't aware that all children go to school. It's a natural progression. Anyway, we were discussing tomorrow's outing, weren't we? Thank you for the invitation. Ned and I would love to go to the antiques centre with you.'

'Need any help packing up the ornaments?'

She almost said no, but gave in to the desire to have company. Joss was always so pleasant and interesting. 'I'd love your help. Sometimes two pairs of hands are better than one.'

'Give me ten minutes to put my food away and get myself a coffee, then I'll be round to help.'

'I'll make you a cup of coffee, and you can tell me what

you think of my orange squash cake.' She put on an affected voice. 'It's just a simple little thing I whipped up.'

He laughed and veered towards his front door. 'See you shortly.'

She put the kettle on and couldn't resist checking her appearance in the mirror. It'd do. Her hair was slightly windswept but it was flattering, she thought. Steven would have hated the tousled look. She didn't use make-up, except for special occasions, and anyway, her cheeks were rosy from fresh air and brisk walking.

Oh, it was so good being with Joss, not needing to think out each remark in advance and worry that she'd upset him. He didn't talk a lot, but she felt comfortable with him, even during the silences.

Some cake having been duly consumed and approved, they moved to the front room, where the cardboard boxes Allie had given her from the shop were waiting, together with all sorts of wrapping that goods had been delivered in.

They sorted out the ornaments into three lots: one group which didn't seem very good, one which might possibly be worth something, and one which seemed older and most likely to be valuable. After wrapping them carefully, they cushioned them in the boxes. Thirty-two ornaments in all, nearly all from the front room.

'I'll come round tomorrow to put the boxes in my car, shall I?'

'They're not that heavy. I can manage. We'll have to put Ned's booster seat in, too. He'll probably fall asleep in the car after a hard morning's playing.'

* * *

They were able to set off by one o'clock the following day, and as Libby had predicted, Ned did fall asleep almost immediately. Trish had told her he was starting to interact with the other children, which was excellent news.

'A penny for them?' Joss said quietly.

'No prizes for guessing: I keep worrying about Steven.'

'We'll cross that bridge when we come to it.'

'We?'

'I'm a trustee . . . and your closest neighbour . . . and, I hope, a friend now.'

She heard her voice soften. 'Yes. Definitely a friend.' She hadn't hesitated to say that, still hadn't worked out what it was about him that made her feel so sure of it. If she weren't in this situation, she'd hope he could become more than just a friend, because she found him very attractive, but she knew – she just knew – that one day she'd have to run or move to a women's refuge. Whatever he said or did, Joss hadn't experienced Steven's bloody-minded stubbornness when he wanted something.

As they began to drive uphill from Littleborough towards the gallery, Joss grimaced. 'This seems a strange place to have an exclusive antiques gallery, don't you think?'

'People may enjoy visiting it as part of an outing, and I suppose he'll be selling stuff online as well. I'm looking forward to seeing it, I must admit, though we'll have to keep an eye on Ned. I'd hate him to break something valuable. Didn't you say it's more than a gallery, though?'

'Yes. It's advertised as an antiques centre, with a main gallery of upmarket pieces belonging to this Edward Chadderley, and another area shared by various vendors.'

'Does the main gallery specialise in anything in particular?'

'I only have a brochure, and that's very general. I don't know enough about the antiques world to say what Chadderley specialises in.'

'What made you want to come here?'

'A friend mentioned it, said it was worth a visit.' Joss wished he could tell her more, hated to fudge the truth with her.

When they arrived, Joss said, 'Let me check the exterior first.' He took a minute to study the sign from the car park. A board ran along the side of the building with CHADDERLEY ANTIQUES on it. It looked very simple, very classy.

It was obvious that the place had once been a pub, but he walked to the upper edge of the car park, from which he could see some connected buildings behind it. He smiled at himself. He still automatically checked places out, as if he were on a case. He rather thought one part of the complex might be eighteenth century, or even earlier. It had an ancient look to it, something about the brickwork maybe; he wasn't an expert on historical architecture.

Libby and Ned came across to join him. 'It's big,' she said. 'Bigger than I'd expected.'

When they went inside, she clutched Ned's hand firmly. The antiques were shown in small groups, with appropriate lighting, and it was obvious that they were expensive pieces. You could just tell.

She was entranced by one group of cranberry glass pieces with silver fittings. She'd seen cranberry glass before, and loved it, but this had that indefinable air of quality. No wonder Joss fancied a piece like that. If she had a stable life, she'd lust after a decanter, too.

She turned away. Beautiful objects like these were not for her at the moment. Perhaps one day.

A woman smiled at them from behind a discreet reception desk to the left-hand side, such a nice smile that Libby smiled back without thinking.

'Do feel free to walk round,' the woman called.

Libby looked down at Ned, who was jigging about in a way that sent a message. 'I think we'd better visit the loo first, if that's all right.'

'Of course. Go to the rear of the second display area and turn right. The loos are just along from the café before you get to the Old Barn.'

When Libby returned, Joss was in a discussion with the woman. He beckoned her over. 'This is Emily. Emily, this is Libby. I've been telling her about your grandmother's ornaments and Mr Chadderley will be happy to value them for you. He'll be back in half an hour.'

'It doesn't . . . cost anything?'

'No. Valuations are free.'

'In the meantime, we can go on looking round. Anything you'd like to see more clearly?'

'That.' Libby indicated a group of 1930s Art Deco figurines, slender women holding graceful poses. Again, she was struck by the high quality of the pieces and the attractive way the figurines were displayed, two of them on little turntables that made them seem ready to leap gracefully into the air. She studied them enviously. 'If I ever get rich, I'm going to buy myself a figurine like these.'

'They are beautiful, aren't they?'

They were intending to go to the Old Barn, where there were stalls with less expensive goods, but when Joss saw the café, where four people were sitting round a table with drinks and snacks, he stopped. 'Aha! Ned and I need something to eat and drink.'

Ned beamed at him and Joss helped him to choose a fruit and nut bar as well as a drink of apple juice.

'You're a good trencherman,' Libby told Joss.

He grinned and picked up a second piece of cake. 'Have to keep up my strength.'

A quick glance into 'The Old Barn' showed them about a dozen generously proportioned stalls with tempting arrays of goods.

'We'll go in there later, or even another time,' Joss said once they'd finished. 'It's nearly time to see Chad. I'd better bring in the boxes of ornaments from the car. Do you want to bring Ned out for a run round the car park?'

'I'd better. He's been good but he's getting a bit restless.'

They were just going back into the centre when a luxury car drew up. Libby bent to listen to something Ned was trying to tell her.

Suddenly a voice behind her said, 'Emily, have you seen—' Then the man broke off. 'Oh, sorry! From behind you looked just like my partner. I'm Chad, one of the owners here.'

Libby smiled at him. 'Emily said you'd be back soon. We've brought my grandmother's ornaments to be valued, if you'd be so kind. They're probably not worth a lot but a few of them seem quite old, so we wanted to check.'

'Happy to oblige.'

They walked inside together, and after greeting Emily with a kiss and a hug, he took them into a side room furnished only with three tables.

'Perhaps you could unpack the ornaments here? I'll be back in a minute.'

'I'll look after Ned; you unpack,' Joss said.

'Thanks.' Libby began to unpack the ornaments, putting them on three different tables. 'I'm sure we're wasting his time, though. The pieces in his gallery are so beautiful.'

Chad came back in just as she was finishing, and she explained about the groupings.

He checked the ones she didn't think were worth anything first, putting most to one side, but taking two of them and examining them more closely. 'These would suit one of the stallholders. I'll call her in afterwards. They're worth about eighty pounds each but of course she won't give you that much. She has to make a profit.'

'I'm surprised.' Libby wrinkled her nose.

He chuckled. 'Ceramic animals are not to my taste, either, but some people love them.'

On the second table stood the ones they thought might have some value. It yielded up four ornaments which Chad said would be sellable for prices between £50 and £100, and three items which he said were worth in excess of £200.

Libby was astonished.

As he was starting to study the items on the third table, a young man peeped into the room.

'Come in, Toby! Tell me what you think of these.'

Libby and Joss exchanged surprised glances, because the young man appeared to have Down syndrome.

Toby went to stare at the ornaments on the third table, head on one side, touching nothing.

Chad put one finger to his lips to signify that Joss and Libby should be quiet.

After a few minutes Toby picked up one ornament, a pretty bowl, and said, 'I like this one best.'

'So do I,' Chad said. 'Well done. You're very clever. You always pick the best piece.'

Toby gave him a beaming smile. 'I like old things. I found something else in town today.' He held out an object wrapped in newspaper.

Chad unwrapped it, shook his head as if in disbelief. 'Emily! Have you a minute?'

She came in to join them.

'Toby's done it again. Where did you find this, Toby?'

'In a little shop near the market. Ashley said it was ugly, but I like it.'

'It's very valuable so look after it carefully.'

Toby nodded, wrapped it up and went off somewhere.

Chad turned to his visitors. 'Toby's got a gift for finding valuable pieces among junk. He's not at all interested in money and valuations, and he's had no training, so it's amazing how good the things he finds are. I must take him to a car boot sale one day soon. Who knows what he'll turn up there! Now, let's get back to your pieces.'

He rearranged the older pieces into two sets. 'I can give you five hundred pounds for these; for the others, three hundred pounds for each piece.'

Libby gaped at him. 'That much?'

'I'll get more for them than that, but unless you have contacts in the antiques industry, you'll find it hard to better the price I'm offering. I'll let you think about it, shall I?'

She looked at Joss, who gestured to her to speak. 'I don't think we need time. We're happy to accept your offer.'

'I'll get Jen in to see the others. She has a booth in the barn.' He strode off, leaving Libby still speechless.

'You've made a good bit of money, so why aren't you smiling?' Joss teased.

She couldn't manage a smile, just said ruefully, 'I can't believe it's real. Life doesn't hand things to me so easily.'

'Maybe your life is changing.'

She shook her head. The Steven problem wouldn't go away. She mustn't be lulled into forgetting that.

When they'd completed their transactions, Libby took a weary Ned back to the car while Joss took a quick walk round the Old Barn, looking down the corridor that led off at the rear left, presumably to the older parts of the building he'd seen from the car park. He liked to get a rough floor plan of a new place fixed in his mind, and that had come in useful at times.

When he looked up at the roof beams, he was amazed at how old the barn really was.

After he came back to the main gallery, he got talking to Chad for a few moments and asked if he could come back another time and look round the older part of the house.

Chad studied him, then nodded as if he'd passed some sort of test. 'Yes, of course. I'll get Emily to show you. It's her house, really.'

'Is it haunted?'

Chad shrugged. 'Some people see ghosts, some don't.'

'And you?'

'I'm never quite sure.'

Clever answers, Joss thought as he said his farewells and walked out to the car.

And clever Leon, to think of this place for a temporary refuge.

When their visitors had gone, Emily tucked her arm in Chad's. 'I had a call from the estate agent. My nephew made an offer on my old house.'

'And you said . . . ?'

'I said he had to pay twenty thousand over the asking price.'

'Good for you.'

She sighed. 'I do wish I could be a fly on the wall when George is given my response. The Americans have a phrase for it: he'll throw a conniption fit.'

Chad laughed. 'He certainly will. Where do you get such lovely phrases from?'

'Here and there. His face will go red; he'll puff up like a bullfrog and sputter with indignation.'

'In other words, he'll throw a conniption fit.'

'I shan't back down, though.'

When they reached Top o' the Hill, it felt to Libby like coming home. She thanked Joss and said goodbye, sighing happily as she put her key in the lock and took Ned inside.

She noticed a red light blinking on the phone and stopped

in surprise. It would be Mr Greaves, probably, because no one else except he and Joss had her phone number. She picked up the handset and pressed the Play Messages button.

Mr Greaves spoke slowly and clearly. 'Could you please phone me back urgently, Libby. I'm afraid your husband got in touch with me today.'

She froze, terror icing her whole body.

Ned was clamouring for a drink and a biscuit, so she gave them to him, but beyond that she couldn't think what to say or do.

Someone moved behind her and she swung round, her heart pounding. It was Joss, but for a moment she lost it and panicked, letting out a scream of shock.

'What's wrong?' His voice was as quiet and measured as ever.

For answer, she pressed the replay button again.

He listened, then shook his head. 'Your ex still won't know where you live.'

'He'll find out. Steven always boasts about how good he is at finding things out on the Internet.'

'Then he'll have to face us both. I won't let him hurt you again, Libby.'

'He might not *hit* me again – in fact, he probably won't because that leaves evidence behind – but he'll find some way to hurt me nonetheless.' Her glance fell on Ned. Steven knew where she was most vulnerable.

Joss's gaze followed hers and his lips tightened. 'I won't let him hurt Ned, either.'

'If a court says I have to give Ned back to him, how can you stop that?'

'I have one or two friends in . . . unusual places. I'll find a way. And we do have the photographs of Ned's injuries.'

'How do we prove Steven did them? It's my word against his.'

'And your neighbour's word.'

'Even she didn't see it happen.' Libby tried to control her emotions, but a tear rolled down her cheek and another one followed. She pulled out a tissue. 'Sorry.'

Joss pulled her into his arms, moving slowly and gently. 'You have nothing to be sorry about.'

She didn't resist, went willingly and stood there, feeling safer.

But she would never feel completely safe as long as Steven had her in his sights. Eventually she pulled away from Joss. 'I'd better ring Mr Greaves.'

'He'll be at home by now. He's not one to work long hours. But I don't think we should wait until tomorrow.' He pulled a pad across the table and scribbled on it. 'This is Henry's home number. Don't use it unless something is urgent.'

He watched her press the little buttons on the phone with fingers that trembled just a little.

'Mrs Greaves? Sorry to trouble you at home, but your husband left me a message to ring him urgently.'

'Ms King?'

'Yes.'

'Hold on. I'll get him.'

Libby waited, tapping her foot impatiently as Mrs Greaves called out her husband's name, then footsteps approached across a wooden floor.

'Is that you, Libby?'

'Yes. I've just got home. Your message . . . worried me. Does Steven know where I am?'

'I don't think so. He was pressing me to give him your contact details.'

'He'll find out, probably by tomorrow morning. It won't be the first time he's spent a night online, searching for information.'

'Please don't run away without letting me know where you are.'

'I might have to.'

'Is Joss there?'

'Yes.'

'Ask him to ring me when he gets home, will you? Trustee business.'

She looked at her companion. 'Mr Greaves wants you to phone him later.'

'I'll phone him now.' He took the handset and clicked on loudspeaker mode, so that she could listen in. 'Henry, I'm here and I don't think we should plan anything behind Libby's back.'

She nodded her thanks and listened carefully to what was being said.

'You'll need to stay close to her from now on, Joss.'

'Obviously.'

'I don't think her husband knows exactly where she is, but it won't take much for him to find out where she'll be, will it?'

'Sadly, no.'

Joss pulled Libby close again with his free arm. 'From

now on, Henry, I'll consider myself on bodyguard duty. Until a suitable solution is reached. I'll get back to you tomorrow.'

She was tense and rigid in his arms, and her voice was low and shaky. 'Thank you.'

'I won't let him get you. Or Ned. I'll make up a bed in your front room, if that's all right, and sleep here from now on.'

'That'd be good. But Joss, what if Steven persuades Social Services that he has a right to access, and they try to arrange a visit with Ned?'

'We'll cross that bridge when we come to it.' He ran his fingers through his hair, thinking hard. 'I have a useful set of contacts, and I'm prepared to call them all in if I have to.'

'I'm more worried about my son than myself. Ned is my Achilles heel and Steven knows it.'

Chapter Eleven

When Joss went next door to pack, he phoned the unit. He needed to stand down from duty with them until he'd sorted things out for Libby. He got the usual artificial voice telling him that Leon would ring him back in a few minutes.

When this happened, Leon didn't waste time on greetings but asked, 'How did it go at Chadderley's?'

'It went well, I think. I had a good excuse to go there, so I don't think the owners realised I was connected to you. It's a beautiful gallery, isn't it?'

'Beautiful but a bit spooky. Did you explore the rest of the buildings at all?'

'No, but I've arranged to go back next week for a guided tour.'

Leon's voice went very quiet. 'I wonder, was that wise?'

'Wise or not, it'd sound strange now that it's arranged if I were to back out. Besides, I want to see the rear outbuildings. I have a feeling I might need to know my way around there. Don't ask me why I feel that. Call it a police instinct, honed over the years. Call it spooky. There's a strange feel to the whole place, as if it's waiting for something, ready for something.' He bit off further words, afraid he'd made a fool of himself.

Leon sighed. 'Oh, hell, they haven't caught you up in their woo-woo already, have they? Don't be surprised if you start seeing ghosts and strange lights in corners next time you visit. Emily does.'

'Do you see that sort of thing when you go there, Leon?'

Silence. Then: 'I don't believe in it but . . . yes, it is a bit spooky and yes, I've sensed . . . something; seen lights.'

His frank answer surprised Joss. It was the last thing he'd have expected such a capable and intelligent man to admit. He realised Leon had said something else. 'Sorry. What was that?'

'Did you meet the tenants of the units that Chad and Emily have built at the rear?'

'I met Toby, if that's who you mean.'

'Yes. Clever lad, in his own way, our Toby. Has some surprising gifts.'

'Finding antiques at flea markets, do you mean?'

'No. Communing with ghosts. You'll see.'

'You sound as if you know the place well.'

'I've known Emily for a long time, so I'm bound to visit, aren't I? I visited when she took over and I went to the grand opening earlier this week. Tell me more about this Libby and her son. Do you realise how your voice softens when you talk about her?'

'Does it really? I haven't . . . That's none of your business'

Leon let out one of his soft laughs. 'Most people wouldn't notice. Bit risky, though, involving a child in our sort of business.'

'Well, I can't get involved myself for a while, I'm afraid. Libby needs protection at the moment, and so does Ned. She's just left an abusive husband, but she's terrified he'll come after her. We were hoping it'd take him a while to find out where she is, but he rang her lawyer yesterday demanding contact details, so he knows she's in this area. I'm one of the trustees for the legacy, and . . .' He took a deep breath and said something that surprised himself, 'I'm involved with her.'

'Hmm. Well, no sane man can stand wife-beaters and I consider myself extremely sane, so you can sort Steven Pulford out with my blessing.'

'You know his name. You already knew about Libby.' It wasn't a question, but a flat statement of fact.

'Oh, yes. I have a rather good information-gathering system. If you need to find anything out to help your Libby, be my guest. Though actually, it looks as if we might welcome some feminine involvement in your first case. Something's blown up out of the blue. It won't put Libby in danger. Could you offer her a job without giving away exactly who we are?'

'Probably.'

'Do it. Promise her a fair payment for accompanying a woman who is also escaping an abusive situation.' He named a daily sum, waited a moment or two. 'Will you do the job for me still? Or should I find someone else?'

'How soon?'

'Probably tomorrow.'

'All right. But the new bathroom won't be ready for a while.'

'That's the last thing she'll care about.'

'Fine by me. But I'll have Libby with me at all times.'

'Libby's presence will reassure the poor woman. Look, I'd put another operative on this job if I had a woman operative available. But I don't. Not for a week or so. Let's hope Libby's ex doesn't get in our way. If he does, I'll be on his tail.'

'Stand in line after me. I'm almost hoping he will need his attitudes correcting.'

'Go for it. This woman is a small but important piece of a larger matter that impinges on national security. I'll get back to you about her soon.'

The phone went dead and Joss was left staring at it, wondering at the way everything seemed to be happening at once.

Alone in the quiet room, with dusk softening the world, he grinned. He'd forgotten how much he enjoyed thwarting villains. You weren't supposed to care about that sort of Boys' Own stuff in this greedy, cynical modern world, but he did. He always had.

Then he realised Libby would be worrying about him and rushed round gathering his things for tonight. Thank goodness he had an air mattress. He was too old to sleep on couches.

He was pleased to find the front door locked. He knocked. 'It's me, Libby.'

The door opened and she let him in, locking up carefully again.

'Sorry to take so long. I had an important phone call to make. Is Ned in bed?'

'Yes. It's been a busy day for him.'

'And busy for you, too. You look tired.' He reached out to touch the dark circles under her eyes and couldn't help caressing the last traces of the bruise on her face. 'It would make me very happy to mark your husband's face.'

'It'd make *me* very happy if neither of us ever saw Steven again.'

'Is it likely?'

She shook her head. 'No. He'll not stop till he finds us.'

'I'll sleep here every night and I'll be around most of the time during the day.'

'What about your new job?'

'Can we sit down with a coffee or something, Libby? I have a few things to tell you.'

'How about a glass of wine? I'm more in the mood for that.'

'Perfect. And let's sit in the front room. It's comfier there.'

She led the way but stopped in the doorway. 'How will you manage, sleeping in here? It's only a two-seater couch.'

'I've brought an air mattress. I'll be fine.' He sat on the couch and when she would have taken a chair, he pulled her down beside him instead. 'There are some advantages to a two-seater couch.'

'I can't think of my own wishes at the moment.'

'I'm not intending to ravish you, Libby. I just want to sit and talk, maybe hold hands, maybe even kiss you goodnight. Is that too much?'

There was a long silence during which she stared at him,

solemn as an owl, then she gave him a tremulous smile. 'No. That definitely isn't too much.'

He hadn't realised he'd feel so relieved by her answer. This had happened so quickly and it felt so right. 'Good. I'm glad. I really like you, Libby. And I find you very attractive.' He realised he was twisting his fingers in his hair again, a stupid habit he had when he was tense. He tried to smooth out the tangles, was vain enough to hope she hadn't noticed the occasional grey threads.

She smiled and removed his hand, tidying his hair for him with her fingertips, her soft, gentle fingertips.

He breathed slowly and carefully, but even that slight touch had roused him further. 'Right. We'll take it slowly and see where we go.' He laughed suddenly. 'I feel as shy as a lad courting his first young lass. Stupid, isn't it?'

'No, not stupid. I feel . . . surprised more than anything. But attracted too. Only, I need to get rid of Steven officially before I can move on. It would seem dishonest to do anything else.'

'He doesn't deserve treating fairly.'

'It's not for him; it's for me, so that I feel right about . . . us. Now, what did you want to tell me?'

It took him a few moments to gather his scattered wits. He set his wine glass down on a small table and took hold of her hand again as he spoke.

'I've been offered some occasional work. I don't know how to describe it. Escort work for people needing to disappear quietly would be the closest, perhaps. I can't tell you about the department that organises it. Very hush-hush. But they sometimes welcome the presence of a woman, to make another woman feel safe. Or even a child, to make a group look like a family. They wondered if you might be interested in working with me every now and then.'

'Is it dangerous?'

'At the stage where I'd take over, not very. But there's no part of life where anyone can feel perfectly safe these days, is there? For you, I think it'd be safer to be involved in one of the transfers, than to be left here on your own. Safer for Ned, too.'

'It all sounds very James Bond.'

'Not nearly that exciting. Probably quite boring in fact; just passing a person on to the next stage in a sort of underground railway till they reach somewhere safe further down the line. What do you think?'

'I think you're right. I'd feel safer being involved in that than sitting here alone waiting for Steven to erupt on to the scene.'

'Is he likely to do that? Erupt?'

'Yes. Now that I've defied him, he'll be furious.'

'Mmm. Well, I can be very decisive about dealing with him, believe me. Oh, I forgot one thing. These people are prepared to pay you for your involvement.'

When he told her how much, she gaped at him in shock. 'That much! Wow, I'd welcome the chance to earn some money. They do pay well.'

'They pay for your silence as well as for the inconvenience, because our services can be required any time, day or night.'

'I'm happy to be involved, especially if it's a woman who needs help.'

'Good. And Libby . . . do not run anywhere except to me.'

'I'll try not to. But if Steven turned up while you were out, I'd have to do what was best for Ned.'

'Fair enough.'

The phone rang at Emily and Chad's flat early the next morning. Chad was in the shower, so Emily grabbed it.

'Leon here.'

She sat upright in bed, feeling at a disadvantage lying down, even though he couldn't see her. 'You're an early bird today.'

'Needs must. I have someone in transit who needs shelter for a night, maybe two nights max. She's had a rough time, been held captive and drugged.'

Emily sighed. She'd been in that position herself, and couldn't turn down the chance to help someone escape. 'OK.'

'That easy?' he teased.

'You know damned well you pushed the right button with me.'

'Yes, I did.'

'Who is she?'

'She'll be using the name Jane Dawson while she's with you. I haven't decided what to call her next.'

'Who'll be bringing her, Leon? Anyone I know?'

'No. He's a newcomer to our chain of contacts. You met him yesterday when his partner was selling Chad some china.'

Emily was startled. 'Joss is one of your men!'

'Intermittently. Retired police. Injured in the line of duty, hates the thought of a desk job.'

'And his partner? She seemed familiar, I don't know why.'

'I haven't met her, only seen photos of her and her son. They'll come to you as a family group. Our lady, whom we're calling Jane, won't leave the centre with them. She'll stay for maybe a couple of days, before moving on again.'

'You don't often use children.'

'No, I don't. But Libby won't go anywhere without her son. And he'll make excellent cover.'

'When exactly are we to expect our visitors?'

'When did you arrange to show Joss round?'

'Next week.'

'Could you make it a little earlier? On Sunday, perhaps. Better to have this happen on one of your busier days, with quite a few people around at the centre. Oh, and Joss is staying with Libby. You'd better phone him there to change the appointment. This is the number.'

'OK.' She put the phone down and looked up as Chad returned from his shower. 'That was Leon. He needs us to shelter someone for a day or two. Is that still OK with you?'

'Yes, of course.'

'You take everything in your stride, don't you?'

'I try to. I'm grateful to be alive, grateful to have you in my life.' He gave her a mock punch. 'But I'll be even more grateful when you agree to marry me.'

* * *

Des studied all the houses carefully as he strolled along the street, making imaginary notes on his clipboard. But there was only one house in which he was really interested.

No one was making any attempt to keep its garden tidy. It being June, weeds were springing up everywhere with happy abandon. Des had already found out that Pulford didn't do the gardening or housework. So was his wife no longer with him? He sauntered along and got talking to an older lady a couple of houses along, who was dead-heading her roses.

After a few minutes, she gestured to the clipboard. 'There's nothing written on that, just squiggles.'

He was annoyed at himself for letting that show. He wasn't usually so careless.

'You stayed in front of the Pulfords' house for longer than the others. Can I ask why or should I call in the police to ask you?'

'You're a sharp one.' He studied her. 'Are you a friend of the Pulfords?'

'*He* doesn't have any friends, for obvious reasons.'

'Then you're a friend of Mrs Pulford.' At her nod, he said, 'Oh, good! I've been hired to find her.' He pulled out a business card and handed it to her, also pulling out an article from a newspaper in which a Police Chief Inspector was commending him for his assistance in solving a tricky case.

'This doesn't look much like you,' she said, looking from the newspaper photo to him and back again.

'I'm glad to hear that. In my line of business, anonymous is good. I was smiling like this and had my hair differently, if it's any help.' He smoothed his hair straight back and put on his official smile. The combination was deliberately calculated to change his face.

'Ah. Clever, that.' She handed the article back to him. 'Who would want to find Mrs Pulford?'

'Her birth mother.'

After a moment's silence, Mary said, 'Why employ you? Can't they contact Libby directly?'

'They tried. Someone responded to a letter which would have arrived a few days ago. The reply was posted last Monday with her signature. We're not sure she was the one who replied, though. If it was, and she really doesn't want to contact her birth mother, this will go no further. If it wasn't . . .'

'If this letter was posted last Monday, she couldn't have been involved. She left the previous Tuesday and hasn't been back since.'

'Very useful information, that. Thank you. So someone else must have signed the form and ticked the box for refusing all contact.'

'It could only have been her husband. There's no one else living there now. It'd be just like him to do that. He's a cruel devil!'

Des waited.

'I don't know what Libby would want to do, but I'm pretty sure she'd have told me if she'd heard from her birth mother. We chat sometimes and I knew she'd written to an organisation which arranges reunions. But her husband always picks up the mail from a PO box near his office.'

'He's not at work at the moment. Do you know why?'

'He told another neighbour he has to catch up on his annual leave. He's hardly taken any for a good few years.'

'Workaholic, eh?'

She nodded.

'Could you get a message to his wife from my client? You don't need to tell us how you do it.'

Mary shook her head. 'I don't know where she is exactly, but I can tell you the name of her lawyer, if that's any help. Since her husband already knows that, I'm not giving anything away that he can use to catch her.'

'Catch her?'

'Come in and have a cup of tea. It'll be less obvious.'

Des opened the gate and followed her inside the house. His luck was holding, he thought, feeling pleased with himself. He was often lucky like this on investigations – didn't know why.

But when he wasn't lucky, he didn't mind bending a few rules. He did whatever it took to help people in need. He had enough money not to have to take on cases where he didn't like the protagonists or what they were trying to do. He was sorry his parents had died young – very sorry, missed them still – but inheriting their house meant he didn't have a mortgage. That had made all the difference to his working life.

'Do you have a photo of Mrs Pulford?' he asked as he took a seat at a small table in the kitchen and watched Mary put the kettle on.

'Yes. I'll get one out.' She rummaged through a folder and came up with a photo of a tense-looking young woman and a small boy. 'That's her son, Ned.'

'Nice looking kid.' Des frowned. 'But they both look . . . repressed.'

'Yes. Years of domination by Pulford. I don't know where she found the courage to leave him, but I'm glad of it. If you go looking for her, keep an eye out for *him*. He'll be going after her. Nothing is surer. I pray he doesn't catch her and hurt her again.'

As Mary started to put the other photos back, the folder slipped and he caught it for her, gasping as he saw another image: that of a woman who'd been beaten.

'He did that to her?'

Mary gave him another of her assessing looks. 'I don't know how you've wriggled your way under my defences, but yes. He did that.'

'Maybe you trust me because I'm telling the simple truth. I usually find it works best.'

'Are you going to carry on looking for Libby?'

'Yes. But I won't be approaching her. I'll leave that to her birth mother.'

'I think she could do with a mother now. Her adoptive mother was a weak straw and married a bully. She's dead now. The stepfather is still alive, but he's a drunken lout these days. *He* gets on well with Pulford, which says a lot about him.'

When she'd given him the lawyer's details, Mary showed him to the front door, but stopped dead after opening it and made a gesture to go back. He moved down the hall obediently, taking a couple of steps sideways to look out at the street through the front-room windows.

Pulford had come out of his house and was standing on his drive scowling at the garden.

'He's missing his domestic slave,' Mary said. 'He never lifts a finger about the place normally, indoors or out.'

They waited, but Pulford opened the garage door and hauled out a wheelbarrow, before starting to pull out the worst of the weeds.

Mary said thoughtfully, 'He looks as if he's settling in to work. He's a bit obsessive about tidiness so I suppose that's making him do menial work. I think it'd be better if I drove you away from the street. You can get into my car in the garage and crouch down in the back as we go out. If you want to remain a complete stranger to him, that is?'

'Good idea. Thanks.'

She dropped Des two streets away, where he'd parked his car. 'Might as well do my shopping. It'd look strange if I returned straight away. Good luck with your search.' She drove off in another direction.

He looked at the lawyer's details on the scrap of paper. The man's offices weren't very far from where the birth mother was living. He wondered what Libby would do about contacting the woman. And vice versa. He'd met Chad before, had worked for him a few times, but he hadn't yet met his partner face to face. He'd phone Emily on Sunday evening. Before he did anything else, he wanted to make sure she still preferred him to see the lawyer on her behalf.

If she did, he'd drive up north on Monday morning and see Mr Greaves as soon as he could.

He didn't want to upset Emily or her daughter. These adoption reunions could be very sensitive.

He sighed. He had no other cases pending. Looked like being a quiet weekend. Too quiet. He really must make time to get out and meet people, perhaps try a dating site on the Internet.

Perhaps.

Chapter Twelve

On the Saturday, Leon rang his newest recruit again. When he couldn't get an answer on Joss's mobile, he rang Libby's phone number. No answer to that, either, so he left a message asking Joss to contact him immediately. He didn't say who he was or give a number, naturally. He flattered himself that they would recognise his voice.

When they came home from their walk, with a tired Ned riding on Joss's shoulders, Libby saw the message light winking on the phone. She tensed immediately. 'Someone phoned, only no one is supposed to know I'm here except Mr Greaves, you and Allie.'

Joss slid Ned down from his shoulders. 'I'll attend to it. You give the lad that biscuit he's been demanding.'

But she waited to hear who it was.

When he lifted the phone, Leon's cultured tones rang out.

Libby looked at him. 'Do I know this guy?'

'I do. It's your new employer.' He pulled out his mobile. 'Ah, someone's left me a message too. Yes, it's him.' He dialled the number he'd memorised, and which he would never put on quick dial or write down anywhere. 'Joss calling Leon back.'

She looked at him in surprise when he ended the call immediately.

'He always rings you back. You can never get straight through to him. I must give you that number, in case . . . Well, just in case you need help, of any sort. Better to be prepared.' He recited the number and she repeated it several times, memorising it carefully.

Joss's mobile phone rang. 'Hi, Leon. Yes, she's here. We went for a little walk.'

'Something's come up and I need to deliver your package tomorrow morning, Joss. Can you pass it straight on to our friends? Before three o'clock tomorrow, maybe?'

'Yes, of course. Any details I should know?'

'The package has been around the tracks and could fall to pieces at any moment. Handle it carefully. You'll recognise the people delivering it. This should be a quick transit.'

'OK.' The call had already ended.

He looked up and smiled at Libby. 'So, we have to deliver a woman to the antiques centre before three o'clock tomorrow, and we already know that Leon thinks she'll feel happier to have another woman in the party. All right with you?'

'Ned won't be in any danger?'

'I doubt it. He'd be in more danger if you stayed behind on your own.'

'OK. It isn't even a long drive, after all.'

'I know. But they do like to change the routes and the people handling the packages. It seems to work well. Leon has a reputation for getting the job done, or even, once or twice, rescuing someone from a failed transit. Not many people even know he exists.'

The following morning at dawn, a car drove up the hill and parked at the little church at the top, a couple of hundred yards up from the cottages.

Joss came fully awake when he heard a vehicle chug up the hill so early.

He got up from his air mattress, stretching and yawning, and slipped into his jeans and a tee shirt. He turned as he heard footsteps coming down the stairs. 'Did you hear it too?'

'Yes. It's a bit early in the morning for visitors to the church, don't you think? It won't even be open yet.'

Ten minutes later three people strolled along the little lane, not hurrying. An older woman was walking rather stiffly. Her two companions were kitted out for hiking.

'How about putting the kettle on,' Joss suggested. 'A cup of tea or coffee says welcome in just about any language.' He went to open the front door, then moved back.

The three visitors walked straight in, shutting the door immediately behind them. The two younger ones were people Joss had met during his visit to London. They exuded health and energy. The older woman looked exhausted and unhappy.

'I'm Nina,' the younger woman said, giving a different name from last time Joss had met her. 'This is Paul and our friend is Jane. Do either of you speak French?'

'I do,' Libby said, 'though not fluently.'

'I speak it very badly,' Joss said, smiling at the older woman. '*Bienvenue, madame!*' He gestured to a chair, watching as she nodded and sank down on it with a sigh, her whole body sagging. Her dark eyes would have been beautiful if there hadn't been shadows beneath them. He'd guess she was of Middle Eastern origin, from a former French colony perhaps.

'We've been up since midnight, so Jane is very tired,' Nina said. 'If she can lie down somewhere till it's time for you to leave, that'd be good.'

'*Du café ou une tasse de thé, peut-être, madame?*' Libby asked.

'*Du café, s'il vous plaît.*'

Libby brought out the instant coffee and made a mug, to which the woman added three spoonfuls of sugar. She took a sip, cradling the mug in her hands, as if needing the warmth more than the dark, fragrant fluid.

'I'll just go and put fresh sheets on my bed.'

'No need,' Nina said. 'Jane is so tired, she could just about sleep standing up. We don't want extra washing on your line.'

'Well, a clean pillowcase at least. And perhaps a bath.' Libby went upstairs.

No one attempted to make conversation while she was gone.

When Jane had finished her coffee and a piece of cake, Libby took her upstairs, half-opened the door of Ned's room to show the sleeping child, putting one finger to her lips in a shushing gesture.

The sight of the little boy sprawled sideways in the bed, still clutching his teddy bear, won a half-smile from their visitor.

The sight of the bath and a big, fluffy towel pleased her too, so Libby showed her into the bedroom and left her to her ablutions.

Paul, who like his companion had used another name, leant forward to say quietly to Joss, 'Jane won't want to chat, won't want to do anything except get as far away from her pursuers as possible. I hope she can sleep a little. She's like a car running on empty at the moment. However, if she collapses, do not take her to a doctor, just get her to the antiques centre any way you can. I mean that.'

'OK.'

'Oh, and these are her things.' Paul handed over the smaller rucksack. 'We didn't want it to look like anything except a casual day out, so it's not much.'

Nina drained her mug and stood up. 'Thanks for the coffee. Is there any way we can get back to the church without using the lane? We're off for a hike across the moors, in case anyone saw us drive up here. We'll call in at the village shop on the way back.'

She grinned suddenly. 'I won't mind a brisk walk in the sun, actually. It's been a bit hectic the past couple of days.'

'I can take you back to the church via a path that twists along the side of the hill.'

'Is it visible from the village?'

Joss frowned, trying to figure that out. 'I don't think so.'

'Good.'

Libby came down and looked at them questioningly.

'I'm taking them to the church the back way,' Joss told

her. 'I'll be back in a few minutes. Keep all the doors locked and don't open to anyone you don't know.'

'I'm well aware of the need for care,' she said sharply. Did he think she was stupid? But when he'd gone, she shivered and hoped he wouldn't be long. Ever since Steven's phone call to Mr Greaves, she'd felt that danger was hovering.

Where was her ex now, she wondered. It was only a matter of time before he struck.

Ned accepted that they had a visitor who was a friend of Joss's. He was more interested in his breakfast, after which he demanded to play ball outside, something he loved doing. He accepted that he couldn't without the tantrum a child his age would usually throw when thwarted.

When Joss returned, she asked him to take the little boy out to the back, and he spent some time tossing a large soft ball to him. Ned tried valiantly to catch it, but mostly missed, for lack of practice. He chased after it laughing and threw it back, more or less, sometimes having to throw it twice to get it the five or so yards to Joss.

Libby stood at the kitchen window watching, enjoying her son's pleasure and rosy cheeks.

Emily picked up the call on her mobile, looking at the caller ID. Her sister. She sighed. She wasn't feeling very charitable towards Liz at the moment, still hadn't forgiven her for bringing George to the opening.

Still, she couldn't go on refusing to speak to her sister. 'Hello.'

'Emily. I've caught you at last. You're so busy.'

'Yes, well, we have a new business to run.'

'Um . . . you're selling your house, I gather.'

Emily tensed. 'Yes.'

'And . . . George is interested in buying it. He really liked living there.'

'Mmm.'

'Only the estate agent says he has to pay extra if he wants to buy it.'

'Yes. To pay for the rent he should have given me when he moved in while I was in hospital.'

'He was just looking after it for you.'

'And now I'm just looking after my finances.'

'Oh, Emily, can't we let bygones be bygones?'

'Certainly. As long as George stays away from me.'

'You won't . . . let him pay the asking price?'

'Nope. He has to pay extra if he wants it.' She heard her sister begin to sob. 'I have to go now. Got a lot to do. Bye.'

She smiled as she switched the phone off. She was sure George had been in the room, prompting his mother.

If he wanted to buy the house, he could accept her terms.

What a nephew to have! He was a horrible, grasping creature. She sighed. What would her daughter be like? Would they ever meet?

No, she mustn't let herself grow pessimistic. She must trust that they *would* meet.

And even if her daughter wasn't what she hoped, surely no one could be as bad as her nephew!

At eleven-thirty Libby went to wake their guest but found Jane lying staring into space. She explained in her best schoolgirl French that they had to eat now then leave for the antiques centre.

'*Bien*.' Jane got up and straightened her clothes.

Once again she ate very little, but when Joss suggested gently that she needed to eat more, she forced down another half sandwich, then pushed her plate away with an apologetic look.

As they drove through the village, Jane slid down without being told, so that she wasn't visible, and she didn't sit up again until Joss assured her it was all right.

'I thought I was nervous,' Libby murmured, 'but she's utterly terrified. I wonder what's happened to her.'

'I doubt we shall ever know.'

At the antiques centre, they got out of the car and Joss hoisted Ned up on his shoulders. Libby offered her arm to Jane, who took it with a nod of thanks. They'd already agreed to call Jane *maman*.

There were about a dozen cars parked outside the centre, and another one drove up as they walked towards the front door.

Jane stiffened, but when a family got out of it, with two children of about ten, she relaxed a little . . . not completely, though. Her eyes kept turning here and there, searching, checking.

Inside the centre, they pretended to look at the displays until Emily came across to greet them. 'I've found one of those ornaments you've been looking for, *maman*. *Viens le voir.*'

Jane nodded, still clinging to Libby's arm.

Libby turned to Joss. 'Can you look after Ned for a few

minutes? I'll meet you in the Old Barn as soon as I can, eh?'

'The stuff in there is at least less valuable if he breaks anything.' He smiled, pleased that she had enough sense to make their reunion in another part of the centre, where hopefully people wouldn't remember the other member of the party. He watched how Jane clung to Libby, how she patted the older woman's hand occasionally.

Emily led the way to the rear of the Old Barn, stopping a couple of times to point out exhibits which they dutifully studied.

'Beautiful,' Libby said. 'But not quite . . .' She shrugged.

When Emily led them through another door, she dropped all pretence of selling them antiques. 'Any trouble on the way here, Libby?'

'None at all. Do you speak French?'

'Oh, yes.' She launched into a greeting, offering Jane the assurance that all would be well from now on. Libby was pleased that she'd remembered enough words to follow most of this. Emily was clearly fluent in the language.

'We have a room prepared, Jane. Come and look at it.'

Libby stepped back. 'I should go and find Joss.'

But Jane still clung to her arm, still looked terrified.

'You'd better come with us till she's settled,' Emily said.

As they walked along the corridor, a light appeared at the other end, and Emily stopped dead. A figure walked across from one doorway to another. Only when they got to the 'doorway' there wasn't one on the left, only on the right.

Jane stopped dead and, like Libby, she looked at Emily in shock.

'You both saw the apparition, didn't you?' her hostess asked.

Libby nodded.

'*C'est un revenant?*' Jane asked.

'*Oui*. There used to be a door there. We have one or two ghosts, but they're friendly ones, so you needn't be afraid.' She repeated that in French.

Libby tried to hide her surprise at the casual way Emily referred to the figure. But she'd seen something that couldn't be explained in any other way, knew she hadn't been imagining things, so she didn't protest.

'Actually, it's a good sign that you've seen the lady,' Emily told her.

'It is?'

'Yes. It means you've been accepted.' A young man came out of a nearby door. 'Oh, Toby, we have a visitor who'll be staying for a while.'

He came forward, smiling as usual.

Jane's face crumpled and she reached out to touch his cheek. '*Mon fils était comme lui. Il est mort, mon pauvre Louis.*'

Emily turned to Toby. 'She had a son like you.'

'He's walking behind her.'

There was dead silence, then Emily translated.

Jane smiled sadly. '*Oui. Je le sais.*'

Emily turned back to the young man with the child's innocent face. 'Toby, our visitor needs to stay in the secret room. There are some bad men chasing her. We don't want them to know she's here.'

'I'll take her there. I won't let the bad men find her.' He took Jane's hand and led the way.

'He quite often surprises us by understanding people's feelings,' Emily murmured.

'She was very comfortable with him, I could tell. Perhaps I should go back now.'

'Tell her goodbye first or she'll worry.'

So Libby moved forward and said her farewells, accepting Jane's thanks.

Then Toby set off again.

This was the strangest place Libby had ever visited. And yet, she felt very much at home here. Safe. Emily was such a lovely person. And so was Toby.

She found Joss in the Old Barn, with Ned still on his shoulders. He waved at her from across the room.

What would her life have been like if she'd married a man like him, she wondered as she made her way past the booths filled with beautiful things. Happy, that's what.

Carina said she'd been carefully conditioned and she was not to feel ashamed of staying with Steven – but she did, oh, she definitely did!

Emily picked up the phone on Sunday evening, tired after a busy weekend. 'Chadderley's.'

'Des Monahan here. Have you a few moments to chat?'

'Yes.' She went to sit down, her heart thudding at the sound of the PI's voice. Had he found her daughter?

'I've found where your daughter used to live and seen her husband. A neighbour said she left him recently, taking her son with her.'

'She has a son? I'm a grandmother?'

'Yes. He's four. The woman knows your daughter and

speaks well of her, seems fond of the boy, too. But she didn't
like the husband. And your daughter ran away before the
letter from the reunion people arrived. So that means Libby
couldn't have filled in that form saying she wanted no
contact with you.'

'But who . . . ? It must be the husband. How cruel
of him!'

'Yes.'

'Thank goodness it wasn't my daughter who filled in
the form!'

'Even so, it would be better not to get your hopes up
until we know more. There's no guarantee that she'll want
to meet you.'

'No, but there's still a chance, at least, isn't there?'

'Yes. Of course.'

'Do you know where my daughter has gone?'

'Not exactly, but I know the name of the lawyer handling
her affairs. Strangely enough, he's in Rochdale.'

Dead silence, then, 'Good heavens! Does that mean she's
living near me?'

'Again, I have to say not necessarily. It's just her lawyer
who's in the area. Do you want me to contact him?'

Another silence heavy with emotion. 'Yes. I think
you'd better. I get upset a bit easily about this. It's been a
rollercoaster ride, trying to find her.'

'I'll drive up on Monday morning. No, I can't come
then. I've got an appointment I can't break on Monday
afternoon. Tuesday morning, then.'

'You'll tell him how much I want to see her? That I
didn't give her away for adoption, she was stolen from me?'

'Yes. I'll tell him.'

'Thanks.'

If Des wasn't mistaken, she was weeping.

Chad came into the flat and found Emily crying, so gathered her in his arms and shushed her gently. He'd only ever seen her weep about one thing.

'More news about your daughter?'

'Yes.'

He pulled a bunch of tissues out of a nearby box and pushed them into her hand. 'Here.'

He waited till she'd calmed down to ask, 'Is it bad news?'

'No. Neither good nor bad.' She explained. 'Well, perhaps it does offer a bit of hope.'

'Then let's be optimistic. Let's believe that you will find her again.'

She nodded and another tear rolled down her cheek.

'Oh, my darling, I can't bear to see you so upset.'

She blew her nose, sniffed and blew it again. 'I can't help it. When I thought my baby had died, I was sad. When I discovered she'd been stolen from me, it hurt all over again and it hasn't stopped hurting since.'

'You hide it well. Most of the time.'

'Yes. It wasn't anyone else's concern and I learnt to have one face for work, another for my personal life. With you, they both seem to have merged into one.'

'Good. I love you just as you are.' He kissed her cheek to prove it, then enfolded her in his arms. 'Des is good at what he does. If anyone can find her, he can. You have to believe that.'

'Sometimes I can believe I'll find her. Other times, I feel quite despairing.'

'I feel very hopeful.'

When she was calmer she went down to sit in the rear courtyard. The rain had stopped for the moment and she didn't care if the bench was damp, because the air was so fresh and cool.

While she was sitting there, she remembered the young woman who'd brought Jane to the centre. She'd had a little boy of about the right age. And she'd reminded Emily of her mother as a young woman.

What if she was . . . ? No, that would be too much of a coincidence.

Toby came out to join her and sat down next to her. 'Don't be sad.'

Emily tried to smile at him.

He patted her hand. 'The lady says you'll find her again.'

'Find who?'

'Your daughter. She came here before. She has a little boy.'

Emily sat in amazement as he walked away. Sometimes it was downright eerie the way Toby seemed to know what you were thinking, not to mention the way he spoke so familiarly about the resident ghost.

He'd said she'd find her daughter. That she'd been to the antiques centre. It couldn't be true, could it? That young woman couldn't be her daughter?

If she was, it would make that beautiful little boy her grandson. Oh, the joy of that thought.

She tried to be sensible, but hope crept into her heart and lodged there.

Perhaps miracles did happen sometimes.

She wouldn't say anything, though, even to Chad. She would just . . . hope.

Chapter Thirteen

Steven spent Monday doing some research online and fumbling his way through the washing and ironing. He refused to dress like a slob! But the need to undertake such menial tasks and the annoyance that he couldn't do them to the same high standard as Libby kept his anger simmering.

On the Tuesday morning, he set out very early to drive up to Lancashire, intending to visit the lawyer in person. He wasn't going to be fobbed off by a mere secretary if he telephoned. Even if he didn't find out where Libby was, it would send a further message to her that he wasn't giving up. However there just might be things he could only winkle out if he was there in person.

At a last resort, he'd pay the extortionate charges of a website he'd found, which claimed to be able to find ninety per cent of people being sought. He'd rather not do that. He worked hard for his money, needed it there behind him.

He'd been trying to remember where the old grandmother lived, because the lawyer hadn't mentioned any addresses in his letter. It seemed quite possible that Libby might have taken refuge in the old hag's house.

No, with such a mean little legacy, the house must have

been sold. He tried the online phone directories, but there was no Rose King listed there. He searched the electoral rolls online, but people could opt out of being listed and she must have done that. Damn her!

He even left a message on Libby's stepfather's phone, asking if he knew the old woman's address, but Walter didn't get back to him. Too busy drinking himself into an early grave.

No, it would be best to go up to Lancashire in person.

Steven set off soon after four o'clock on Tuesday morning, half-listening to the usual rubbish on the radio. He even hummed along with one or two favourite songs because he was feeling better for having some purpose to his day and there was no one there to hear him and criticise his singing. He stopped at a motorway services for some breakfast, enjoying a cup of surprisingly good coffee.

As he got closer to Rochdale, it began to rain and he cursed because he didn't like getting wet. He kept an umbrella in the car, naturally, but if he walked round the streets, as he'd intended, his trouser legs would get soaked, umbrella or not. That wouldn't make a good impression on people, and he hated to look anything less than immaculately turned out.

He parked in the town centre next to a shopping complex, scowling as the rain beat down against his windscreen. It wasn't easing up at all, so he got out the umbrella and made a dash for the shops.

As he walked through the centre, he could see that the town was going through some hard times. Some shops were empty; most looked as if they needed sprucing up. The paintwork was faded, the floor scuffed and shabby, in need of a refit, and the goods mostly suitable for the cheaper end of the market.

He despised the northern accents of the passers-by. So crude. He hated their cheerfulness, too, and the way they smiled at people. What the hell had they to be cheerful about?

He threaded his way through the complex and peered out into the town centre. Thank goodness! It had stopped raining. He bought a coffee in a fast-food outlet and took the opportunity to pull up the street map of the town on his phone.

The app said it would take him ten minutes' brisk walking to reach the building where the lawyer's rooms were located, so he went back to get his car. Who knew where he'd want to go next?

He drove into the parking area of the building and stopped to study the brass nameplate which said simply 'Greaves and Hallibourne' in neatly incised letters. At least this place wasn't unkempt or shabby.

The lawyer's rooms were right next to the entrance.

A woman looked up from behind a large desk in the reception area, smiling. 'May I help you?'

'You may. I'd like to see Mr Greaves.'

'And your name is . . . ?'

He stared at her, the sort of stare he'd found to be intimidating when he used it on women, but this old bitch didn't seem to be intimidated, so he said simply, 'Pulford.' Ah, that had got her!

Her smile vanished completely. When he took a step

forward, she pressed a button and a siren began to sound.

He looked at her in shock as he heard running footsteps. A door at the rear of the reception area burst open. The man who rushed in was older, but very smartly dressed and he was followed by a younger man. They both stopped to stare suspiciously at Steven. Which one, he wondered, was Libby's lawyer?

'Trouble, Mrs Hockton?'

'Could be, Mr Greaves. This is Mr Pulford. I wasn't giving him a chance to hit *me*.'

'I haven't threatened you in any way,' Steven pointed out, pleased that she'd just proved she'd actually met his wife.

The woman stared at him defiantly. 'I didn't say you had. But since I felt nervous, I called for backup.'

Steven made a scornful noise to show her what he thought of her, but didn't allow himself to continue arguing the point. If he ever got the chance, he'd make her sorry she'd treated him like that. But at the moment his main need was to find out exactly where in this town Libby and Ned were hiding.

'Pulford, I've already told you I will only deal with you in writing,' Greaves said. 'You are not one of my clients. Please leave the premises and do not come back.'

That made Steven even more angry. 'Not very civil of you.'

'I spoke very civilly . . . considering.' He let that word hang in the air between them.

'I'll leave as soon as you tell me where to find my wife.'

'She doesn't wish to see you. She's asked me to set matters in train for obtaining a divorce.'

'Oh, has she? Well, she won't be getting one. She's my wife, the mother of my child and that's how it's staying. Which brings me to the other thing I came for: I want to see my son. I have a father's right to access.'

'So that you can hit him again? We have photographs of the results of your last encounter with Ned.'

The anger at being treated like this was burning so brightly now, Steven knew he had to leave. He might be tempted to punch this fool as he deserved. 'I did *not* hit my son.'

'Sorry, my mistake, *kick* was the word I should have used.'

Steven had to breathe deeply and wait a minute or two before he could speak calmly again. 'Tell Libby I'm here. Tell her I insist on seeing her and my son to sort this ridiculous nonsense out. I won't be leaving the district until I've done that. I'll let you know where I'm staying when I find a hotel.'

'You're wasting your time. She still won't wish to see you. And I definitely won't be giving you her address.'

'She can't hide for ever.' Again he took a step forward, smiling to see the way the old man took a hasty step backwards, thinking he was being threatened. Timid old fool! As if Steven was stupid enough to hit him in front of witnesses.

Tired of this useless confrontation, he turned round and strode across to the door, stopping to say loudly and slowly, 'I *will* get Libby back, you know. And there will *not* be a divorce.'

He went out and used his phone to find a hotel, glad

he'd had the forethought to pack an overnight bag. Now that he was here, he might as well stay until he'd sorted this mess out.

There was nothing to return home for, after all.

If he had to knock on every door in the town, he'd find her.

There were other ways of getting information besides the official directories.

That same day, Des Monahan also set off early to drive up to Lancashire. He reached Rochdale about eleven o'clock and let his satnav guide him through the town and up towards the moors.

Chadderley's was just outside Littleborough, nestled in a hollow that looked as if it had been scooped out halfway up the moors to fit the former inn. Des drove into the car park and stood admiring the place, which had been tastefully renovated to keep its old-fashioned styling. It looked well cared for, the sort of place where you found quality antiques, not rubbish.

Inside, he stopped yet again to study the displays in the area near the front door. A young woman was dusting the items, working slowly and carefully, with such concentration that she didn't even turn to see who had come into the room.

He was wondering whether to interrupt her task when a woman came down the stairs at the side of the room.

She studied him for a moment or two, then moved towards him and asked, 'Are you Des Monahan?'

'Yes. You must be Emily Mattison.'

'I am.'

She held out her hand and he shook it, amused by the careful, assessing look that accompanied the handshake, typical of strangers about to work together.

'I'll just ask my colleague Rachel to keep an eye on the showrooms and call me if anyone needs help. I doubt we'll get many customers on a wet Tuesday afternoon, though.'

He watched her walk towards the rear. When she disappeared from sight, he turned to study the next exhibit. Beautiful glassware, sparkling in the overhead display lights. No prices, but he'd guess such delicate beauty was way beyond his purse.

Emily returned. 'Shall we go upstairs, Mr Monahan?'

'Just call me Des.' He followed her into a flat with a luxurious living area. One or two beautiful pieces of glass or china were to be seen and there were a couple of paintings on the wall that he'd have loved to spend time examining. He guessed these were things they owned, rather than stock. Well, Chad had done well for himself in London, had a name for high-end stock and his ability to find exactly what a customer wanted. Such success couldn't happen to a nicer man.

'Chad?' she called. 'Have you a minute? Des is here.'

Chad came out of another room, more casually dressed than Des had ever seen him before and radiating happiness. After shaking hands, he gestured to a comfortable armchair upholstered in a subtle purple velvet.

'Tell us again what you found out, Des,' Emily prompted. 'All the details you can remember this time.'

He described his visit to the street where her daughter had lived and his chat to her neighbour, then the photos.

Emily looked aghast. 'She'd been badly beaten? By her husband?'

'I'm afraid so.'

'There's too much of that sort of thing,' Chad said. 'Who the hell do fellows like him think they are?'

'We contribute towards a women's refuge,' Emily put in quietly. 'It's always busy and they have to have a roster of people willing to give emergency accommodation for when their own rooms are all occupied.'

Des waited for a moment to continue. 'So. Do you still want me to see the lawyer for you?'

'Yes. You can tell him what you've found.' Her voice wobbled. 'I don't think I'd be calm enough.'

Chad took hold of her hand and patted it.

Des wished suddenly that he had someone to comfort him when things went wrong. 'I'm happy to do that for you, Emily. Is it all right if I tell the lawyer who you are?'

'Yes. Actually, we know him slightly and he came here for the opening. It's a small world. I didn't realise he was representing my daughter.'

'I'll phone him for an appointment now.' Des frowned. 'No, it'd be better to go and see him, I think. Even if I can't talk to him today, I can present my credentials and suggest he contacts you for verification that I really am representing you. Would that be all right?'

'Do you want me to give you a letter on headed notepaper saying you're representing me?' she asked.

'Good idea.'

'I'll write it now.' She went into the next room.

He heard the sound of her blowing her nose several times

during the next few minutes and guessed she was still crying.

He looked at Chad. 'These cases can be very upsetting. Let's hope we get a good result this time.'

'I think Emily's been hiding her grief about her daughter for years, and now that it's all out in the open, she's finding it hard to cope with her emotions.'

A few minutes later Emily came back with a letter on exquisite headed notepaper, and a matching envelope. 'Would you check this, see if it's all right?'

Des read it quickly and nodded. 'Excellent. But I have to say, if he has anything about him, her lawyer won't take my word for it, or even trust a piece of headed notepaper.'

'We'll be in all day, if Mr Greaves wishes to phone us.'

Des arrived at the lawyer's rooms just as a man was coming out, a furiously angry man, by the looks of him. He opened his umbrella, even for the short walk across the car park, so his face was hidden. When he bumped into Des, he hurried on without a word of apology. He got into a large silver Mercedes, slamming the door on the world.

What a boor! Des stood watching the car drive away. That Mercedes must have cost a fortune, which only went to prove that having a lot of money didn't necessarily make you happy. Or polite.

It was only as the car passed him, narrowly missing the gatepost, that Des realised who the man was: Steven Pulford. What was he doing here? Chasing after his wife, presumably.

Des hoped the poor woman was well hidden, or well protected. Or both. She didn't need another beating.

A cool, damp breeze made him shiver and reminded him that he was standing out in the rain, so he went inside the building and turned into the rooms of Greaves and Hallibourne.

The woman behind the big desk was looking angry, so he guessed Pulford had not made a good impression.

She pulled herself together with a visible effort and forced out a smile. 'How may I help you, sir?'

'I'd like to see Mr Greaves on behalf of a client of mine. I realise it's probably too late to get an appointment today, but I've come from near London, so I'd be grateful if you could fit me in by tomorrow at the latest.'

She frowned at him as if he'd said something that made her suspicious. 'Could I ask your business, sir? And your name?'

'Certainly. I'm Des Monahan and I'm an enquiry agent.' He took out his card. 'Please keep this confidential, but obviously you and your employer will need to know. I'm working on behalf of Emily Mattison, who is one of the owners of Chadderley Antiques.'

'The new centre on the edge of the moors? Mr Greaves said they had some beautiful pieces for sale.'

'That's the one.'

He took out the unsealed envelope Emily had given him. 'I'm sure Mr Greaves will wish to verify that I'm telling the truth. Ms Mattison said she'd be happy for him to phone her. She's at home today.'

The woman scanned the letter quickly. 'I wonder if you could come back in an hour, Mr Monahan? Mr Greaves is with a client at the moment, but he should be finished in half an hour, then he can phone Ms Mattison.'

She was giving Greaves time to check up on him and he didn't mind that at all. 'That's fine by me. Is there a café nearby? I didn't get time for lunch.'

'Go to the end of the street in that direction.' She pointed. 'Turn left there, then right at the traffic lights and you'll find a row of shops. One of them is a café. It's not fancy but they do a nice cup of tea. The coffee is good, too.'

'Thank you. I'll come back in an hour.'

Mrs Hockton waited until the client had left before taking a cup of coffee in to Mr Greaves. 'I had a caller who said he was a private investigator working on behalf of Emily Mattison.'

'Delightful woman. What would she be enquiring into?'

'He didn't say.'

'What did you think of him?'

'I liked him. He has the sort of face you trust instinctively and excellent manners. A big contrast to that Pulford creature.'

She went out, shutting the door quietly behind her.

He read the letter and reached for the phone. 'Is that Emily Mattison?'

'Yes.'

'Henry Greaves here. I believe you sent a private investigator to see me today.'

'Yes, I did.'

'Could you give me some idea of what this is about?' He heard a sniff and she blew her nose. Was she crying?

Someone else took over the call. 'Chad here.'

'I'm sorry if I upset your wife – um, partner.'

'It's not you who upset her, Mr Greaves. Let me explain.' He outlined the bare bones of the situation.

Henry listened, amazed. 'Are you sure this young woman is Emily's daughter?'

'Des is pretty sure. We sent him to see you because it upsets Emily to talk about it. Besides, he's the one who's found the daughter, so he can tell you exactly what he knows and show you the proof. Then perhaps you can communicate with your client and see if she would agree to meet Emily.'

'I'll definitely speak to Mr Monahan. Thank you for being so frank. It's not an easy situation for your partner, I do understand. It's just that my client is having difficulties with her ex-husband at the moment, so may not be able to arrange a meeting yet, even if she wants to. She might have to go into hiding, though we hope it won't come to that. I'll get back to you in a day or two with her response.'

'Thank you.'

Henry put the phone down and strolled into the outer office. 'When Mr Monahan returns, could you please send him straight through to me, Mrs H? He's quite bona fide.'

'I didn't doubt it. I can always tell.'

He smiled as he walked back to his room. She was right. She was the best judge of human nature he'd ever met.

When Des returned to the lawyer's rooms after his belated meal, he was shown straight through to Mr Greaves. He held out his ID card. 'I assume you contacted Ms Mattison?'

'Yes. She's . . . um, rather fragile about this, so I spoke to Chad mainly.'

'Yes. Who wouldn't be upset? I've brought the case folder along. I thought it might save us both a lot of trouble if you looked through it first. Start at the back.'

'Thank you.'

While Mr Greaves read carefully through the documentation, Des studied the office. It belonged to someone who liked to live well, he'd guess, not a legal go-getter hunting for the big cases and huge sums of money.

Eventually, Mr Greaves put the documents back into a neat pile in the folder. 'Amazing, the things that happen sometimes. I've met the husband. He's an extremely difficult man. He made Mrs Hockton so nervous she pressed the panic button.'

'He upset her that much?'

'Yes.'

'I saw Pulford when I was investigating the case. And he was walking out of your building when I came here earlier on. He looked brutal. How do you wish me to refer to your client? I doubt she'll still be calling herself Mrs Pulford.'

'She's Ms King now. It's her maiden name.'

'Look, if she needs protection from that fellow, I'm happy to offer my services. I'm sure Emily would approve of that and pay my expenses.'

'Thank you, but Ms King has a neighbour who is an ex-policeman. He's keeping an eye on her. We're hoping that'll be enough.'

'It might not be. I asked around about Pulford. I managed to speak to a couple of his work colleagues and they were glad to blacken his name. They detest him and hinted at nasty tricks, though neither would specify what he'd actually done.'

Des hesitated, adding, 'And I saw the photos of Ms King and her son's injuries when I was speaking to the neighbour who took them.'

'I saw her face the next day.' Mr Greaves shuddered. 'Pulford said he was going to stay in the town, find a hotel room. If he lingers, we may have to take out a restraining order.'

'Do you think that'll stop him?'

Mr Greaves looked shocked. 'You think he's that dangerous?'

'I don't know him well enough to say for certain . . . yet. But he probably is.'

'Could you give me a call tomorrow, Mr Monahan? I'll speak to my client and see what she wants to do.'

When he went to show his visitor out, Mrs Hockton was looking annoyed again.

'Something else wrong?' Mr Greaves asked.

Des paused beside him. Even the tiniest scrap of information could be of use.

Mrs Hockton said in a tight voice, '*That man* rang to tell us where he's staying and he *ordered* me to inform you that he expects his wife to contact him at the hotel.'

Des said quietly. 'Give me the address of the hotel and I'll take a room there. I have to stay somewhere and it wouldn't hurt to keep an eye on him.'

They both looked at him in relief. He felt sorry for them. A lawyer who usually dealt with house sales, wills and other domestic matters was the last person to have the expertise and experience to handle a case like this.

'Let me give you the number of my mobile phone,' he suggested.

'Good idea!' Mr Greaves said. 'Then I'll phone my client and bring her up to date.'

When Des had left, Henry said, 'I like that young man.'

'So do I.'

He looked at her with a wry, twisted smile. 'We're out of our depth here, aren't we, Mrs H? Oh well, we can only do our best. Could you get Libby on the phone, please?'

But Libby didn't answer her phone and he was reluctant to leave a message. In the end, he got his secretary to type a note and left early to see if Libby was back. If not, he'd push the note through the letter box. That way he'd be sure she'd been warned about her husband.

Chapter Fourteen

When they got back from the antiques centre, Joss went to shower and change in his own house, and found a couple of messages waiting for him. One was from Leon's unit, asking to be given the details about the package as soon as he got back, so he rang that number straight away.

Leon's second-in-command rang back. 'We're just checking. No trouble with the package?'

'The delivery went very smoothly. Ms King was helpful in caring for the package.'

'Good. I'll put her on the payroll. Are you up for another job?'

'Not at the moment, I'm afraid. Ms King is in danger from a violent ex-husband and I'm riding shotgun here.'

'Who's the husband?'

'A guy called Steven Pulford.'

'Want me to check him out?'

'I don't think that's necessary at this stage. His wife can probably fill me in on any details I need. He's a macho, bullying workaholic.'

It was a while before he went back next door and when he did, he found Libby looking anxious.

'What's the matter?'

'Mr Greaves has twice tried to phone me. He didn't leave a message. I wonder what he wants.'

'Only one way to find out.'

'I rang his rooms, but they were closed for the day.' Libby sighed. 'I'm wondering whether I should pack our bags, in case we're forced to leave suddenly.'

'Wouldn't hurt to have your things ready.'

'What if Steven's already found us? What if he comes here?'

'Then he'll have to walk through me to get to you.'

'He's rather good at walking through people.'

'He'll be facing you *and* me this time, Libby. Two to one. I'd say we have the advantage.'

But she didn't look convinced.

Joss knew something about the psychology behind these situations and wondered if she'd be able to break her conditioning to fight back if Pulford attacked her again.

As they were preparing an evening meal, Joss held up one hand. 'Shh!'

The sound of a car coming up the hill from the village echoed clearly in the damp evening air.

Without a word, Joss put down his chopping knife and went into the front room. Libby watched him anxiously.

What if it was Steven?

What if there was a fight?

Who would win?

She shivered at that thought and for a few seconds

couldn't move. Then she thought of Ned and told herself not to be a coward, so followed Joss into the front room, standing close beside him, feeling the warmth and strength of his body.

The car turned off towards the cottages, and she held her breath. Then it came into sight and she recognised both the vehicle and the driver. Mr Greaves. Oh, thank goodness. Thank goodness!

Ned started shouting for his mother.

'I'll let Henry in,' Joss said quietly.

'Bring him into the kitchen. I have to keep an eye on Ned, see he eats his tea.' If they had to flee, it was even more urgent that her son get a good meal into him.

He went to open the front door.

Mr Greaves didn't look at all happy. He waited till he was sitting in the kitchen, where a sleepy Ned was just finishing some fruit and ice cream.

'I'm afraid your ex is in Rochdale, Libby. He came to see me today.'

Libby closed her eyes, feeling sick. 'I'll leave at once.'

'He doesn't yet know where you live.'

'He'll find out. Anyone can check phone directories or the Electoral Rolls.'

'Rose chose not to be listed publicly in either of them. She said old ladies were safer remaining anonymous. And we haven't had time to register you.'

She considered this, but shook her head. 'That'll only delay him a little. He'll go online and find someone to help him illegally. No one can stay anonymous these days. I'm sorry. I'll have to forego the inheritance and leave. Would you . . . let me keep the money I've had so far? I'll pay you back one day, I promise.'

Joss took her hand. 'There's a provision in the trust for us to allow you to leave here, if we're unanimous. What do you think, Henry? Should we let her go?'

Mr Greaves nodded vigorously. 'Yes, of course.'

'I think you'd be safer staying here for the moment, though,' Joss said. 'I'll be with you and there are a few guys from the village within call. If you're among strangers, well, they can ignore someone needing help.'

She bit her lip. 'I don't know.'

'At least wait until morning. We need to make a plan.'

Mr Greaves nodded approval. 'If you need more money, Libby, let me know. In fact, let me know what you're doing at all times. I've told Pulford not to come to my rooms again. If he pursues you, we can take out an injunction to prevent him approaching you.'

'As if he'll pay any attention to that.' She sighed. 'But I don't want to spend my life running, so I'll . . . see how it goes. For a day or two, at any rate.'

'There is something else I need to tell you about.' Henry looked at her as if this wasn't going to be pleasant.

Ned chose that moment to snuggle his head against his mother, with his thumb in his mouth.

She looked down to see his eyes closing. 'Could whatever it is wait a few minutes while I put him to bed? If I force him to stay awake, he sleeps badly and gets very grumpy the next day.'

'Of course it can wait.' Mr Greaves turned to Joss. 'Perhaps a cup of coffee might be in order?'

'Or a glass of wine?'

'Sadly no. Not when I'm driving and haven't yet eaten.'

'Coffee it is, then.'

Steven sat in his car, wondering if he was wasting his time. No, he was just checking out all possibilities, as he always did when he was working on a project. Besides, he had time to spare these days.

He sat a short distance along the street from the office building for over two hours, getting more and more irritated at what he was forced to do to get his own wife and son back. Oh, to hell with it! This was a stupid idea.

He started up the car but just as he was about to pull away, that old twit of a lawyer drove out of the car park.

Steven's car was facing the wrong way. He managed to turn round quickly, annoying another motorist whom he held up, but he didn't care. His need was urgent.

When he got to the end of the street, he thought he'd lost the lawyer, but saw him across the road, filling up the car at a petrol station. He slid into a no-parking zone, alert for police or parking officers, but his luck held and no one bothered him.

Once the car was filled, Greaves set off again, driving out of town.

That made it more difficult, because he might realise he was being followed. Luckily, there was enough traffic on the road for Steven to stay one or two cars behind him.

Greaves skirted a place called Todmorden, after which he turned off on to a side road that wound its way up the hill. He was the only one to turn, so Steven turned off and stopped, sitting at the end of the side road in his car, worrying. If he followed, he'd stand out like a sore thumb. If he didn't, he'd lose the trail.

Then he saw a sign and laughed aloud. THIS ROAD LEADS TO TOP O' THE HILL ONLY. It was a dead end. He got out and found a gate to stand on, watching for glimpses of the lawyer's car winding its way up.

When it disappeared from sight among the houses, Steven got back into his car. He had to take the risk of following.

A Land Rover came down the hill. Steven flapped one hand, telling the other to back away, but the woman just folded her arms and waited. No way was the stupid female going to let him through. Then Steven saw a GIVE WAY TO ONCOMING TRAFFIC sign and realised he was in the wrong, so he backed the car until he reached a passing place.

With a triumphant toot on the horn, the Land Rover sped off down the hill. Steven made a vulgar sign at it and continued upwards.

The village was tiny. What a shabby hole! He slowed right down, looking right and left, but not seeing the lawyer's car. There was only one road leading out of the village and it seemed to lead to a church tower right at the top of the hill, so he went up there.

Dammit! There were no cars parked at the church. Where the hell had Greaves gone?

Steven drove slowly back towards the village and saw an unmarked track with what looked like a grey slate roof beyond the bend in the track. He stopped to consider the best thing to do. If he went down the track and there was only one house, he'd have shown his hand.

It took a five-point turn to get a car as big as his pointing back up the hill, then he drove up to the church again. He'd walk down and spy out the land.

Greaves might not be there, of course. But it was worth a try. There weren't many other choices.

He climbed over another of those damned drystone walls, catching the sleeve of his suit on a projecting piece of sharp metal which some fool had stuck in a crack. It not only tore his sleeve but his shirt too, scratching his arm so that a few drops of blood trickled out on to his shirt to add insult to injury. Muttering a curse, he crept carefully on towards the house.

As he got closer the upper storey came into view, then the tops of the front doors. So it was a group of four cottages. Tiny places and . . . Ah! He'd hit gold. Well, possible gold. There were three cars parked at the right-hand end of the row. One belonged to Greaves. Whose were the others?

Disappointment ran through him like acid. Libby's old heap wasn't one of them, so she couldn't be here.

It looked as if he'd be searching online again. And paying through the nose for information.

He waited, because he couldn't leave until after the lawyer had gone, in case the fellow recognised his car.

Well, he could be very patient when he wanted something. He stood under one of the scrubby little trees near the wall and through its sparse branches watched the end houses.

Come on, you old fool. Go home, then I can get back to the hotel.

Libby came downstairs smiling. 'Ned fell asleep straight away. He looks like a little angel now. Thanks.' She accepted the mug of coffee from Joss and took a sip. 'Lovely. Now, Mr Greaves, what's the something else you need to tell me about?'

'Your birth mother is looking for you.'

She stared at him in shock.

Joss whistled softly. 'One thing after another.'

'She's been looking for you for a while now,' Mr Greaves said quietly. 'And you registered to find her, I think.'

Libby opened her mouth but no sounds came out. When she tried again, her voice was scratchy. 'How do you know that?'

'The man who found you for her has just contacted me. She wants to meet you.'

'I'd like to meet her, too. Oh, I would! That's why I contacted the agency. Only I haven't had a reply.'

'They did write to you. Twice. They got no answer to the first letter, but the second time someone filled in the form and signed it to say no contact was wanted.'

She turned so white, Joss went to stand behind her, his hands on her shoulders. For a minute she leant back against him, closing her eyes, then she moved away. 'I'm all right now. I was just . . . shocked. I didn't think even *he* would do that when he knew how important it was to me.'

'Men who want to control someone usually want

complete control. He wouldn't have wanted you to have anyone else to turn to,' Joss said quietly.

'But he *encouraged* me to contact the agency when I wondered about it.'

'Clever. I bet he said you'd probably never hear from your birth mother.'

'Yes. Yes, he did.' She took a deep breath that sounded very close to a sob. 'I've been so very stupid, so easy to fool, as well as cowardly.'

Joss squeezed her hand. 'You've escaped now.'

'Have I?' She turned to Mr Greaves. 'Who is she?'

'I'm not yet authorised to reveal her details, but I can tell you how you came to be adopted, if you like.' He explained how her mother had been fooled into thinking her baby had died, while the baby had actually been sold to some parents longing for a child.

When he'd finished speaking, Libby sat staring down at her hands, which were clasped tightly together in her lap.

Neither man interrupted her.

At length she looked up. 'It makes me feel better that she didn't want to give me away. Silly, isn't it? After all these years.'

'Not at all silly.' Joss wished he dare hold her close and comfort her more openly; she looked so anguished.

'How did my birth mother find out I hadn't died?'

'She was working for . . .' He hesitated. 'There's a man called Leon. I don't know his second name. Your mother used to work for him.'

Joss said quietly, 'We know Leon. I work for him sometimes too, and Libby just did a small job for him.'

'Goodness! It's a small world. But it makes it easier for you to understand. This Leon found out about your mother's child when he was investigating the group running this scam. It can be a very lucrative trade, babies, and this group had grown into quite a large international operation. It went on until they were stupid enough to place a baby with a rather important couple. Then one of their operatives tried to blackmail him and his wife, which would have caused a very unwelcome scandal.

'The authorities had to act and who better than Leon's unit for such a delicate situation?'

Libby nodded a couple of times, still feeling the warmth of knowing she hadn't been given away. 'I'd very much like to meet her. It'd be so good to have a blood relative. I don't count my stepfather, and Grandma Rose is dead, so I'm completely on my own in the world.'

'Shall I arrange a meeting?'

'I wish I dared meet her, but it depends on what Steven does. I may not be here for much longer.'

'Can I tell her who you are? Mention Ned, perhaps. She'd love to have a grandson, I'm sure.'

'No names yet. I don't want to risk this getting back to Steven. And . . . I don't want her to see me as an abused wife. You could tell her I have a son, though. Does she live locally? Is that how you come to know about this?'

'Yes, she does live nearby. She's being as cautious as you. The man who found you for her contacted me on her behalf.'

'There's another reason to wait for this business with

Steven to be sorted out before I meet her. I don't want to put her in danger.'

'Very well.' He glanced at his watch and stood up. 'I'd better get home now. If you have to leave suddenly, keep in touch with me.'

Joss stood up. 'I'll show you out, Henry.'

As they stood beside Henry's car, he said in a low voice, 'If her husband is half as bad as she seems to think, she's right to be cautious. I won't leave her side, I promise you.'

He stood waving goodbye to Henry, then went back into the house to find Libby standing staring out of the kitchen window. She turned to Joss. 'I don't know what to do next.'

'Why don't I call Leon and tell him about Pulford? They've already offered to investigate him if you wish.'

'Why would they do that?'

'Because you helped them get Jane to a safe refuge and you may be useful to them in the future.' He snapped his fingers as something occurred to him. 'If anything does go wrong – if for some reason we're separated and you have to flee – go to the antiques centre. Emily and Chad will be happy to help you, I'm sure. They'll keep you safe. And I'll know where to find you.'

'All right.'

He gave her a hug. 'But that's only the worst-case scenario. My intention is to stick to you like glue and keep you safe.'

She leant against him and they stood for a while, not speaking, just being together. When this was over, she wanted to get to know Joss better. She wasn't going to rush into anything, but she wasn't going to let her experience with Steven put her off finding another partner, either. Well, even with her husband, there had been some good times in the beginning.

Her ambitions weren't unrealistic. She wanted, had always wanted, a proper home and family, the small pleasures of daily life with someone she was fond of. Perhaps more children. Three or four even. A real family.

Was that too much to ask?

Steven continued to watch the cottage and eventually Mr Bloody Greaves came out, escorted by a tall, thin fellow. They chatted for a short time, after which the man went back inside and Greaves got into his car.

Steven frowned as he studied the house. He was assuming Libby was somewhere around here, because she'd talked about her grandmother living in a small village on the edge of the moors, but what if she wasn't? What if the lawyer's visit was about something else? Neither of the two other cars was hers, after all.

His elation faded. He'd have to check, which meant waiting here in this cold, damp field until darkness, trying to catch a glimpse of the occupants of the house. Or should he go back to wait in his car? No. He'd wait here. He had to know.

When it began to rain, he cursed, but stayed where he was.

It was well over two hours before the light faded enough for him to approach the group of houses. He made his way round them, climbed over another damned drystone wall and approached the rear of the buildings from uphill.

His shoes were muddy, he was cold and his clothes were damp, but the anger burnt brightly enough still to keep him there.

Whatever it took!

When he reached the rear of the house, he found they'd drawn the curtains in the kitchen and cursed under his breath.

But luck was with him, because a movement upstairs showed Libby in a lighted bedroom, just about to draw the curtains.

He laughed softly and moved back up the hill, easily finding his way to the church car park. He'd done it! He'd found her!

He started the car, hoping they wouldn't notice it, and drove slowly down to the village. The shop was closed but there was a brightly lit pub. He was tempted to go in and see what he could find out, but he didn't want to give his presence away by asking questions. And anyway, he was wet through.

He turned up the heater, shivering still, and found his way back to Rochdale, stopping to buy some fish and chips. Luckily the rain had stopped, so he could eat them standing outside the car. He couldn't bear to have it smelling of grease and food.

There was an off-licence nearby, so he bought a bottle of whisky and took it back to the hotel. He wasn't in the mood for sitting in a public bar; he needed to think.

Just a nip, he told himself, enjoying the warmth trickling down his throat. But the bottle was half empty before he realised it.

He forced himself to stop and put the top back on the bottle. He mustn't drink too much. He didn't want to end up an alcoholic like Libby's stepfather.

After taking a hot shower, he got into bed. He still hadn't made proper plans, but the long day had taken its toll and he fell asleep before he could work anything out.

Chapter Fifteen

The following morning, Steven woke knowing exactly what to do. He visited a magistrate, pleading an emergency. He explained about his wife, how fragile her emotions were, how she'd taken their son and run away, leaving her anti-depressant medication behind.

He obtained a letter requesting Mrs Pulford to appear before the magistrate with her son at the earliest possible opportunity to answer the claims her husband had made against her.

That wasn't enough, so Steven emphasised that he was worried about his small son's safety. 'She has been known to beat him,' he said sadly, shaking his head and sniffing as if close to tears. 'I can't bear him to be hurt again. Or worse.'

Steven knew there had been a case recently where a father had killed his child rather than let the mother take him back after a parental visit. As he had expected, the magistrate erred on the side of caution.

An officer of the court was sent with him to deliver the letter, make sure Mrs Pulford received it and see that she presented herself to the magistrate immediately, with her son.

This time Steven drove openly up the hill, smiling at his own cleverness, followed by the official.

The two cars were still outside the cottages, thank goodness. Where the hell had she got a new car from? He got out and saw a figure in the downstairs room. The figure left the room immediately, but it had been a woman. Well, Libby couldn't get away without her car, could she?

He turned to wait for the official, who was standing by his car fussing with some papers. *Come on, you fool*, he thought. *Get a move on!*

When Libby heard a car, she rushed into the front room and peered out of the window. 'Joss, come here! It's Steven!' she yelled, moving to the back of the room. 'And there's someone with him.'

He came running to take a quick look. 'The other guy looks like an official.'

'I won't be able to get away now that they're here. What am I going to *do*? If Steven gets hold of Ned, I'll have to go back to him, for my son's sake. I bet he's relying on that.'

'Let's see if I can help you escape by a little trickery. Take Ned out the back way while I keep them talking. Will he stay quiet?'

'He will if I tell him his father is here.'

'Right. Wait at the corner of the house till I invite them inside. I'll make sure they come through into the kitchen. Then get in your car and drive away as quickly as you can.'

'What about our suitcases?'

'No time for them. You know where to go. I'll meet you at the antiques centre and bring the cases if I can.'

The knocker sounded and she grabbed Ned. 'Your father's here, but we're going to run away. Shh. We'll go round the back way.'

He had gone rigid, looking afraid. He'd not make a noise, she was sure. She put her finger to her lips and led him outside.

Joss closed the back door quietly, waiting until the visitors knocked again before yelling, 'Coming!'

He took his time about opening the front door and looked at the two men politely. 'Can I help you?'

'I'm Libby's husband and I want to see her. I need to make sure my son is all right.'

'Of course he's all right. He's just having his bath. If you're who you say you are, I suppose you'd better come in, but I'm going to insist you produce some ID first.' He closed the front door, trapping them in the hall.

The official fumbled in his pocket, producing a laminated card.

Joss took his time about studying it, then handed it back and turned to Pulford. 'And you? You say you're Libby's husband, but how do I know that? I need some ID from you, too.'

'Oh, for heaven's sake! She'll be able to identify me all right.'

'I'm not letting you near her till *I* am sure.'

'What are you, her lover or her bodyguard?'

'Her bodyguard. I'm an ex-policeman and her lawyer has asked me to stay with her because she's afraid you'll beat her up again. The bruises from last time have only just faded.'

The official looked at him sharply. 'What? You're sure of that?'

'I saw the bruises myself.'

'She's lying if she said I hit her. She's mentally unstable and harms herself. Oh, very well. Here's my driving licence.' As Pulford started to take out his wallet, there was the sound of a car engine starting at the front of the houses.

Joss blocked his way for a moment, then heard the car move away, so stepped sideways and let his unwelcome visitors pass him.

Pulford threw open the front door in time to see Libby's car leave the parking area and vanish down the lane.

Joss grabbed his keys and raced out to his own car before the other two men had realised what he was doing. He knew he had no chance of evading both of them, but if he possibly could, he was going to prevent them from following Libby and her son.

In the morning, Des watched Pulford eat his breakfast in the hotel dining room before following him to the magistrate's court. He was surprised when another man, an official by the looks of him, came out of the court and drove along after him out into the country.

As he followed them, Des debated phoning the lawyer's rooms and leaving a message to say that he was keeping an eye on Pulford, but decided to wait a little. He would be able to intervene if necessary. And if that guy was an official, there would be an impeccable witness to any wrongdoing.

When the two cars left the main road and took off along

a narrow road that led up the hill, Des stayed where he was, checking his satnav.

That road was a dead end, leading to a village called Top o' the Hill.

He waited to follow them till the two cars had reached the top.

But there was no sign of them in the village. Damn! He turned his car round in case he had to follow them again, and waited.

He sighed. You did a lot of waiting in this job.

Libby slowed down a little as she drove through the village, but speeded up again as she made her way down the hill. She kept an eye on her rear-view mirror but couldn't see anyone following her.

When she had to stop to give way to someone coming up the hill, she moaned in despair, but the other driver had already started up the narrow one-lane part of the road, so she waited for him to pass.

She'd expected her husband's car to appear behind her, but there was no sign of it. How had Joss managed to stop Steven pursuing her? She hoped he hadn't done anything that got him into trouble.

When she turned on to the main road, she looked back at the road up the hill, but there was no sign of any vehicle.

Feeling she had a good chance of getting out of sight before anyone came after her, she set off for the antiques centre, murmuring, 'Thank you, Joss. Whatever you did, thank you.'

She hoped she'd remember the way and that whatever

Joss had done worked for long enough to let her get herself and her son to a refuge.

If the owners had given shelter to Jane, surely they wouldn't deny Libby temporary asylum until she could contact the women's refuge and ask to be taken in and hidden?

Joss drove along the narrow track like a bat out of hell. He didn't slow down as he went through the village because there was no one out on the street, but he sounded his horn several times. He was aiming for the far end, where the road began to narrow as it started to wind down the hill.

When he got there, he chose his place carefully and used all his driving skills to go into a deliberate skid, fishtailing the car and stopping with it turned sideways. Since there was a drystone wall on either side, he was now completely blocking the road.

'Get past that if you can!' he muttered.

He waited as the two cars pursuing him stopped and Pulford began to sound his horn, hammering it again and again.

The official, who was behind Pulford, came up to Joss's car and banged on the window, asking him to move his car. But he shook his head. He was waiting, giving Libby time to get away.

People had come running out of the houses, and to Joss's relief, Pete ran out of the shop and along to the front car. He stopped dead at the realisation that it was Joss's doing.

Only when his friend was standing there did Joss unlock

the car door and get out, locking it again and slipping his keys into his inner pocket.

'What's up?' Pete asked.

'I'm trying to stop that wife beater from catching Libby and hitting her again.'

Pete turned to glare at Pulford. 'Ah. Allie told me about her friend's problems. So that's him, is it? I want to see this.' He leant against the car, folding his arms, and they both stood there calmly amid a babel of voices.

Pulford came right up to Joss and yelled, 'Get that damned car out of the way!'

'You're blocking a public highway,' the official said.

When Joss merely smiled and made no attempt to move, Pulford kicked the car. 'Move it, damn you!' He kicked the car again, denting it.

'Pete, will you bear witness that this man, whose name is Steven Pulford, has just damaged my car on purpose?'

'I certainly will. What's up with the fellow? Has he run mad?'

'I think he's been mad for a long time.'

Joss tensed, ready to duck, as Pulford bunched up a fist. 'If you hit me, you'll be had up for assault as well as the damage.'

'Now, now, gentlemen, we don't want any trouble,' the official bleated, edging away from Pulford.

For a moment or two there was a standoff, then Pulford breathed deeply and dropped his fist.

'That's right,' Joss taunted. 'I didn't think you'd hit someone your own size. You usually save your punches for your wife, or you kick little boys like your son. When she ran away, you must have missed having them around to use as punch bags.'

The official frowned at him. 'Who exactly are you and why are you doing this?'

'My name's Joss Atherton. I'm an ex detective inspector.' He pulled an ID card from his wallet and held it out.

'Do you have proof of what you're claiming about this man?'

'I don't possess any proof myself, but I've seen it. I can take you to the wife's lawyer who has photos and also testimony from a neighbour, who heard Pulford beating his wife and son just before they left . . . and saw the results. The neighbour took some photos as well.'

'He's lying!' Pulford yelled. 'And you're letting him delay you. Do something!'

Joss ignored him. 'When the lawyer saw the injuries, he arranged for the Domestic Abuse Unit in town to take another set of photos and hear her story. After that Mr Greaves asked me to keep an eye on her.'

'Indeed.' The man turned to Pulford, not speaking nearly as politely now. 'I must ask you to come back with us while we look into these claims. It goes without saying that I cannot help you gain access to your wife if what Mr Atherton says is true.'

'Well, it isn't true. It's a pack of lies. She bangs her head on things to try to incriminate me and injures the boy for the same reason.'

Joss laughed. 'Is that the best you can do? Your neighbour heard the quarrel. Ach, you're a pitiful excuse for a man. A real coward.'

Pulford lashed out at him suddenly with a clenched fist, but Joss was too experienced to be taken by surprise. People like this one didn't realise how much their eye movements gave away before they took action.

He ducked the punch and knocked his opponent down, stepping back immediately. 'I'll defend myself if I have to, but I do not wish to get into a fight.'

Pete and another man from the village helped Pulford up and kept hold of him.

'Could someone please call the police?' the official asked quietly. 'I need to take Mr Pulford to see the magistrate again, and if you wish to press charges against him, Mr Atherton, you'd better come with us.'

'Happy to.'

Pulford didn't struggle. His lips had lost their colour from being pressed tightly together and his expression was now stony. He looked across at Joss and said slowly and sharply, 'I'll find Libby. However long it takes, I'll find her. She's *my* wife and Ned is *my* son. And if you've been in her bed, you'll regret it.'

The official's frown grew more pronounced.

Joss said quietly, 'You have a low opinion of your wife if you think she'd hop into bed with a near stranger.'

Des saw a car whiz through the village, noted that it contained a woman and small child, then realised belatedly that it was her – Libby. He was about to start his motor when he heard another car approaching. No, several cars.

What the hell was going on?

He watched the encounter with great enjoyment. He'd have intervened if it had been necessary, but the tall guy was doing a great job of blocking the departure of Pulford and whoever it was from the village.

Des settled back to enjoy it, jeering when Pulford kicked the car, laughing when he attacked the tall guy, who dodged beautifully and knocked his attacker down with one good punch.

There was a standoff and they were clearly waiting for something. The police, maybe. Someone must have called them by now.

Des went into the shop again and bought a sandwich, chatting to the shopkeeper, who had been standing in the doorway watching the exciting goings-on. He described the car with the woman and child, and she said that it was her friend Libby.

When a police siren sounded, they both went to the door again to watch.

It didn't seem as if Libby King needed another protector, Des decided. The one she had was doing a great job of keeping her husband away from her.

But someone had to keep an eye on Pulford.

The two men from the village stayed next to Pulford until a police car drove up the hill.

Only then did Joss move his vehicle out of the way and greet the dark-skinned officer by name. 'Hello, Lance. Long time no see.'

'What's been going on, sir?'

'I'm not your boss any longer. I've retired from the force. Could we move away for a minute?'

When they were several paces away from the others,

he said quietly, 'I've been doing a bit of protection work, keeping an eye out for that fellow. He'd beaten his wife and their four-year-old, and they'd fled. He followed them. Now he's claiming *she* is the danger and has got a court order for her to bring the boy in.'

'Is there any proof either way?'

'Definite proof that he thumped her from a neighbour and photos of the results at the Abuse Centre. What's more, I've spent a few days watching over her and she seems a very devoted and loving mother, to me.'

'They don't often fool you, Mr Atherton.'

'No. I hope not.'

Lance scanned the group. 'Where is she now?'

'I don't know. I blocked the road to let her and the boy get away.'

'Was that wise?'

Joss shrugged. 'Who can tell? Gut instinct says she's telling the truth and I was afraid Pulford might con a magistrate into letting him take the boy. When I wouldn't move my car, he kicked it and tried to punch me. I have witnesses to that, so I'd like him charged with the damage. That'll put his violent nature on record nicely.'

Lance smiled. 'It'd take a more skilled fighter than him to get the better of you in a one-to-one fight. We've missed you, sir. Glad to see you looking so well again.'

'Thank you. Give everyone my best. Now, you'd better question the others about this incident.' He was itching to leave and find out whether Libby had made it to the antiques centre. He glanced at his watch. No, there hadn't been time for them to get there yet.

Did she have his mobile phone number? She didn't have a mobile of her own yet. They should have remedied that. Well, he had the number of the antiques centre. He could phone to check she'd got there.

But he couldn't leave till he'd seen the magistrate and brought Mr Greaves in to protect Libby's interests.

She'd be all right, though. He was sure Emily and Chad wouldn't turn her away.

Only . . . what if she'd gone somewhere else? No, surely she wouldn't do that!

Libby glanced in the rear-view mirror at regular intervals, but didn't see any car that she recognised, or notice any car staying behind her for more than a minute or two. She lost her way twice but eventually found the road up to the moors, feeling like sobbing in sheer relief as the car started to climb.

Ned was getting fidgety so she said brightly, 'Nearly there now.'

'Where's Boo-Bear?'

Oh, heavens, she'd forgotten his bear. He'd be lost without it.

'I want my Boo-Bear.'

'He's looking after our house for us. He'll be waiting there when we go back.'

Ned began to cry. 'Want Boo-Bear now! Want my bear.'

She didn't reply. There was nothing she could tell him that would console him. Everything was so strange to him, and he'd clung to his bear even more than usual since they ran away.

The antiques centre came into sight just then, thank goodness. 'We're here, darling.'

But he was scowling as she unbuckled him, his lower lip jutting out ominously.

She went up the steps into the centre and hesitated just inside the doorway, keeping tight hold of Ned's hand. There didn't seem to be anyone around.

She walked forward to the café area and to her relief found someone there. 'I need to see Chad or Emily. It's really urgent.'

'They're down in London, I'm afraid.'

Libby stared at her in horror. She hadn't even considered this, had no contingency plans at all.

'Is something wrong?'

She looked at the woman. 'Do you . . . work here?'

'I have the café concession. I'm a friend of Emily's from way back.'

Libby tried to think what to do and suddenly tears began rolling down her cheeks and she couldn't stop crying.

A man came into the café and hesitated.

'Oliver, can you take over for a while? I'm going to take . . .' She broke off to say, 'I'm afraid I don't know your name, but I'm sure I've seen you before. I'm Rachel by the way.'

'We – a friend and I – brought some goods here to sell a few days ago.'

'Is your business to do with that?'

'No. It's to do with a friend of Emily's, Leon.'

The woman stilled and studied her with eyes narrowed, as if she recognised that name. 'Let's go and talk somewhere else. Would your little boy like something to drink?'

'Yes, please. An apple juice and one of those big biscuits.' Libby fumbled in her purse.

'No charge. How about a coffee for you? I'm having one.' She turned to the man behind the counter. 'Oliver, two coffees to go. We'll take them upstairs. Libby and I had better discuss this in private.'

He nodded and Libby waited numbly for their drinks, then followed Rachel upstairs into Emily's flat.

'Are you sure it's all right, us coming in here, I mean?'

'Yes. Emily gave me a key. And if this concerns Leon, it's definitely not for public consumption.'

'No. But it only concerns him sideways. I . . . um, helped him with a job recently.'

'Ah! You and that guy brought Jane here.'

'Yes. Is she all right?'

'She's fine. She's – um, gone to stay with friends.'

Libby took a deep breath and said in a rush, 'I was hoping Emily and Chad would let me stay here for a day or two. I'm running away from an abusive husband. He followed me up to Rochdale and found where I was staying. Joss – the guy who helped with Jane – works for Leon and he was keeping an eye out for me, in case Steven tried to attack me again. He stayed behind to prevent Steven following me. He seemed sure Emily and Chad would help me.'

'I'm absolutely certain they will, so I'll stand in for them and find a bedroom for you and Ned. They'll be back late tonight or early tomorrow.'

It took a moment or two for the words to sink in. Libby

closed her eyes and let out a long, shuddering sigh, burying her face in Ned's back as he sat on her knee. 'Thank you.'

'Do you have some luggage to bring in?'

'No. Not even Ned's favourite toy. We had to leave in a hurry, like within seconds. And I daren't go shopping, just . . . daren't. My ex is staying in the district, you see.'

'We'll make up a list of what you need and I'll nip out to the shops for you.'

'You're being incredibly kind.'

'I don't believe in abusive husbands getting even half a chance to find their prey. I had a friend who suffered for years. And if you've been working for Leon, you're all right. I don't know much about what he does, but I know how greatly Emily and Chad respect him. Now, let's make up a list.'

But first Libby had to take Ned to the toilet, where she washed both their tearstained faces. Then she supervised as he ate the biscuit and drank the apple juice.

When it came to the list, her brain seemed to have fragmented and she had trouble working out what she needed. She managed the clothes for Ned, then decided she needed a change of underwear.

'I'll find you some of Emily's things. You're about the same size.'

'I can't just take her clothes.'

'She won't mind at all, believe me.'

After the list was finished, Rachel found Ned some paper and a pencil so that he could entertain himself by drawing, and left to go to the shops.

'Don't worry,' she said as she left. 'I won't be long.

But you'd better not answer the phone while I'm gone.'

'What if Joss rings up? He'll worry.'

'I'll be back in half an hour, an hour at most. Oliver can answer the phone and let him know you're all right.'

Libby sat limply in the chair, willing herself to calm down. She'd found an asylum, as Joss had said she would.

But the fear still lingered, fear that Steven would find them and take Ned away from her.

What if he went to the police? He could be so convincing.

When she looked, Ned had lain down on the floor beside the little table and was fast asleep, his head on a cushion, his thumb in his mouth.

Her heart melted with love for him. She was *not* going to let Steven get custody of their son. And, somehow, she would make a happy life for the child.

Chapter Sixteen

Henry abandoned a client to come rushing round and have a quick word with the magistrate, who was a friend of his from way back.

While they were waiting to see Mr Corby, Joss initiated charges for damage to his car.

When he was questioned about this, Pulford shrugged. 'Sorry. I lost my temper. I'll pay for the damage.'

Joss could do nothing but accept this. 'Very well.'

The magistrate fitted them in shortly afterwards, but it took over half an hour for the facts to be sorted out, after which Mr Corby decided to rescind his previous letter and asked for it back.

'I've lost it,' Pulford said.

'I saw you put it in your inner pocket,' the official who'd accompanied him said indignantly. 'Do you think I'm stupid?'

'Give it back to me, Mr Pulford,' Mr Corby said, his tone sounding weary. 'And do not lie to me again, or you'll be in trouble officially.'

Pulford's eyes were bright with fury as he pretended to search for the paper and eventually pulled it out. Afterwards he kept very still, too still for a man with such suppressed rage in every line of his face.

If Joss hadn't been so worried about Libby, he'd have enjoyed the way these quiet, elderly men were frustrating Pulford's attempts to pull the wool over their eyes.

The magistrate turned to Joss. 'Do you have any idea of where Mrs Pulford may have gone, Mr Atherton?'

'I do have a couple of places in mind. I'll have to check them out. She doesn't have a mobile phone, unfortunately. And by the way, she's using her maiden name now: Ms King.'

One tight little sound escaped from Pulford at that information.

'Let her name change be duly noted,' Mr Corby told his clerk. 'When you find her, Mr Atherton, please tell her she's released from her requirement to report to me. For her own safety, she can reside where she chooses. However, she must keep in touch with her lawyer at all times. I'll communicate with her through Mr Greaves as needed until this matter is settled once and for all.'

Joss nodded. 'I'll tell her. I'm sure she'll comply.'

Mr Greaves cleared his throat. 'One more thing. I'd like to apply for an injunction requiring Mr Pulford to stay away from his ex-wife.'

'*What?*' Pulford caught the magistrate's eye and snapped his mouth shut again.

Joss was hard put not to chuckle as Mr Corby chose to mistake the meaning of this exclamation.

'Don't you understand what an injunction is, Mr Pulford? I can explain, if you wish.'

'Of course I understand. But I don't think it's necessary.'

It seemed to Joss that the fellow was permanently angry underneath the stiffly composed exterior. Because of Libby? Or was the anger there all the time?

'We think it's very necessary,' Mr Greaves said. 'You've already attacked and hurt her once. I'm hoping she'll press charges about that.'

'She won't do that. Not to me. I'm her husband and this is just a misunderstanding which we can sort out if you'll only let me speak to her.'

Joss didn't like what he was hearing. He'd bet anything that Pulford wouldn't obey the injunction.

'I still need access to my son. A father has rights too.'

'My client would like to extend the injunction to cover her son,' Mr Greaves said quickly. 'The child has already been hurt by this man.'

'That was an accident!' Pulford roared, taking a hasty step forward. He caught the magistrate's eye, and stopped, but his fists remained clenched tightly.

'We'll grant your client the two injunctions for the moment, Mr Greaves, then we'll reassess the situation in a week's time.' The magistrate turned back to Pulford and said slowly and clearly, 'You are not to go near your wife or your son until I lift the injunction. Do you understand?'

'Yes. Am I free to go now?'

'You are.'

When Pulford had left, Corby leant across to whisper to his clerk, who hurried out of the room. When he came back, he nodded.

The magistrate smiled and turned to the others. 'I mean it about your client keeping in touch, Henry. We need to do this officially and properly.' He turned to Joss. 'Off the record, I assume you know exactly where she is.'

'Yes. I'll stay with her, but I'd better have Mr Greaves' mobile number,' Joss said.

'And I'll need yours.'

The magistrate nodded. 'You can give them both to my clerk as well. And Mr Atherton . . .'

'Yes, sir?'

'Please try to stay out of trouble. Do not go looking for Pulford.'

'I won't. But I'm worried he'll follow me when I go to look for Libby.'

Mr Corby smiled. 'I think you'll find that Pulford has been – ah, delayed. You should take advantage of that and leave quickly.'

'Thank you.' Joss hurried out, wondering what was going on. The magistrate was a wily old fellow.

He paused for a moment in the car park when he saw Pulford on the other side of the road, standing next to his car, arms folded, foot tapping, while a parking officer wrote on his pad.

Brilliant! Joss could get right away while Pulford was otherwise engaged.

He doubted the other man would find her at the antiques centre.

When Steven went outside, he headed straight for his car, which he'd left on the street. Whatever they said, he had a *right* to see his wife and child, and he intended to follow Atherton until he found them.

To his intense annoyance, he found a parking officer standing beside his car, writing on a pad.

'What's the matter?' he asked as he hurried up to the man.

'You parked in a fifteen-minute pickup zone. You've been here nearly an hour.'

'I'm so sorry. I do apologise. I had urgent business with the magistrate and just nipped in to see him. I didn't realise it'd take so long. Look, I wasn't paying as much attention as I should have done to the time limits, and I apologise. It won't happen again. Surely you can let me off with a warning this time? I'm a visitor to this town and—'

'The ticket's been started now, I'm afraid, sir.' He continued writing. 'I'll only be a couple of minutes.'

Steven glanced at the door of the magistrate's court. No sign of Atherton yet. If this fool would just hurry up, he'd be all right. What mattered was finding Libby.

At that moment a policeman came strolling along the street and stopped beside Steven's car. 'Does this vehicle belong to you, sir?'

'Yes.'

'We're doing random checks in the town centre today. Can you please wait with me while I check your registration and a few other things?'

Steven stared at him in shock. 'But it's all in order and I need to get somewhere quickly.'

'Sorry, sir. I've just put your registration number into the system, so we'll have to complete the check now. Will you please wait over there till I get the information?'

Steven moved away from the policeman and began to pace to and fro. They were doing this on purpose, banding together against him, he was sure.

A young man was standing a few paces away fiddling with a motor bike. He looked at Steven sympathetically and when his pacing took him nearby, the man said in a low voice, 'Hard luck, mate. They're very sharp on parking in this area. Just say "yes sir, no sir, three bags bloody full sir," or they'll keep you here for ever.'

Steven didn't reply and was about to turn away when Joss came out of the building opposite. How the hell was he going to keep tabs on Atherton now?

Then he had an idea and turned back to the young man. 'Want to earn a hundred pounds?' He pretended to be admiring the motor bike, patting it.

'I'd love to. As long as it's legal. I'm not breaking the law, though, because I'm on probation.'

'You see that fellow over there. I don't want to point. He's just getting into that silver car.'

'Oh, I know him. Atherton nicked me once.'

'Can you follow him without him finding out you're doing it? I need to know where he goes.'

'Can do. I'll need something on account, though, to prove you mean what you say.'

Steven fumbled in his inner pocket, where he kept some loose money, and managed to twitch a £20 note out. He slipped it to the young man when the policeman wasn't looking.

'How do I find you again, mister?'

'I'll be at my hotel.' Steven gave him details. 'My name's Pulford. What's yours?'

'Just call me Ken.' The young man started his motor bike and set off after Joss's car. They both disappeared round the corner.

When the parking attendant came to give him his ticket, Steven said, 'That's a great motor bike, isn't it?'

'I'm not fond of them, myself. Here.'

As the man walked away, the policeman stopped talking into his radio and came back to join Steven. 'I've got the details of the car, sir. Have you proof of your identity?'

Holding his temper under control, Steven answered the questions and at last was allowed to leave.

He went straight back to the hotel, hoping the young man was to be trusted. But if he wasn't, then there would be some other way to find Libby.

He wasn't giving up. She was his and she was staying his. Once she understood that their son would be the one to suffer if she didn't, she'd toe the line. She was besotted with the brat.

Joss set off for the antiques centre, but took a roundabout route and kept a careful eye out for pursuit.

At one point he thought a motor cyclist was following him, but the fellow took a left turn, and though Joss saw a couple of motor cycles of the same type, neither of their drivers were wearing the same clothes or helmet.

When he set off up the hill to the antiques centre, he made very sure no one was pursuing him, whether in a car or on a motor cycle. But the only vehicle chugging up the hill, apart from his, was a heavily laden truck which slowed him down all along the last stretch to the antiques centre since there was no chance to overtake it safely.

He parked round the corner of the car park, in an overflow parking area which was hidden from the road, and went inside.

There was no one in the showrooms, but he found a man he recognised from the opening day looking after the kiosk. A couple of Japanese tourists were sitting at a table, happily chatting away as they drank their cups of tea.

'Have you been here for a while?' He tried to remember the man's name, but couldn't.

'An hour or so.'

'I'm looking for a woman and child. We arranged to meet here.'

'What's your name and have you ID to prove it?'

Joss nodded and produced it.

'She said you'd be coming. I'll take you to her.'

He led the way back towards the showrooms but turned up the stairs and knocked on a door.

It opened slightly, then there was a gasp and it was flung wide open. 'Joss! Oh, Joss! You're here. Come in quickly. Thanks, Oliver.'

When the door closed, Joss took Libby in his arms and held her close, because she was shaking.

As he explained how he'd prevented Steven from following her, then went on to describe how a policeman had run a check on her ex's car, she began to relax and even smiled. But she shook her head about the injunctions. 'He won't obey them.'

'I don't think he will, either. He's obsessed by you.'

'Not by me – by controlling his wife and son. We're only

components and possessions to him, not individuals in our own right. Want a cup of coffee?'

'I'd love one.'

'What now, Joss?'

'We wait here for Emily and Chad to return.'

'Rachel says they won't be back till tomorrow.'

'Then we'll wait here for them. The only other place you'd be safe would be the women's refuge, and I think you'll be a lot more comfortable here.'

'And you? Will you be comfortable?'

'I can make myself comfortable anywhere.' He took her hand and kept hold of it. 'I know this isn't the time, but after we've sorted everything out, I want to get to know you better. Is that all right with you?'

She gave him one of her sudden glorious smiles. 'Oh, yes. I'd like that very much.'

The smile soon faded, though.

Des hung around, waiting for the various players to move on.

He watched Atherton leave the magistrate's court and turned his attention to Pulford, amused by the fuss with the police checking his car. When that was over, he followed the fellow, but Pulford only went back to the hotel.

Des decided not to hang around there, but to go and see the lawyer again, to find out whether Libby's guardian angel would be staying with her. If so, Des would be superfluous to requirements and could probably wind up this case.

Mr Greaves had a couple of clients to see, so Des arranged to come back later in the afternoon.

He went for a brisk walk. Sitting around on surveillance

wasn't much good for keeping you fit. He noted that Pulford's car was in the hotel car park when he started out and was still there when he got back.

Then it was time to see the lawyer.

He explained to Mr Greaves what he'd seen. 'You said Libby has someone watching over her. Is he still with her?'

'Yes. And he's very experienced.'

'So I'll get back to my client and explain what's happened then sign off on the case. I've other people wanting my services.'

'You seem to have done a good job.'

They shook hands and Des left. This case had been pretty straightforward. He'd soon be able to wind things up.

Ken waited till the silver car was out of sight before following it. He was shivering by the time he reached the first place on the hill where Atherton might have parked because he'd taken off his jacket to change his appearance, changed helmets to his passenger lid, and even taken off his sweatshirt, leaving only a tee shirt. He'd have bloody earned that money.

He nearly missed the car he'd been following, but saw it as he was turning his bike in the car park, ready to move on. It was parked out of sight of the road.

If the cop was stopping here, so was she, Ken decided. He looked for somewhere to hide his bike, and found a place where gravel was stored behind a low wall. Not really part of the car park, but who was to stop him? He could always say he was worried about his bike getting pinched.

He wondered whether to go inside, but he was cold

and soon got fed up of waiting around, so decided to risk it. He combed his hair into a more ordinary style, one his mother would approve of, but his friends would laugh at, and put his sweatshirt on over his tee shirt. There. He looked respectable now, like a boring little office worker or something.

When he entered the centre, he saw sparkling lights and all sorts of gleaming stuff. They'd have CCTV here, he was sure, because the place screamed 'valuables' – but hey, he wasn't doing anything wrong, was he? Anyone could look at the goods in a shop.

Then he saw a sign at the back saying CAFÉ and sighed in relief. An excuse for being here.

The man serving there didn't seem in the slightest bit interested in chatting, so Ken just said he was cold after riding over the moors and ordered a coffee and a cake.

He chose a seat in a corner, from where he could see all round him and most of the front showroom too. Taking a newspaper from a rack, he settled down to read. He could pass a pleasant hour here whether he found out anything else or not.

Just as he was wondering whether to leave, who should come down the stairs and into the café but Mr Bloody Atherton himself. Ken lifted up the newspaper to cover most of his face, but listened hard.

'We were wondering about something to eat, Oliver.'

'There are only snacks here, I'm afraid, though we do have some rather nice little packets of soup.'

They discussed what the little boy would like to eat and Atherton walked back upstairs with a loaded tray.

Ken folded up the newspaper and left, feeling very pleased with his own cleverness. That Pulford fellow ought to give him a bonus.

Rachel came back from the shops with some clothes for Ned, and a couple of cheap plastic toys too, as well as a pork pie and some other bits and pieces of food.

'Since Chad and Emily won't be back till tomorrow, I'd better show you which bedrooms to use.'

'You're quite sure they won't mind us staying here?' Joss asked.

'Certain.'

Libby was exhausted after the stress of the day and let the others make the arrangements. She accepted the loan of some of her hostess's clothes and did her best to keep Ned occupied, but he was bursting with energy.

'Shall I take him out for a play in the car park?' Joss asked, but answered his own question. 'No. Too risky. I'll ask Rachel if there's somewhere at the back where we can play with a ball.'

'If there is, I'll come out with you. I could do with some fresh air.'

He guessed she didn't want to let Ned out of her sight, but didn't say so.

When he came back, Joss took them down and Rachel let them out into the private rear courtyard.

'Visitors aren't normally allowed here,' she said. 'We have two young people living in the units at the back. They're special-needs folk. They might come out into the courtyard but they won't be any trouble.

'Toby's out doing one of his gardening jobs at the moment but when he gets back, he likes to sit outside in the evening sun. Oh, and Ashley sweeps the yard at least twice a day, she's so obsessive about cleanliness. She dusts our displays and she's brilliant, now she knows what's required. Never seen anyone as careful to get everything perfectly dust free.'

Rachel went back into the centre and Libby sank down on the bench, sighing with pleasure as she turned her face up to the late-afternoon sun.

'Want to play ball, Ned?' Joss asked.

The little boy nodded and was soon running round happily, though he kept an eye on his mother, as if he only felt safe when she was nearby.

When Joss had had enough of throwing the ball, he joined Libby on the bench. 'You all right?'

'As all right as I can be at the moment.'

A young man came into the yard at that moment, accompanied by Rachel.

'This is Toby. Toby, these are friends of Emily and Chad, but no one must know they're here.'

'Are they hiding?'

'Yes. A bad man is chasing them.'

'They'll be safe here. This is a good place.' He nodded a greeting and went past them through a door, but came out after a short time to sit in the sun on another bench.

He seemed to bring an air of peace and quiet happiness with him, and Libby could feel herself relaxing. He was right. This place did feel good.

A little hope crept into her heart. Maybe things would

work out all right. After all, she wasn't on her own now. She glanced at Joss, caught him looking at her warmly and blushed.

He grinned.

And before she could think what she was doing, she was smiling foolishly back. She was in danger of falling for him. She shouldn't do that, but how could you stop yourself from being attracted?

After a while Toby stretched and stood up. 'I'm going to get my tea now. Ashley and I have tea together. We have to clear up carefully. She doesn't like a mess.'

He disappeared through the door into their quarters.

Libby yawned. 'I suppose we'd better get something to eat as well, then I'm going to put Ned to bed. You've tired him out nicely.' She looked at her son, who was examining a rose bush which had three perfect blossoms on it. He didn't try to pick them or destroy them – well, he hardly dared touch things, let alone damage them – but he stroked one fingertip along the velvety surface of a petal and bent his head to smell the flower, smiling at it.

When they went inside, they found Rachel getting ready to lock up the centre, which had now closed for the day.

'I was just coming to get you,' she said cheerfully. 'I need to lock all the outside doors, because of the security system, but I'll give you a code that will let you go outside at the back if you don't go near the display cases, and here's a key to the back door. You may want to go outside in the morning and I don't usually get here till nine o'clock.'

'I want my Boo-Bear,' Ned said suddenly.

Here we go, Libby thought. 'Boo-Bear's waiting for us at home.'

Ned plumped down on the floor and began to sob and thump the ground. 'Want my Boo-Bear. Want my Boo-Bear.'

'We left his teddy behind,' Libby explained to Rachel. 'I knew we'd have trouble getting him to sleep without it.'

'There's a stall with teddy bears in the Old Barn,' Rachel said. 'They're antiques, so they're a bit more expensive than bears usually are, but they have some very small ones and a few other soft toys too.'

'Could we have a quick look, do you think?'

The big room at the rear was full of shadows and the stalls were covered up. It looked eerie. Rachel switched on the overhead lights and turned the cover back from a stall to one side. 'I know they have a bargain shelf here. Yes, here it is. Ned, come and look at these toys.'

He let go of his mother's hand and went to study that shelf. On it was a small, woolly lamb. As he picked it up and stroked its head gently, light seemed to gather around him and he relaxed.

Libby blinked but there was definitely a light haloing her son.

'He's nice,' Ned said. 'He's lost his mummy, but he could come and live with me and Boo-Bear.'

Libby looked at the price and gulped, but Joss had already taken out his wallet.

'Let me buy it for him.'

'I shouldn't.'

'I can well afford it and he's been so good today, he

deserves a treat.' He picked up the lamb. 'Let's take his ticket off, Ned. He wants to live with you.'

Rachel moved closer to Libby. 'You saw it, didn't you? The light, I mean.'

'I'm not sure what I saw.'

'It's a sort of friendly spirit. It won't hurt Ned. It seems to appear to people who need help.'

Libby blinked in surprise, not knowing what to say to this.

Ned beamed and crushed the woolly lamb against himself as Joss weighted down the banknotes and ticket on the counter.

'I'll tell Gillian about the sale in the morning,' Rachel offered.

He looked round, studying their surroundings. 'If we had to get away suddenly, is there a back way out? Where does that door lead?'

'Only to the units. Oh, and to the earliest part of the building, which is not for public use. I'm afraid you'd have to go out into the rear courtyard and round the side, then clamber over the rough ground of the moors to get away from the centre any way but via the car park.'

'I see. Still, it's useful to know the layout, isn't it? I don't expect we'll have any trouble tonight. Thank goodness Pulford doesn't know where we are.'

When Emily and Chad had delivered Jane to the next link in the escape chain, they went for an Indian meal and sat chatting.

'We should find a B&B,' she said at last. 'I doubt there are any decent hotels round here.'

'Yes. It is a bit isolated, isn't it? Or we could drive home. I'm not sleepy. Are you?'

'No. I was on the alert, too concerned to make sure Jane got there safely to relax. It'll take me a while to come down from that. Anyway, I infinitely prefer my own home to a B&B. Once you've slept in a six-foot bed, four foot six seems tiny. I must be getting old and set in my ways.'

'So am I. If we hadn't had to wait until after dark to deliver her, we could have been well on our way back by now.'

'We should buy some bottles of water and a snack in case we get thirsty in the middle of nowhere. But it's mostly motorway down to Lancashire from this part of Scotland, so it should be straightforward enough. We can stop further south at a services for some coffee to help us keep alert.'

As she drove, she stayed silent for so long, he asked, 'Something wrong? Changed your mind? Or would you rather I drove now?'

'No. I'm fine to drive for the first hundred miles or so. But it's just . . . Well, to tell you the truth, I have a strong feeling we're going to be needed at home.'

'One of your psychic feelings?'

'Yes. I don't get them often, but when I do, they're usually worth paying attention to.'

They found an off-licence that hadn't yet closed, bought some fizzy water and sweets, and set off again. When Emily glanced sideways, she saw Chad dozing gently in the front passenger seat.

She turned her attention back to the road, which unfurled

before them in the light of the headlights, beckoning her on through the dark landscape.

The feeling that she would be needed at the centre persisted. She couldn't understand why.

Then there was a loud bang and the car skidded suddenly, dragging sideways, hard to control.

Chad came awake with a jerk.

'We have a flat,' she informed him as she brought it to a halt.

'Damn! I hate changing tyres.'

'I can do it.'

'Is there anything you can't do, woman?'

'Lots.' She opened the car door and got out, shivering in the cool night air. 'I don't enjoy changing tyres in the dark, though. I'm glad I'm not on my own.'

'Nice to know I have some uses.'

'Stop fishing for compliments and get out the spare tyre.'

Chapter Seventeen

Ken went to Reception and asked for Mr Pulford, giving his first name and explaining that he was expected. The woman phoned through to the room and told him Mr Pulford would be down in a minute.

He came hurrying down the stairs and took Ken into the hotel bar. 'Did you find out where she is?'

'Yes.'

'Well?'

'I'm hungry and thirsty. Aren't you going to offer me a drink, even?' He waited and as the minutes ticked by without even an offer of a half of beer from the miserable sod, he took his revenge. 'That information will cost you a hundred pounds on top of the twenty you've already paid me. Payable in advance.'

'Tell me where they are!' Pulford's voice was so loud people turned to stare at them.

'Not till after you give me the money.' Ken waited again, not liking the vicious expression on his companion's face. He was beginning to wonder if this guy was a bit of a fruit loop.

'Very well.' Pulford pulled the money out of his pocket, but kept hold of it. 'Where are they?'

Ken twitched the money away from him. 'In an antiques centre halfway up to the moors, on the road to Todmorden. Chadderley Antiques, it's called.'

'Don't even think of moving till I've found it on my satnav.' He got out his smart phone and fiddled around. 'It isn't known.'

'It used to be called The Drover's Hope. Used to be a pub.'

Ken waited, not because he couldn't have escaped, but because he didn't want any trouble.

More fiddling, then: 'Ah. There it is.'

'Can I go now?'

'How do I know you're not cheating me?'

An outstretched arm prevented him from leaving without causing a scene. Ken kept his cool. 'Look, Mr Pulford. I've done what you asked and I've told you the truth. You'll have to take my word for it, I know. But I'm *not* lying to you.' He crossed his heart mockingly.

Another minute's scrutiny, then: 'Very well.' Pulford stood up. 'Not a word to anyone.'

'Do you think I'm crazy? I'm keeping my head down till I've finished my probation.'

Ken walked out of the hotel as quickly as he could without attracting attention to himself. He was glad to be away from that sicko. He didn't envy the poor wife when the guy found her and felt a bit guilty for pointing the finger.

Then he touched the pocket with the money in and shrugged. You did what you had to.

Once back at his hotel room, Des tried to ring Chad's mobile, but got the same mechanical voice telling him the service wasn't available. Was there something wrong with the phone or was Chad somewhere with no coverage?

He didn't like to go home again till he'd wound things up with his client, so he went back to his hotel room. He was sick of the sight of it. He checked that Pulford was still in the hotel, had a meal and went down for a drink in the bar. He was about to call it a day when Pulford came into the bar with a scruffy young fellow.

Where had he seen the younger guy before, Des wondered? Somewhere. He couldn't figure out where, though.

He couldn't get into a position from which to lip read so found it very frustrating to watch them. He could see enough to tell that the pair were not on good terms, however.

When the younger guy left, Des followed his gut instinct and walked out after him.

On the street he caught up and said quietly, 'Want to earn some money?'

The guy spun round. 'You're the second person to ask me that today.'

He looked about to run for it, so Des spoke quickly. 'I saw you talking to Pulford, and all I want to know is what you were talking about.'

'How much are you offering?'

'Fifty quid.'

'Fine. Would you buy me a coffee, too?'

'Sure. Let's go in that café over there.' When they were seated, Des paid for a coffee and a piece of cake.

'Well, you're more generous than Pulford, I'll say that

for you. And I need to do less to earn the money. I'd like to see the cash first, if you don't mind.'

'I don't blame you.'

'Who are you? Police?'

'Private investigator.'

'Licensed?'

'Fully licensed. Do you want to see proof?'

'Yes. I don't want to get into any trouble with the police.'

Des pulled out his ID card. 'Here you are. And I like to stay on good terms with the police, so I won't be leading you into any trouble, I promise.'

After a careful study of Des's face and the ID photo, the young guy said, 'What do you want to know?'

'What you're doing with Pulford. Every single detail. And . . . I might be even more generous if the information is useful. But I'm good at telling when someone's lying.'

'Fair enough. Who needs to lie? I only met the fellow tonight. He's not a friend or anything.'

The young guy started talking. Des prompted him a couple of times, asked questions and was satisfied he was being told the truth. He pushed the fifty pounds across the table, followed it with another twenty. 'Thank you.'

'My pleasure. Been a good day for earning a bit on the side.'

'Don't go back to Pulford. He's trouble.'

'Can't stand the fellow.'

'Oh? Why not?'

'He's a fruit loop. Something wrong up here.' He tapped his forehead.

'Why do you say that?'

'I don't know. He just . . . makes me feel uncomfortable.' He looked at the menu. 'I might grab a meal while I'm here.'

Des returned to the hotel. Pulford's car was still there. He wondered whether to disable it, but decided against it. He doubted the fellow would leave and go after her tonight. Bit difficult stumbling over the moors in the dark.

No, he'd get up early and follow Pulford discreetly.

He tried Chad's mobile phone again, but there was still no answer, so he went to bed.

After his informant had gone, Steven started to go up to his room, then changed his mind and found a quiet corner in the bar. He ordered a single malt. As he sipped it, he checked the area around the antiques centre on his satnav.

The place seemed to be on the edge of the moors, away from other habitations. If he could park somewhere out of sight, he could perhaps approach it from behind and break in. Then he'd drag Libby and Ned home, where he'd make sure his wife agreed to give a statement to the police saying they were now reconciled.

But he mustn't get caught. The trouble was, the antiques centre was bound to have a good security system. How was he to get round that? What the hell did he know about electronics? He could use gadgets like his smart phone but he didn't know how they worked, let alone how to break into a security system.

So he'd have to wait until dawn and hope someone got up early and switched the security off so that he could get inside.

It wasn't a good plan. He needed a lot of luck if he was

to get near her. But time was on his side. He had plenty of that, too bloody much, so he could hang around in the area as long as he had to. Days, if necessary.

If he didn't die of boredom first.

He drained his glass of whisky and left the hotel, going out to an off-licence he had noticed on the way here, which was also a minimart.

He passed a café on the other side, then stopped and moved back, still keeping to the other side. Yes. That was Ken and he was talking to a man who looked familiar. Steven studied him carefully. He'd been in the hotel. On his own. Strange that he was talking to Ken, who wasn't staying at the hotel.

When the man paid money to Ken, Steven's suspicions were further roused. Something was going on here. It might not be connected to him, but there again, it was best to be sure.

When the guy came out, Steven nipped into the café and sat down at Ken's table, smiling at the young fellow's shock. 'If you want to earn another fifty pounds, come to the hotel car park in quarter of an hour.'

He saw Ken hesitate, so added, 'If you don't turn up, I'll call the police and lay a complaint against you for picking my pocket.'

'Hey, man, chill! I'm always happy to earn more money.'

Steven arrived back at the hotel in time to see the stranger put something into a car and go up in the lift.

He took £50 out of his wallet, then waited in the car park until Ken turned up. Steven had been sure he would come.

Ken greeted him with, 'Show me the money.'

Steven pulled the money out of his pocket. 'Tell me about the guy you were talking to.'

He listened in annoyance, handing over the £50 when he was satisfied all had been explained. 'Do not – go near – that guy again.'

'Definitely not. I'm outa here.'

He watched Ken hurry out of sight, then studied the stranger's car. Not now. Later.

He carried out his original plan and bought some supplies from the minimart in case he had to hang around near the antiques centre. He left them in the car.

At the hotel, he rang the bell at Reception, rousing a sleepy clerk from the rear office to pay his bill on the excuse that he'd had an urgent message and needed to leave really early in the morning.

Then he went to bed, to get what sleep he could.

He slept like a baby, waking at 3 a.m. as the radio alarm clock next to the bed went off. He wanted to reconnoitre the area round the antiques centre before anyone was stirring and it got light early in June.

It took him only a few minutes to shower and dress, after which he stopped in the hotel kitchen to pick up a sharp knife. There were plenty of them, so he doubted anyone would notice.

He slung his things into his Mercedes, then dealt with the car of the private investigator. He enjoyed disabling it.

'Now try to follow me!' Steven told it with relish.

He set off through the dark town, making his way up to the moors. No other vehicles were going in his direction and only two lorries came down the hill.

He drove slowly past the centre, looking for somewhere to park. He hadn't passed anywhere suitable on his way – well, not in the last couple of miles – but luck was with him and he found a lay-by about half a mile up from the centre. He parked there, put on his trainers and set off across the moors, cursing the rough ground and the tussocky grass.

Grey light was filtering into the landscape now, even though it wasn't yet dawn. His eyes quickly grew accustomed to the pre-dawn dimness and he had no trouble finding his way. It felt as if he was an actor in an old black and white movie.

He circled the antiques centre from about half a mile away, climbing over a drystone wall at one stage. But to the north and east there was only one wall. He couldn't see any farms in that area and the land rose quite steeply at one point. He went south-westwards as far as the next wall, which was round a large private house in a little hamlet just down the hill. Yuppie tree-huggers, probably.

After standing for a moment, thinking hard, he moved closer to the centre. It had a lot of outbuildings at the rear, which might or might not be an advantage. It depended on whether they were included in the security system.

He'd read about Chadderley Antiques on their website. Why the hell had a big London dealer moved up here? It didn't make sense. The man could have made far more money in London.

As the light increased, Steven found a few stones, the remains of some small shelter, and sat down on them.

He didn't want anyone to notice him standing up like a sore thumb. He wanted to observe what went on.

Libby slept badly and woke feeling as if she had a hangover, which she couldn't have, because she'd not had anything alcoholic to drink last night. Worry. That was what was giving her a dull headache.

In other words, Steven. She knew he wouldn't give up, not without a much better reason than an injunction. She was a possession to him, not a life partner.

It wasn't yet light and Ned was still asleep. He'd sleep for a couple of hours yet, because he rarely stirred until after seven o'clock. She, on the other hand, felt restless and unable to go back to sleep.

She had a sudden urge to go down and sit in the small courtyard. She could watch dawn creep across the sky and maybe think up an alternative plan for getting away, in case Steven did find out where they were.

Would Joss be able to keep them safe? He seemed to think so. She wasn't as sure. He was too kind – not nearly as ruthless as her ex.

On that thought, she got up, unable to lie in bed for another second. She put on her borrowed undies, jeans and a top, then went to the foot of the stairs. After she'd keyed in the security number, she was able to walk round the side of the display area, which was still electronically armed, and get out into the rear courtyard.

It was chilly outside and she wished she'd put a cardigan on, but she'd only stay here for a few minutes because she didn't want to leave Ned on his own for long. She couldn't see the dawn horizon to the east, because it was on the other side of the main road. She didn't want to go so far away from the door.

But the air was cool and fresh, making her head feel better, so she sat down on the nearest bench.

Suddenly she thought she saw a light in one corner of the courtyard, as if someone was out there with a torch, and jumped to her feet, ready to dash inside. But the light slowly faded and there was no sign of a figure in that area. She must have been mistaken. It was probably a reflection of one of the security lights inside the buildings.

She sat down again, wondering whether she could meditate. No, she was far too agitated to do that. Besides, she had to keep watch at all times.

She'd just sit here quietly for a few minutes, before going back and waiting for Ned to wake up.

In the morning Des woke early, as usual, and decided to do a quick check that Pulford's car was still there. Since his room was at the back, he couldn't see the car park, so had to go down and look out of the front door of the hotel.

The car was gone.

Damnation! He should have kept better watch.

He would, he decided, go up to the antiques centre himself. And he'd set off as soon as he'd packed and paid his bill. He had a bad feeling about this.

When he took his case outside to his car, he stopped dead and cursed. Someone had hacked at his front tyres. Made a good job of it, too.

On a sudden suspicion, he went to peer into his exhaust

pipe and could see something blocking it. Someone had been very determined to stop him driving.

Cursing, he wondered if it was Pulford, or someone else.

Would the young guy have done it? No. He didn't look the type. It took a lot of physical strength to hack at modern tyres. It must have been Pulford.

How had he given himself away?

It would take a while to get this sorted out. He went into the hotel and reported the vandalism, asking that they call in the police.

He tried Chad's mobile phone again, but got the same lack of response. He wondered whether to call the antiques centre, but when he phoned, there was no answer, so he could only leave a message asking Chad to get back to him as soon as possible, since he had something to report.

After that Des was kept busy for quite some time, first with the police, then with sorting out repairs to his car.

In the end, since he hadn't heard from Chad, he decided to hire a car and drive up to the antiques centre.

He hoped Pulford wasn't causing trouble there. But he'd not bet on it. That fellow had trouble written all over him. He was, as the young guy had said, a fruit loop.

Steven moved very carefully along the rear of the antiques centre. This part was really old and should have been knocked down years ago. Those Heritage people had a lot to answer for, preserving unimportant ruins like these at enormous cost.

There was a shoulder-high drystone wall running right round the complex. Fat lot of good that would be for keeping people out. He climbed over it easily, annoyed with himself when he knocked out a loose stone and it fell with a loud clatter.

He paused, listening carefully, but no one came out to investigate. It probably hadn't been loud enough to be heard inside, had just seemed loud out here in the morning stillness.

He carried on round the top end of the outbuildings. When he'd nearly reached the front again, he found a kind of three-sided courtyard, enclosed by the wings of the house.

And then – he couldn't believe his luck – he saw Libby sitting on a bench looking weary and worried. So she should be, the trouble she'd caused, the bitch!

He nearly ran across to grab her, but stayed mainly hidden by the corner of the wall to make sure she was alone. Besides, she was about thirty yards away from him and she might run back into the building and lock the door on him before he got close enough to grab her. He didn't want her screaming for help and bringing other people running. There was that damned injunction to think about.

Still, if she came out like this every morning, he might find a way to get close enough to grab her and cover her mouth.

He let out a sniff of near laughter. Perhaps he could make a noise like a cat and see if she came to investigate. As if! That sort of thing only happened in cartoons.

A minute later, he congratulated himself on his caution, because someone came out of the rear building, near where he was hiding. He pressed even further back against the wall. It was a young man with a big moon face, who was yawning and stretching.

Steven could hear their conversation quite clearly.

'Hello, Libby.'

'Oh, Toby. Hi. I hope I didn't wake you up.'

'I heard a noise. It wasn't you. It came from behind our units.'

'Perhaps it was an animal.'

He frowned. 'No. Sheep can't climb walls. And we don't have a cat.'

'Do you want me to come with you to look? Could it have been a bird?'

Damn you, no! Steven thought. *Stay where you are.*

'There are birds on the moors. I like to watch them.'

'So do I.'

'I think I'll go back to bed.' Toby yawned again. 'I'm still tired.'

'Yes, so am I. Bye.' She went back into the centre.

She was inside so quickly, Steven could only watch her and listen to what sounded like a lock clicking into place. He glared at the building. So near – and if it hadn't been for that idiot, he might have had her.

Now he'd have to hang around and wait for another opportunity. Perhaps she'd come outside the following morning. But that would be a long time to hang around in this godforsaken place.

He heard the sound of a car engine and watched as a white BMW came down the hill and turned into the centre. Who the hell would be turning up at this hour of the morning?

* * *

Chad stopped the car and rolled his shoulders. 'Well, that was an annoying thing to happen.'

'It only delayed us for a short time.'

'Nearly two hours by the time we'd stopped at a services to clean ourselves up. And fancy me treading on my mobile! I'm not usually so clumsy. It's ruined. I'll have to buy a new one.'

'Never mind. We're home now.'

He looked at the car park. 'Looks like someone else is here, too. Who can that be? I don't recognise the car.'

She shook her head. 'Perhaps we weren't the only ones to break down yesterday. There was that car in the layby just up the road as well.'

'I'd have stopped to offer help if there had been anyone in it, but there was no sign of the driver. If it's still there later today, I'll call the police. No one would just dump a luxury car like that.'

'Unless they'd stolen it.'

'Yeah.' They got out of the car and went into the antiques centre, disarming the security system.

'It was already partly disarmed,' Chad said, frowning at the control panel near the door.

Even as he spoke a woman peered at them from part way up the stairs. She looked as if she'd recently got out of bed, her hair still tousled.

He recognised her at once; it was the woman who'd sold him some pieces of china and helped bring Jane to them. 'Libby King, isn't it?'

'Yes.'

As they moved slowly forward towards the stairs, a man

appeared above her. 'Rachel let us sleep here last night. I hope that's all right.'

'Joss Atherton,' Emily said.

'Yes. I thought you might give us shelter till I can ask Leon for help.'

'It's all my fault. I was running away from my husband,' Libby said. 'He found out where I was.'

Emily stared at her. Toby had been right. She wanted to blurt out that she was Libby's mother, but the young woman was looking so strained that the words died in Emily's throat. Instead she said cheerfully, 'Why don't you put the kettle on and you can tell us about it over a cup of tea? And maybe make some toast? We're both dying for something hot to drink and we're ravenously hungry. We had a flat tyre on the way back or we'd have been here a few hours ago.'

'Not much fun, changing tyres in the dark.'

'Tell me about it. My phone slipped out of my pocket and I trod on it.'

'Tough.'

Libby let the owners pass and go into the master bedroom. She went into the kitchen of their flat, put the kettle on and got out some mugs and the makings for toast.

By the time Chad and Emily had dumped their luggage, used the bathroom and joined them, she had a pot of tea brewing.

'I feel terrible being in your home like this,' she said. 'Only I had to get away from my ex.'

There was a sound at the door and they turned to see a small boy standing there, looking anxious. When he saw

Libby, he ran across the room, avoiding the strangers, and clinging to the side of her clothes.

She put an arm protectively round him. 'This is my son, Ned.'

'Pleased to meet you, Mr Ned,' Emily said, the first words she'd ever spoken to her grandson. She was aching to cuddle him.

He looked at her solemnly, relaxing a little. 'I'm not Mr Ned, silly. I'm just Ned.'

'Oh, yes. Sorry. I'm Emily and this is Chad.' She watched Joss move to stand near Libby and the boy. He looked protective, as if he cared for them.

'You must be tired,' he said. 'Sit down and I'll make the toast.'

'Butter and jam are in the fridge.' Emily took a seat and smiled at Ned again. 'Is that your lamb?'

He nodded.

'What's he called?'

'Lamb.'

She laughed. 'That's a very good name for him.'

Ned nodded solemnly and the whole atmosphere lightened still further.

By the time they'd toasted and eaten the whole of a loaf between them, the tale had been told.

Emily laid one hand on Libby's. 'Of course you must stay here. You'll be quite safe. If Chad and I can't help Joss keep one man away from you, we've lost our touch.'

'Thank you. I'll try not to be a nuisance.'

But Emily could tell that Libby was still worried.

* * *

As Steven was making his way out to the moors again, he found an old lean-to at the back of the older buildings. It had a door, but no windows, and was empty. Clearly it wasn't being used for anything at the moment. He looked up. The roof seemed watertight.

He nodded. This would do as a hiding place. When he'd finished here, he could get out on to the moors easily from his hideout, without anyone seeing him.

In the meantime he was hungry. He'd go back to his car and have something to eat, then find another place to park.

He didn't know who had turned up at the centre. Probably someone who worked here, given the early hour. No, it had been a luxury car. Perhaps it was the owner. In any case, there was no use hanging about at the moment. He knew the layout, had a vague plan and was prepared to wait for his moment.

He was glad to find his car still in the layby, untouched. Well, there wouldn't be vandals around up here, would there? But still, you never knew who was driving past.

He drove slowly off, smiling as he saw another layby on the other side of the road, only a few hundred yards further up.

He drove right to the top of the slope, where there was a lookout with a gravelled space for cars to park. He'd stay here for a couple of hours, he decided, before reconnoitring again. If the centre got busy, he might even go inside it and wander round. He could claim that he didn't know his wife was there.

He listened to the news and an interesting business report, watching the road get busier. But there was only a stupid chat show after that, or classical music on another channel. Miserable stuff it was, too. He should have brought something to read.

He didn't feel at all sleepy, so simply sat there, bored and irritated . . . waiting.

All this was Libby's fault, damn her. He'd teach her not to run away again. Oh, yes.

Chapter Eighteen

Libby found the hours passed slowly. She felt like a prisoner and was bursting with unused energy. There were only so many games you could play with a small child who hadn't got many toys, so Ned was fidgety.

Joss took over playing with him from time to time, but it was obvious that he too was chafing at the inaction.

It was a relief when Ned fell asleep in the bedroom during the afternoon.

'Let's go and sit in my bedroom,' Joss whispered. 'We can chat and we'll hear him if he wakes up. I think Chad and Emily deserve a little privacy, and I wouldn't mind some time with you.'

Joss gestured to the bed and went to sit on a chair beside the window, staring down at his loosely clasped hands. When he looked up, he asked, 'What are you going to do afterwards, Libby?'

'I don't know.'

'Will you stay in Rose's house?'

'If it's safe, I'd like that very much.'

'I love living out there. I like the views, I enjoy walking on the moors and I find the people in the village friendly in the best of old-fashioned ways. What do you usually do in your spare time?'

'I used to be so busy keeping the house immaculate and looking after Ned that I didn't have time for hobbies.'

'Before you were married, then?'

'Oh, I was very active. I swam and hiked, played netball for my school. I loved any sport, come to that.'

He looked sad and she went over impulsively to take his hands. 'I'm sorry. I was forgetting your leg.'

'It's OK for walking and activities where you don't have to jerk around at speed. I'd be getting a bit old for rough sports now anyway. I miss being able to kick a football around – that's too risky. I like to go to the cinema or watch movies on DVD, and I enjoy reading.'

'Is that enough to fill your life?'

'No. But I'm hoping Leon will give me something interesting to do.'

She realised she was still holding his hands and tried to pull away, but he drew her gently down to sit on his knee.

'Stay with me.'

She did as he asked and when he kissed her, she kissed him back. Oh, she'd wanted to do that, wanted to feel cared for again, desired.

They stayed there, hardly saying a word, kissing occasionally until they heard Ned's voice calling for his mother.

'That was a good time,' she said quietly as she stood up.

'Very good,' Joss corrected. 'To be continued.'

'Definitely.' She raised her voice. 'I'm coming, Ned.'

That quiet hour was the highlight of her day. She wasn't going to make love to Joss until she was free of Steven. It wouldn't feel right. At this stage it would be more a way of sealing their growing feelings for one another than out of lust, anyway.

She really hoped they could nurture their relationship. At the moment she was too anxious about other things to lose herself in sex.

She could forget Steven for a few minutes, but that was all. She was so sure he was coming after her. So sure there would be more trouble.

In the late afternoon, Libby decided to take Ned to play ball in the rear courtyard while Joss made a couple of phone calls. She was halfway down the stairs when a man entered the antiques centre. He looked frazzled and his clothes were wrinkled, even though he'd clearly made an attempt to tidy himself up.

She stopped to watch him and he stopped, too, staring at her so openly she had to wonder if there was something wrong with her appearance.

Then Chad came out of the ground-floor offices to the left of the entrance, beaming a welcome at the newcomer. 'Des! I saw you drive up. What happened to your other car? Have you traded down?'

The newcomer scowled. 'Someone trashed it, hacking the tyres. I've hired that slug of a car because it was the only thing available today.'

No wonder he looked angry, Libby thought, surprised when once again his eyes slid towards her. He looked as if he recognised her, but she was quite sure she'd never seen him before in her life.

He followed Chad into the office and the door closed behind them, so she continued towards the Old Barn. 'Hold my hand, Ned.'

'Don't want to.'

'If you don't, we'll go back to the bedroom.'

For a minute he looked at her, bottom lip jutting out, then he took the hand she was offering.

He cheered up immediately as they went into the huge room. As it was Tuesday, there were only a couple of customers there and some of the stalls were covered. For a while they enjoyed looking at the stalls, particularly the toy stall. She wished she could buy him something but didn't dare spend any money.

After a while, she took Ned out into the rear courtyard and let him chase the ball around. He laughed and shouted as he ran to and fro, full of energy.

Toby and Ashley came to the door of their units to watch him, smiling.

Then Ned missed the ball and let it roll round the corner. He chased after it, shouting happily. Suddenly his voice cut out and there was only silence, not even the sound of footsteps.

Something was wrong. She started running across the courtyard, yelling, 'Toby, fetch Joss. Fetch Joss quickly.'

He stood staring at her.

Ashley said, 'I'll go.'

Round the corner, Libby stopped dead.

Her worst nightmare had just come true.

Steven was standing there, holding Ned in his arms, his hand firmly across their son's mouth.

Ned was rigid with terror.

'Not a sound, unless you want me to hurt him.' Even though he spoke very quietly, Steven's voice rang with menace and he looked different from usual, wild and angry, as if he'd let his temper off its chain. She froze, terrified of what he might do in this state of mind.

'Follow me, and don't make a noise.'

If she followed him and they got as far as a car, who knew what he'd do to them? Whatever happened to her, she wasn't going to let him hurt Ned, so she had to stop him and let her child escape.

She walked forward as slowly as she dared, pretending to stumble on the uneven ground.

'Hurry up!' Even though Steven's voice was low, it was sharp.

'Let Ned go,' she pleaded. 'I'll come with you. I won't struggle. But let Ned go.'

'Why should I? He's my son. I've a right to have him living with me. You're both coming home and you're going to tell the busybodies that's where you want to be.'

She saw a tear roll down Ned's cheek and that was the final straw. Not giving herself time to think, she flew at Steven, taking him by surprise and making him stumble. She scratched the hand that was across Ned's mouth then clouted Steven across the head before he recovered from his shock.

'Ouch! You bitch! Stop it!'

She tried to kick him where it would hurt most and in defending himself, he dropped Ned.

'Run to Joss, Ned!' she shouted and began screaming at the top of her voice, till something hit her on the head and she knew nothing more.

Joss looked up as he heard someone running up the stairs, calling his name. He was already at the door of the flat when Ashley arrived.

'Come quickly! There's a bad man. He's hurting Ned. Libby says to fetch you.' Ashley turned and ran downstairs again.

He was after her at once, yelling for help as he clattered down the stairs.

Chad and another man came to the door of the office.

'Libby's in trouble!' Joss yelled.

Ashley ran ahead, taking him across the courtyard.

There was no sign of Toby, and when they turned the corner, there was no sign of Ned – or of anyone else.

'Where are they?' Joss asked.

'They were here. The man was holding her. They've gone.'

'Stand still and be quiet.' He listened carefully and thought he could hear the sound of footsteps from the direction of the outbuildings. 'Shhh!'

He listened again. Yes, that was definitely the faint squeak of a door being closed.

Chad caught up with him just then, so Joss pointed, whispering 'What's over there?'

'Some sheds.'

'I think he's hiding in one.'

Des stepped forward. 'Shall I call the police?'

Joss hesitated. 'We don't know what's happening. There are three of us. If it's only Pulford, we can take him down.'

'And if her abusive husband has got Libby, that might be a hostage situation,' Chad said.

Joss swallowed hard. Dear heaven, how had this happened? Why had he left her on her own? The damned phone calls could have waited. If anything happened to her . . .

'Better safe than sorry. I'll call the police; you go after them. I'll catch up with you.' Des moved back into the courtyard and took out his mobile to dial 999.

Joss nodded to Chad and they began to move forward as quietly as they could.

Cursing his son, who'd run back towards the house, Steven slung Libby's unconscious body over his shoulder and ran along the back of the building to the empty shed. It'd do as a place from which to bargain. They'd have to let him go or . . . or he'd end it here and now.

He was panting by the time he got there and she was stirring.

Dammit, he should have brought something to tie her up with. He hadn't planned this as well as he usually did. That was her fault for upsetting him.

He fumbled through his pockets and came up with his handkerchief. That'd have to do. He yanked her arms behind her and tied her hands at the wrists, noting that the back of his hand was bloody where she'd scratched him. The bitch!

Where was the kid?

He thought he heard something outside and opened the door a crack to peer out, ducking back, cursing. Two men. Strangers. They were looking for something – him, probably.

He must have been seen.

'Pulford! We know you're there. Stop this now. Don't make things worse.'

The door creaked, so he stopped trying to hide and pushed the door back, dragging Libby forward to show them he wasn't alone. 'Stay where you are. Do not move another step forward or I'll thump her again.'

They froze.

He smiled. 'That's right. Now listen. This is just a domestic dispute. My wife and I can settle it if you leave us alone. She's agreed to come home with me. I'll not hurt her if you let us go.'

She tried to wriggle away from him and he was forced to yank her back by the hair.

'Where's Ned?' she yelled.

Steven glared at her. Always the child. She cared more about the boy than she did about her own husband. That was wrong. 'I've got him safe in the car. You've been unconscious. I came back for you.'

She immediately yelled, 'He says Ned's in the car. Save my son! I don't—'

In desperation, Steven dragged his tie off and fastened it across her mouth, which more or less shut her up. Then he saw a third man join them – that sod from the hotel – and shouted again, 'Stay back or she'll suffer.'

Des crept closer and whispered, 'I've called the police, told them it's urgent. Where's the boy?'

'She just shouted that he's locked in Pulford's car.'

'His car isn't in the car park,' Des said at once. 'I was keeping my eye on him yesterday and I'd have recognised it. Where else could he have parked?'

'Well? Do you accept my terms?' Steven yelled.

'No!' Joss replied at once. 'It's stalemate, so you'll have to negotiate. You can't get away.'

'But I've got Libby *and* the boy. You wouldn't want me to hurt her, would you? If you try to come any nearer, I'll lock the door of this shed, and then who knows what I'll do?'

'What's his car like?' Chad asked suddenly.

'Big silver Mercedes.'

'There was one parked in a layby up the road when we drove down from the moors yesterday. You could go to the road and see whether it's still there.'

Des set off at a run.

'Answer me, damn you,' Pulford called. 'Do I have to hurt her to make you negotiate?'

'We won't do anything till we have the boy back.'

'She was lying to you. He's here, inside this shed.'

Somehow, Joss didn't believe that. 'Prove it. Show him to us.'

Pulford laughed, but it only sounded like a bad stage laugh. 'Why should I?'

'The fellow's lost it,' Joss whispered. 'Listen to him. We'd better tread really carefully here. He's already hurt her and who knows where he'll stop.'

'Are you a trained negotiator?'

'Yes. But I'm way out of practise. And anyway, I'm emotionally involved.'

'You're all we've got at the moment. Do what you can.'

* * *

Des ran through the antiques centre, pausing briefly to yell to Emily. 'We've got a hostage situation. No one's to go outside.'

'Who's the hostage? Not Libby!'

'Yes. Her husband's got her. But we can't see Ned.'

He ran out to the road and stared up the hill. He could see a layby, but there was no car parked in it. He couldn't see the road beyond that very clearly, so clambered up on the wall, holding on to the gatepost. That was better.

There was a car further up the hill, silver, could be Pulford's.

He didn't believe the boy was there because Pulford hadn't had time to get here and back, so he didn't linger.

As he was going back into the centre, he thought he could hear police sirens in the distance, so he asked Emily, who was standing in the rear courtyard, to tell the police where the others were and what was going on. Then he ran back through the front showroom and outside.

Perhaps he could get round to the back and take Pulford by surprise.

Pretending to be only semi-conscious, Libby watched Steven carefully. He was staring out of a small dusty window and jerking to and fro like a mechanical toy that wasn't working properly.

Something was very wrong with him. In the six years of their marriage she had never seen him so out of control, never been so afraid of him, either.

He turned towards her and she managed a small groan. But the tie was partly in her mouth and she couldn't speak.

'You shouldn't have shouted out like that,' he said abruptly. He reached out to hold her face, thumb and fingers digging into her cheeks, forcing her to look him in the eyes. 'I'll have to teach you to do as you're told in future. Do you understand?'

He seemed to expect something so she forced herself to nod and groan again.

He let go of her and turned back towards the window, muttering to himself. Then he yelled suddenly to the men standing guard on them, 'I'm coming out with her and if you don't stay back, I'll hurt her again.'

This time he took out a knife.

She stared at him in terror. Was he going to kill her?

He yanked her to her feet and she staggered more than she needed to. 'You'd better move only when I tell you. Got it?' He pressed the knife tip against her throat.

She nodded very slightly, but it satisfied him.

As he opened the door, she could see Joss standing there, with Chad behind him. There was no sign of Ned. Dear heaven, what had this monster of a husband done with her son?

'Get back,' Pulford yelled.

Joss spoke much more quietly. 'We need to agree on the terms first.'

'No, we don't. *You* need to do as you're told. And so does she.'

There was the sound of a police siren, more like two of them.

'What the hell have you done?' Steven shouted. 'That wasn't necessary.'

'We haven't done anything.' Joss's voice was calm.

'Sounds like the police, but I haven't called them. I give you my word on that.'

'Then *he*—' he jerked his head in Chad's direction – 'can go and tell them to stay clear. This is between me and my wife, no one else.'

'Do as he says,' Joss said. 'Tell them to stay back.'

Chad stared from one to the other, moving away with a sigh.

'She wants to come back to me,' Steven said. 'Don't you?'

With the knife still at her throat, Libby could only nod.

'You see. This is all a lot of fuss about nothing.'

'The trouble is, you're depriving her of her liberty. If she says the same thing after you release her, naturally we'll respect her wishes.'

'She wants me to take her and the boy back home, so that we can make up and carry on with our lives. We were happy before.'

The bleak expression in Libby's eyes told Joss this wasn't true.

As Chad started to cross the courtyard, Ashley intercepted him. 'Toby wants to see you.'

'I'll speak to him afterwards. I have to speak to the police first.'

'He wants to speak to you now.'

Chad was already turning away when she added, 'He's hiding the little boy.'

He swung back. 'What did you say?'

'Toby's hiding the little boy. They're in the secret room.'

'You're sure of that?'

She nodded.

Two police officers peered through the windows then came out of the centre. Chad gestured to them to stay where they were and turned back to Ashley. 'Tell Toby to come out and bring the boy.'

But she only repeated, 'He's frightened. He wants to speak to you.'

'Wait here. I'll be back in a minute.' He hurried across to the police officers, told them quickly what was going on. As the officers moved quietly across the courtyard towards the scene of the confrontation, he turned to Ashley. 'We'll go and see Toby now.'

She nodded and led the way.

When they got to the secret room, he called, 'Toby! It's Chad here. Come out.'

The door began to open slowly.

Steven was looking so wild-eyed that Joss knew he couldn't delay him much longer. The hand that held the knife was twitching and Pulford's other hand was clamped firmly round Libby's arm.

Suddenly Steven dragged the improvised gag down. 'Tell them to let us go, Libby. And tell them I always mean what I say.'

Her voice was husky. 'Let us go. For Ned's sake. *Please*.'

Joss could see that she was terrified for the child and with that knife still close to her throat, he didn't dare detain them any longer. 'I'll move slowly backwards.'

The minute he was out of the way, Steven began to move

sideways towards the perimeter wall, still keeping the knife at Libby's throat.

As they reached the corner of the shed and passed him without seeing him, Des moved quietly after them. Joss saw him but didn't give him away.

Pulford had no idea anyone was behind him until Des grabbed the hand holding the knife with both his, jerking it away from Libby's throat and twisting her attacker's wrist in a way guaranteed to hurt.

Pulford yelled in shock, struggling to keep hold of the knife, but as Des increased the pressure, he fell to his knees and let go of the weapon.

Joss rushed forward to help, but Pulford continued to struggle like a madman.

Libby moved right away from them, shaking in fear and shock.

A police officer joined them and, even then, it was a few moments before they managed to get handcuffs on Pulford.

Joss sat beside him on the ground, panting. 'Where's the boy?'

Pulford smiled. 'Wouldn't you like to know?'

Libby walked over to join them. 'Please, Steven! Ned's your son. Tell me where he is.'

'I've got him hidden away. He might starve to death if you don't let me go.'

A voice called loudly, 'No, he won't.'

She turned to see Chad standing at the corner of the building, holding Ned in his arms, with Toby and Ashley standing a little way behind them looking anxious.

With an inarticulate cry of relief, she ran across to take her son and cuddle him close.

'Daddy's mad at us again,' Ned whispered, clinging to her tightly.

'He's not mad at you; he's mad at me. But he's going away and he won't be coming back.'

But Ned stole a glance at the man the police were helping to his feet and shivered.

'Come on.' Joss put an arm round Libby's shoulders. 'Let's leave him to the police.'

'I'll get out one day. And I'll find you, Libby. Wherever you go, I'll find you!' Pulford yelled.

'The bad man won't find you,' Toby said suddenly. 'He's going away and he won't come back.'

She stopped to stare at him in surprise.

'Toby seems to have some psychic powers,' Chad murmured. 'I hope he's right about this, as he has been about other things. Come on, Libby. Let's get you somewhere comfortable.'

She felt hope curl through her as she walked into the building with Joss, not looking back at the man still screaming obscenities after her.

Emily was waiting for her inside the centre. 'Come up to the flat. I can offer you tea or coffee, or you could join me in a brandy. Here. Let me take the boy.' She smiled at Ned and held out her hand. 'I've got some cake and a drink of orange juice waiting for you, young man.'

To Libby's surprise, Ned went to Emily, smiling at her. 'I'm thirsty.' Then his smile faded. 'My daddy's a bad man.'

'He is. Very bad.'

'But Toby says he won't come back.' He nodded as if that pleased him.

'We won't let him come back,' she said firmly.

He stared at her and nodded again.

They all trailed up the stairs.

Chad turned to beckon to Toby. 'Come and have a drink of tea. You helped us today. You did really well.'

'All right.'

Ashley hesitated. 'Me too?'

'Of course. You're a friend as well.'

She stared at him solemnly, nodded and followed Toby up the stairs.

Epilogue

When they were all supplied with something to drink, Des stood up and clinked his spoon against his mug to get their attention. 'There is something else I need to tell you.'

'I hope it's good news this time,' Joss said.

'I think it is.' Des looked at Chad and Emily. 'All right if I tell them what you employed me for?'

She smiled. 'Yes. But make it the whole tale. I don't want to figure as a woman who willingly gave her baby away.'

Libby went very still and looked across at her.

Des said gently, 'I've already told Libby about her birth mother and how she came to be adopted.' He turned to Libby. 'Emily's been looking for her daughter for several months now, but letters to you have gone unanswered. You never saw them, did you?'

She shook her head, stealing another glance at Emily. Was it possible?

'But you wanted to find your birth mother, didn't you?'

'Yes. Very much. It's not good to be alone in the world, to have no blood relatives.'

'As you must have guessed by now, Emily is your birth

mother and it's more than time you two got together.'

He turned to Emily, who had tears rolling down her cheeks. 'Why don't we go and finish our refreshments in the café, while you and Libby have a long-overdue chat?'

People nodded and began to leave.

But Ned wouldn't leave his mother, so he stayed with the two women.

'I'll explain it to you,' Joss whispered to Toby and Ashley as they left.

Toby looked at him in surprise when he'd finished a simplified version of the tale. 'Emily is Libby's mother?'

'Yes. They've been looking for one another for a while now.'

'My mother died,' Ashley said.

'So did mine.' Toby sighed.

'But now you've got each other. You can be good friends.'

He nodded. 'Good friends. But I have to be tidy or Ashley gets angry.'

'We'll go back to our flats now,' Ashley decided. 'I'll clean up the secret room tomorrow. It's very dusty.'

Chad smiled as they walked off together.

Then he heard the fax machine go, so went to see what the message was.

He wished he could hear what Emily and Libby were saying.

When everyone had left, Emily looked at her daughter. 'I think this has surprised you more than me. I'd guessed you were the one, from things Des said. I remembered Ned.'

Libby stared at her, seeming unable to speak.

'Are you all right about it, me being your mother, I mean?' Libby's smile at this was so glorious, it made Emily want to weep.

'Oh, yes. I'm definitely all right about it. If you are, that is.'

'I can't tell you how happy I am. There aren't words to describe it.' She smiled at Ned, who immediately smiled back. 'Not only a daughter, but a grandson. I feel rich beyond my wildest dreams.'

Ned clambered down and began to rearrange the mugs and plates on the low table.

Emily stood up and held out her arms, and Libby rushed to hug her mother for the first time in her life. Both of them were sobbing.

When Ned began to look anxious, Libby scooped him up. 'It's all right. We're crying because we're happy. This is your grandma.'

He looked at Emily and beamed. 'My friend Jenny has a grandma. And now I have one too.' He seemed so bemused that he didn't pull away as his grandma bent to kiss him, which made more happy tears roll down Emily's face.

After a while, the two women sat down next to one another on the couch and wiped their eyes.

'I always cry when I'm happy,' Emily said apologetically.

'So do I. I so hoped I'd find you.'

'And if you ask me, you've found more than a mother and stepfather lately. Have you seen the way Joss looks at you?'

Libby could feel herself blushing. 'Yes. He's . . . a great guy. But we're taking it slowly. I can't do anything till I'm officially divorced from Steven.'

'In the meantime, I think this calls for champagne, don't you?'

'Yes.'

They cleared the table of cups and called the others in.

Chad went straight to Emily, giving her a big hug. 'I'm so happy for you, my darling.' Then he hugged Libby for good measure.

When he stepped back, Libby saw Joss hesitate, looking uncertain, so she went and put her arms round him.

'My mother said this is a place of hope,' she said softly. 'I felt that the first time we came here and helped Jane along the road to safety. I feel it even more so now that my hopes and dreams have come true. And I haven't thanked you properly, Joss.'

'For what?'

'Putting your life on the line. Steven had a knife.'

'I wasn't going to let him use it on you, but it was Des who grabbed him first. Thank goodness.'

A little later Chad cleared his throat to get their attention. 'I have another piece of good news for Emily.'

She looked at him. 'Oh?'

He grinned. 'George has agreed to pay your price for the house.'

She looked at him, a smile crept across her face, and she let out a loud cheer. 'Serves him damned well right.'

Then they had to explain to the others.

'I have an aunt as well?' Libby asked.

'Yes, but my sister's a bit of a weak reed. And as for George, who's your half-cousin, I absolutely guarantee you'll dislike him.'

'That's what it's like in families,' Joss agreed. 'I have an uncle I can't stand. He's a pompous fool.'

Emily smiled at him. 'I'm going to enjoy being related to you, Joss. I hate people pretending all their relatives are perfect.' She hesitated, then added, 'I'm glad Libby's got you now.'

A little later, while Emily and Chad were talking to Ned, and Des was taking a phone call, Joss asked quietly, 'Are you coming back to live at Top o' the Hill, Libby?'

'Oh, yes.'

'That's good. And . . . are we going to get to know one another better?'

'Absolutely.'

He let out a happy sigh and pulled her closer. 'So I'm now allowed to cuddle you in front of your mother?'

'It's obligatory.'

But as they kissed she felt someone tugging at her skirt. She looked down at Ned.

'Why is Joss kissing you?'

It was Joss who answered. 'Because I love your mother.' Then he scooped up the boy and tickled his stomach. 'And I love you, too.'

Ned leant trustingly against him and Libby felt more happy tears rise in her eyes. She had to be very firm with herself not to cry again.

By the time Joss had put the little boy down, the

champagne was ready and they could raise their glasses in a toast proposed by Chad.

'To families, old and new.'

'To families.'

ANNA JACOBS is the author of over eighty novels and is addicted to storytelling. She grew up in Lancashire, emigrated to Australia in the 1970s and writes stories set in both countries. She loves to return to England regularly to visit her family and soak up the history. She has two grown-up daughters and a grandson, and lives with her husband in a spacious waterfront home. Often as she writes, dolphins frolic outside the window of her study. Inside, the house is crammed with thousands of books.

annajacobs.com

ALSO BY ANNA JACOBS

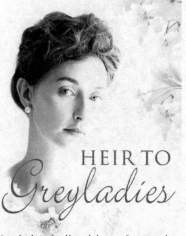

HEIR TO
Greyladies

'Anna Jacobs is adored by a whole army of women readers
for her heart-warming stories of love and life'
Lancashire Evening Post

ANNA JACOBS

With the sudden death of her father, the life of Harriet
Benson changes forever. She is forced into service at Dalton
House, where she becomes friends with the owners' crippled
son Joseph. When circumstances force Joseph to leave the
family home, Harriet accompanies him and breaks free
from the controlling influence of her stepmother.

But Harriet is unprepared for the event which will
alter her life even further: her unexpected inheritance of
Greyladies, a supposedly haunted house in the country.
While Harriet and Joseph grow ever closer, the plots and
actions of both their families threaten to destroy their
happiness. Will their love, and the legacy of Greyladies, be
able to survive?

MISTRESS OF
Greyladies
ANNA JACOBS

'A beautifully told, engaging story with brilliant characters'
Books Monthly

During the First World War, Greyladies is requisitioned by the government as a POW internment centre. The mistress, Harriet Latimer, now has a family to care for, and while they are allowed to stay, tragedy puts their future at the house at risk.

In Swindon, Phoebe Sinclair loses her job when her German employers are interned and the future looks bleak indeed. However, a chance encounter leads her to a new life as a VAD nursing assistant and to a blossoming friendship with soldier Corin McMinty. When she's posted to Greyladies, Phoebe feels like she's come home. Latimer family legend says a new mistress will be found to look after the house, is this the path she was meant to take?

LEGACY OF
Greyladies
ANNA JACOBS

'Anna Jacobs is adored by a whole army of women readers for her heart-warming stories of love and life' *Lancashire Evening Post*

Wiltshire, December 1915. Widow Olivia Harbury has been persuaded by her cousin Donald to live with him and his wife, but tensions soon rise between the pair. Then, much to Donald's disapproval, Olivia becomes involved in starting a new Women's Institute.

A chance meeting brings Olivia to Greyladies, an ancient manor house run by Phoebe Latimer, and she feels as though she's finally come home. But someone is attempting to rid Greyladies of the German internees based there. Their cruel tricks put Phoebe's life and that of her unborn child at risk. Can these two help one another through these troubled times? Or will violent men destroy Greyladies and all it stands for?

Peppercorn Street

ANNA JACOBS

'A beautifully told, engaging story with brilliant characters. What more could you possibly want?' *Books Monthly*

Eighteen-year-old Janey and her baby daughter are disowned by her family and left to fend for themselves. They move into a small flat on Peppercorn Street, meanwhile, Nicole is renting one of the new luxury apartments after walking away from her husband and sons, tired of being taken for granted. Winifred has lived in her huge family home for over eighty years but now feels completely lost. Many of her friends have died and her nephew suggests she should go into a retirement home.

A chance meeting between the three women sparks up a beautiful friendship that will change their lives forever.

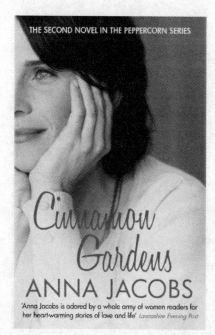

Cinnamon Gardens

ANNA JACOBS

'Anna Jacobs is adored by a whole army of women readers for her heart-warming stories of love and life' *Lancashire Evening Post*

Now her sons are grown up, Nell Chaytor is ready to leave Australia and build a new life for herself in England. She's been left a house by a great-aunt but it isn't fit to live in, so Nell is happy to sell it and allow a builder to create Cinnamon Gardens.

Her elderly neighbour Winifred, however, wants to stay in the only home she's ever known, but someone is trying to frighten the old lady into selling, and to make matters worse, her young friend Janey is being stalked. Can Nell build a new life with a new love? And, more importantly, what can she and her friends do to help each other stay safe?

THE THIRD NOVEL IN THE PEPPERCORN SERIES

Saffron Lane

ANNA JACOBS

Nell has come to feel very at home in her beautiful corner of Wiltshire with her partner Angus. What she could do with, however, is a challenge, and the prospect of bringing life back to an abandoned row of houses, Saffron Lane, is just what she's looking for.

Stacy, lost and alone after a divorce she didn't see coming, is trying her best to start over. And Elise, battling her nieces who would force her into residential care, longs for a home where she can get back to her painting. When their paths cross, the future starts to look brighter although not all goes according to plan.

To discover more great books and to
place an order visit our website at
allisonandbusby.com

Don't forget to sign up to our free newsletter at
allisonandbusby.com/newsletter
for latest releases, events and exclusive offers

Allison & Busby Books
@AllisonandBusby

You can also call us on
020 7580 1080
for orders, queries
and reading recommendations